SAFE HARBOR

Moanna Island Series—Book 1

SAFE HARBOR

Moanna Island Series—Book 1

Kristen Terrette

COPYRIGHT NOTICE

Safe Harbor
Copyright © 2017, 2023 by Kristen Terrette. The information contained in this book is the intellectual property of Kristen Terrette and is governed by United States and International copyright laws. All rights reserved. No part of this publication, either text or image, may be used for any purpose other than personal use. Therefore, reproduction, modification, storage in a retrieval system, or retransmission, in any form or by any means, electronic, mechanical, or otherwise, for reasons other than personal use, except for brief quotations for reviews or articles and promotions, is strictly prohibited without prior written permission by the publisher.

This is a work of fiction. Names, characters, businesses, places, events, locales, and incidents are either the products of the author's imagination or used in a fictitious manner. Any resemblance to actual persons, living or dead, or actual events is purely coincidental.

Scripture quotations marked (NIV) are taken from the Holy Bible, New International Version®, NIV®. Copyright © 1973, 1978, 1984, 2011 by Biblica, Inc.™ Used by permission of Zondervan. All rights reserved worldwide. www.zondervan.com. The "NIV" and "New International Version" are trademarks registered in the United States Patent and Trademark Office by Biblica, Inc.™

Scripture quotations marked (MSG) are taken from The Message. Copyright© 1993, 2002, 2018 by Eugene H. Peterson. Used by permission of NavPress. All rights reserved Represented by Tyndale House Publishers.

The hymn verses in Chapter 14 and 27 were written by Kristen Terrette. All rights reserved.

Cover and Interior Design: Kelly Artieri, Derinda Babcock
Editor(s): Mary W. Johnson, Cristel Phelps, Deb Haggerty

PUBLISHED BY: Elk Lake Publishing, Inc., 35 Dogwood Drive, Plymouth, MA 02360, 2023

Library Cataloging Data

Names: Terrette, Kristen (Kristen Terrette)

Safe Harbor / Kristen Terrette

386 p. 23cm × 15cm (9in × 6 in.)

ISBN-13: 978-1-64949-856-4 (paperback) | 978-1-64949-857-1 (trade hardcover) | **978-1-64949-858-8** (trade paperback) | 978-1-64949-859-5 (e-book)

Key Words: Christian Contemporary Romance; Religious Romance; Clean and Wholesome Romance; Contemporary Romance; Women's Religious Fiction; Women's Christian Fiction; Christian Romance

Library of Congress Control Number: 2023xxxxxx Fiction

DEDICATIONS

For my sweet Jana

ACKNOWLEDGMENTS

Pursuing my dreams of writing and helping other authors achieve theirs is only because of Jesus and my husband. Jesus placed these dreams inside of me and opened doors I never thought possible. Glory be to Him!

And He also gave me my husband, my Ashley, who's been with me well over half my life. He has fully supported me and our family, not only financially, but emotionally as well. There are always days of doubt, but you never doubt me. My writing and career are just as much your success as they are mine. Thank you, honey.

In the publishing world, I have found my people. People who understand my love and devotion to words and stories. Those who enjoy falling asleep to a good book and who are always caught up in their own minds with made up characters. These people bring me so much joy and also make my writing and editing better. Thank you, Allie Millington and Dawn Tolbert. Thank you, editors, old and new, Mary Johnson, Lin Harris, Deb Haggerty, Cristel Phelps, Georgia Woods, and Steve & Ruth Hutson. Thank you, Denise Gallagher, for your beautiful artwork.

Thank you, Writers House, Michael Mejias, Rey Lalaoui, and Jodi Reamer for an amazing learning experience in the Intern Program and for believing in me.

Thank you, Sharlene Martin, for new opportunities and an exciting future.

And, thank you, faithful friends/family, beta readers, sensitivity readers, and visionaries of this story and others: my mom, Donna, Kelly Campbell, Jennifer Slattery, Teri Marsh, Julie Guebert, Amanda Burgos, Kimberly Dobson, Robrenna Redl, Urlynn Francois, Susan Aken, Kayleona Lucero, Denise Gallagher, and Michele Shaeffer. I'm sure there are more!

Thank you, Jana, and your precious girl for inspiring Eva's character in every way.

I love you all, and hope to make you proud.

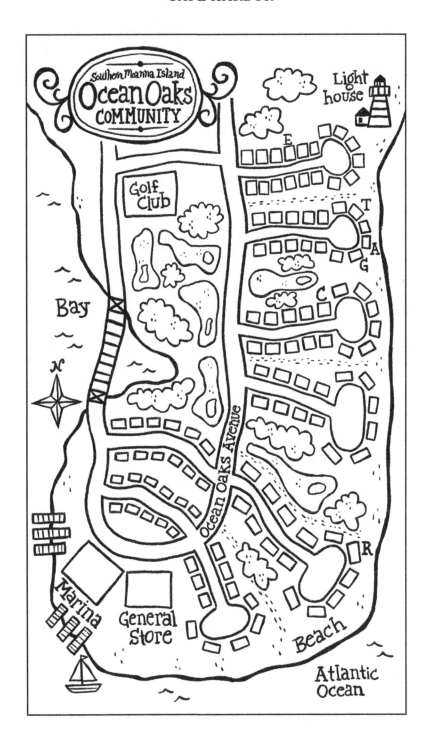

CHAPTER ONE

Early August

Sunday

Eva

I swiped another disobedient tear away.

Good thing Willow was out cold in her car seat. At four years old, she already had superpowers when it came to reading me, and she would've sensed I was crying.

After seven hours, my old Honda's wheels hit the bridge leading to Moanna Island. Our new home, with the best of Georgia's beaches only blocks away.

My phone rang. Definitely Mom. I checked the rearview again to confirm her Camry was tailing me while I tapped to answer. "Hey—"

"Well, you can't back out now."

"I wasn't going to." I totally was. Had flipped-flopped on the decision numerous times in the last few weeks, unconvinced the move was the right decision.

"Well, good. It's officially settled now because we're here. We're here! I'm so excited I can hardly stand it," she yelled into her Bluetooth earpiece.

I glanced at her Camry in the rearview mirror, picturing her wide smile. "Buying a house sight unseen from three hundred miles away will do that."

"I know. Is Willow still asleep?" she asked, her voice lowered as if she might wake her up through the phone.

"Yeah, still zonked out."

"I hate to wake her up, but the second you put the car in park, you know she will." I nodded my head as if she could see me.

"Oh, Eva, I still can't believe I bought a house on Moanna."

We exited the bridge and approached the iron gate into Ocean Oaks, our new community that took up the whole southern tip of the island. "Mom, I'll see you in a bit." I clicked off and started to roll down my window, but the security guard waved me through. The decal on my windshield worked. I took a deep breath going through the entrance as childhood memories of vacationing here flooded my mind.

It looked exactly as I remembered, with its main drag branching off to quaint streets lined with homes. The ones to the left dead-ended at the beach, and the ones to the right dead-ended at the bay. Two incredibly fancy golf courses traversed back and forth, zigzagging over the speck of land. Moanna even had a little marina with shops and restaurants, and a bigger harbor with a lighthouse. Over half of the community residents were retirees, and Dad would have been one of them if the heart attack hadn't taken him. Golfing would have become his day job, and Mom wouldn't have seen him any more than she had while he was working.

The GPS said to take the next left onto White Egret Drive.

We'd never rented a house on White Egret for a family vacation, but its beauty was just like all the other streets I remembered. The grayed asphalt road was completely shaded, even though it was the hottest part of the day when the sun was directly overhead. The front yards of all the homes were full of huge live oak and magnolia trees, dripping with Spanish moss amongst a smattering of pines. The trees' branches reached out to touch every area of the sky, stretching across the road, leaving a rooftop of browns and greens above my car. Each home was painted in neutral grays and beiges, seamlessly blending into an open pocket of space between the big trees, and hidden behind the overflow of wax myrtles, cinnamon fern, and saw palms.

"Wow," I could only whisper, as I pulled into the ranch home's driveway.

Our home.

I parked in front of one of the two garage bays. Mom stopped at the other.

We got out and stared at each other over the top of the car. Both of us blinked away tears, until a little voice cried from the backseat.

"Mama, we're here. Get me out ... please!" Willow said *please* as an afterthought.

We broke into laughter.

"Now, get my granddaughter out, and let's go pick out our rooms."

"Yeah, I wanna see our new house," Willow squealed as I unclipped her seat belts and helped her down to the pavement. She hated not being able to undo herself yet, always wanting to be bigger. I, on the other hand, wished she could stay little forever.

I had to jog to catch up with her as she bounded up the sidewalk and through the heavy wooden door Mom had already opened.

"Mama, it's so pretty." Willow took off down the hall to the left.

"Yes, it is," I called, but she was gone.

The foyer opened into a large family room, its back wall lined with floor-to-ceiling windows and a sliding glass door leading out to the pool and patio area. The pictures of the kitchen to my right hadn't done it justice. The former owner spared no expense renovating it with the latest stainless-steel appliances, white Shaker cabinets, marble countertops, and a gray quatrefoil tile backsplash to match the gray veins running through the marble counters. It rivaled any designer kitchen found in the latest home design magazines, and was the top reason Mom chose to buy the house over the other contenders.

I went through the half-hidden door off the breakfast bar area. When I was finished, it'd be our library. The small nook of a room smelled like old mahogany, a scent forever ingrained into the dark-stained shelving covering every horizontal surface. And the cherry hardwood floor was perfect for a cozy rug underneath a comfy chaise or reclining chair.

I ran my hand along the shelves, already giddy about unpacking all my books. Alex always teased me for my love of words and books, but he was actually proud of my English skills. Ones that did me well now. At least on a seventh-grade level.

Alex would have loved to give me a room like this.

"Mama, I've picked my room." Willow's voice from the family room snapped me

back to the present.

"I'm coming." I rushed to find her rounding the corner into the kitchen.

"Mama, come on. I have to show you the cool window."

Mom appeared behind her, biting her lip to hold back her grin. We had hoped to entice Willow to choose the bedroom with the cushioned window seat by highlighting its cool factor. It happened to be the smallest bedroom, and it lay between Mom's room and what was to be mine, which made me feel safer. Looked like Mom had pulled it off without my help.

SAFE HARBOR

"Really? A cool window? Then I guess it only makes sense for that room to be yours."

"Yes." Willow's eyes lit up, and her curly light brown hair jostled around her face as I tucked it behind her ears to keep it out of her eyes. She grabbed my hand and pulled me out of the kitchen and into the hall. We paused at the first bedroom. "This one's yours, right next to me."

"Okay," I said, with only a second to view it before she pulled me once again.

"That's the bathroom." She didn't even stop for it. "And this one's mine." She let go of my hand and spun around the room's middle.

"Beautiful." The closet was small but would work. "You still want to paint it pink?"

"Yup. Bubble gum pink."

"So, a Pepto Bismol-colored bedroom?"

Willow's eyes questioned.

"Never mind. We'll see what the paint stores have." *In lighter pink options.*

Willow nodded and tugged my hand again. Mom moved out of the way as she pulled me through the door at the end of the hall.

"And this is Gramma's room. It's huge!"

Mom leaned down to get on Willow's level, her dark brown bob bouncing. "Yes, it is huge. Did you see the big bathtub? Perfect for bubble baths?"

"Nope." She sped to check it out.

I faced Mom, both our matching brown eyes rimmed with tears. "You did good. Thank you for this ... this place ... this new start."

"Honey, thank your daddy. His life insurance and retirement set us up nicely. You know the last thing he said was to take care of you. Taking care of you and Willow this way—moving to a house on Moanna to start fresh together—I can't think of any way he'd rather have me use the money. The timing just wasn't right until now."

Willow came back and we three hugged. Tightly.

"Thank you. Mom *and* Dad."

"Now you can take me to the beach." Willow looked back and forth between us.

Mom, hand over heart, said, "That's a great idea. Your mom can take you. Y'all find out where the beach walk entrance is. It's supposed to start between a couple of houses down from here, on the other side of the road."

"Mom, c'mon, that's not fair to you. Plus we've gotta unload the cars."

"Eva, take your daughter to the beach while I unload. They're not even packed that full. Just random things, the air mattresses, and a couple of small suitcases." She plunked her fists on her hips. "I just bought a house a football field away from the beach, and I intend to live out the rest of my days seeing the ocean. And I'm not the one who starts her new job in the morning."

Our move had cut it close timewise. I had taken a job at Palmer Middle School, twenty-five minutes inland, and one of the poorest schools in the county. Our preplanning week started bright and early the next day. Still, I persisted. "The moving truck's coming tomorrow. I already feel guilty about not being here to help you."

"Enough." Mom stamped her foot on the hardwood floor. "I can order the movers around and show them where the boxes and furniture go just fine. Now take her to the beach."

Willow repeated, "Yeah, take her to the beach."

Both gave me their best stern faces. "Okay, okay. But no bathing suits today. We'll just go see the ocean for a little while."

This was clearly enough, because my sweet, energetic daughter bolted for the door, once again leaving me to chase after her.

CHAPTER TWO

Eva

We emerged out from under the mangroves and thick palms covering the beach walk into the openness of the ocean and sky. Willow trotted away.

"Wait for me, young lady."

She halted, half-turned toward me with a full smile. "Hurry."

"Sassy girl, I *am*." I bent down to her. "Okay, it looks like a big storm is coming. We'll look for shells for a bit, but stay *out* of the water, understand?"

Willow nodded.

"Kick off your sandals here."

She flung them off with her toes. "Mama, let's *go*."

She took off down the beach, and I kicked off my own flip-flops and trotted after her. Her childish enthusiasm tickled me into a belly laugh.

I cruised slowly, watching the water wash the sand, as Willow ran ahead searching for shells. The sun hid behind the ever-increasing clouds as it grew closer to setting. We'd have to go in soon. Still, the beach here was lovely.

I hope this was the right decision, after all that's happened. Moanna might be a good place to live. And to forget.

"Mama!"

The gurgling, panicked voice snapped me out of my musing. I spun and saw a flash of tanned skin and muscles dive into the water, heading in her direction.

"*Willow!*"

I ran and dove, but she was too far, and between my strokes and pulls, I watched my baby roll and tumble, unable to gain footing.

"Willow!" I screamed, though the water hitting my face muffled the sound as I kicked harder, my adult body fighting hard against the waves. I would not lose anyone else.

The man, only a blur ahead of me, snatched her up. I planted my feet as he gained his balance, hugging her to his bare chest.

"Baby! Is she alive?" He rushed to shore, his giant frame unmoved by the powerful undertow. I chased after him, horrified. Out of reach of the waves, he laid her down on the sand.

She sputtered a cough as my knees hit the ground. "Willow! Are you breathing?"

The man sat back to give her space, and I got down close. She tried to talk but couldn't through her coughing.

"Turn on your side so you can breathe better." The man pushed on her shoulders, prompting her to roll over. "That's it. Take a deep, solid breath, and try to let it out slowly." His husky voice settled over us.

She recovered some and locked her blue eyes with mine.

"Yeah, Mama," she said softly, though a sob was beginning to take over, "I'm ... I'm breathing." She coughed again, though it didn't have so much force behind it.

I pulled her to me, and she gripped me tight around the neck.

"Willow, my goodness, you scared me to death!" I closed my eyes to ward off tears, but it was useless. The ocean's utter vastness had always unnerved me, and now my very worst fear had nearly come true. I took a deep breath. "I'm sorry, honey. I didn't mean to sound so mad. I was scared, really scared. But I'm not mad at you, okay?"

She nodded into my neck. I looked up and locked eyes with Willow's savior. He wore a happy grin. Through my range of emotions—panic, relief, and even anger—I now had to add off-balance as his smile shot through my heart.

He laughed. Hearty. Manly.

"You know, I didn't want us to meet like this." When I frowned, he added, "Never mind." His country accent didn't fit this dark-skinned, completely drool-worthy man who looked like a Hawaiian native. He stood and offered his hand.

I took it, gripping Willow tight with the other, as he heaved us up. He was so tall. His frame hovered above me. My eyes stared right at his chest. His bare chest.

"Th ... th ... thank you," I rambled. "I'm not sure how I could ever properly say thank you for"—I squeezed Willow, now resting on my hip—"rescuing my girl."

"Well, you just did. And don't worry about it. I'll take any excuse to get in the ocean." He laughed and ran his fingers through his shoulder-length, almost-black wavy hair.

"We were *not* planning to get wet." I held out my free hand to refer to our drippy clothes.

He cocked his head and looked at Willow. "Oh, that's not your bathing suit?"

She giggled. "No, my bathing suit is hot pink with ruffles."

He smiled and looked at me. "Are you and your husband new to the island?"

"Uh, no husband." In an effort to cover my flush, I stuck my hand out for a shake, even though we'd technically clasped hands when he heaved us off the sand. The husband question was one I always dodged. "I'm Eva, by the way, and this is my daughter, Willow."

"I'm Thad." His hand lingered in mine a moment before letting go. Heat inside lit more than just my fingers. He had an easy way about him, a peacefulness.

What's happening?

A flash of lightning hit the ocean. I was grateful for its ominous interruption. "We better get going."

"Good idea."

"Thanks again."

"You're welcome," he said, with another killer smile. "And Willow, you be careful. The ocean is a beautiful thing from God, but also very powerful, okay?"

"Okay." She smiled back at him, already smitten with her hero.

"Willow, can I put you down? Are you okay to walk?"

"Yeah. I'm tough."

"Yes, you are." I gently placed her on her feet but grabbed her hand as we started toward the dunes. "Well, it was nice meeting you."

He called out, "Yeah ... so I'll see you around?"

"Um, sure."

Oh my, hopefully not.

I picked up the pace as the first sprinkles of rain fell, using sheer willpower to keep my eyes ahead and not looking back at the man who'd saved my daughter—the man who had the most genuine smile, yet appeared capable of taking on five guys in a bar brawl. The man with many tattoos who had probably been *in* a bar brawl. The man who unnerved me, and yet ...

I liked it.

Seeing Thad again would be a bad idea. For Willow. For me. Even for *him*.

SAFE HARBOR

"C'mon, Willow, we gotta beat the rain." I pulled her into a jog and the sounds of the rain overtook the sounds of the crashing waves.

CHAPTER THREE

THAD

I watched Eva and Willow disappear underneath the beach walk overgrowth, standing in the rain like a lovestruck idiot before I walked across the sand to the gate of my beachfront house. My heart still raced, both from watching the little girl get swept into the waves and feeling the force of my instant attraction to her mother.

They equally came out of nowhere as I'd longed for the last of the beachgoers to disperse with the storm approaching.

I grabbed my surfboard off the sand, having discarded it in a flash when I rose to seek out the two girls.

It was like I was pulled to them.

Like God had needed me to pay attention.

Thank you, God, for stirring me to move.

I rinsed off my legs and the board in the outdoor shower by the pool and trotted up the back stairs to the covered porch—Dad's and my own favorite spot of the house.

"Dad?" I called, as I went inside.

"Coming," he responded from his main-floor master bedroom. We'd made a new and snazzy second master bedroom upstairs by combining two of the previous rooms and baths. I'd let Dad stay on the main floor. Couldn't let the old man walk up and down the stairs every day. He was retired, after all.

So are you.

The devil liked to remind me of my shame and heartbreak. Like I needed the reminder.

Dad came into the room, heading straight for the fridge, while I toweled off my rain and ocean-soaked body. "What are we having for dinner?"

"I guess a pre-packaged something." They were delivered every week and considered healthier than fast food. I hoped they were because they cost a fortune, but it was either them or starve.

"You really need to learn how to cook." I tried to say it seriously.

"*You* really need to learn how to cook," Dad countered.

"Maybe one day."

"Yeah, one day." We both glanced at each other before we broke into laughter. He put a meal in the microwave.

I sat on a barstool as Dad leaned against the counter to wait, his wire-rimmed glasses sliding down his nose a bit. He was finally starting to look more his age. I always said he was like Denzel Washington—never looking a day over forty-two. But his short black hair had grayed in the five years since Mom passed, and fine lines creased the edges of his brown eyes. Squinting all day on Moanna's golf courses probably didn't help those.

Though his skin was a darker walnut than mine, my skin tone and caramel eyes were the only things I had which slightly resembled my five-foot-ten, lean-as-a-string bean dad.

But it didn't make him any less mine.

He met my eyes. "What's wrong, son? You look ... scared or something."

"More like or something."

SAFE HARBOR

Dad's cocked head prompted my explanation.

"I just pulled a little girl out of the ocean. She was close to drowning."

"Oh my gosh. What? How?"

"Her and her mom were walking the beach. The girl—her name is Willow—got too close to the water, and a big wave just snatched her right off the sand. It was terrifying."

"I bet. I'm glad you were there."

"I know. That's the thing. It's like God orchestrated it. I'd started to follow them—and yes, I know that could be considered stalking—but her mom and her, they were so adorable, and I just moved. I can't explain it. But then, I was there and able to save her."

"Sounds like divine intervention."

I harrumphed.

Dad added, "To make today a little weirder, I need to tell you something. Becca may have called earlier."

"What? Why do you think that?"

He took a deep breath. "Well, the house phone rang as I was coming in from my golf game, and only telemarketers ever call that line. I looked at the caller ID. It said California … so I went ahead and picked it up. The lady asked if Damien was home. I hesitated and said no. I asked if she wanted to leave a message, and the lady said no. It sounded like it could have been her, but I was never around her that much. Anyway, I got the *feeling* it was her."

"Huh, that is weird." I slumped into a bar stool. "It's been four years since I've talked to her."

"I know." The patter of rain on the tin roof grew louder in our silence.

Why would Becca be calling?

What could she have to say? We hadn't called off our engagement on great terms, and Dad knew it. He didn't have to say anything for me to know what he wanted to ask.

"Don't worry, I'm not planning on calling the number back. If she needs to talk to me, she'll find a way."

The microwave dinged, and Dad turned to pop open the door. "Well, wanna watch some football?"

He didn't have to look my way to know I deadpanned him.

"You're going to need to, one day," he said. "Probably help you heal. I know you miss it sometimes—"

"I'm going to shower." *And watch something else besides football.*

Dad nodded but didn't say anything else.

I headed upstairs with a more controlled heartbeat, but my mind wandered back to Eva. I certainly wouldn't mind seeing her *and* Willow again. Probably wouldn't happen, but maybe ...

CHAPTER FOUR

WEDNESDAY

THAD

My favorite worship song blasted through my earbuds, drowning the noise from the leaf blower strapped to my back. But the tune couldn't hold my attention. I let go of the handle, letting the machine's nozzle fall to my side. It purred in idle while I took my phone out of my pocket to mute the music. Sweat everywhere, so I stuffed the phone back into my jeans and pulled out a rag to wipe the mix of it along with grass and dirt off my face.

Man, the field is beautiful.

I tucked the rag away again, admiring the incredible football field. The smell of gasoline mixed with fresh-cut grass stirred memories of taking over the lawncare duties when I was old enough to handle the walk-behind, and the satisfaction I felt once I finished. Plus, there were memories from endless days in heavy pads, helmets, and mouthguards. All representing *home.*

I leaned over the chain-link fence, imagining my team of rowdy seventh grade boys sitting on the bench lining the field. Their first game would mark my third year of coaching, and they'd be the third set of players coming through our little homegrown junior football league. And we were making an impact, seeing the results of what providing an after-school extracurricular activity could do to keep these kids out of trouble and their grades up. Every new season brought more and more youths out in the brutal summer heat. With Dad by my side, we taught them about sportsmanship, respect, and hard work.

Weird how even being surrounded by people all the time can still leave you lonely.

A prayer bubbled inside, pushing away the lie the devil was feeding.

God, I'm sorry I don't always feel enough love for this beautiful life you've given me. Your plans here in Palmer are big, and I want to do your will. Sometimes I just feel alone.

Eva flashed through my mind, her chocolate eyes finding their way into my thoughts more often than I'd ever admit. I figured God had needed my attention to be alert and ready to jump in to save the child. I didn't expect to relive the images *after* the rescue. I replayed the magic between the two girls as they held each other close. I longed for that. Finding out she was single seemed like a sick joke.

I grunted. Time to snap out of my pity party.

I cast one last look around the field. Two and a half hours of manicuring a middle school's football field was plenty long enough to have it in good shape for ball. I grabbed the blower's handle, squeezed the lever, and made my way back to the parking lot, blowing the remnants of grass and dirt off the sidewalk.

Eva

I pushed through the school's doors and out into the bright sun. It felt refreshing to feel the warmth after being inside all day setting up my new classroom. Things were

SAFE HARBOR

now coming along nicely, considering I'd only had two days so far. Monday was a wash—a day full of meetings with the other seventh grade teachers on my team and a full staff meeting that lasted for hours.

Only one vehicle remained with mine in the parking lot. A lawn maintenance company, apparently. A trailer holding a large brand-new-looking riding mower hitched up to an old model dark blue Bronco, not one of the new fancy ones. The shiny equipment looked out of place riding behind the beat-up truck.

What am I talking about? The Bronco's probably the same age as my Honda.

By the time I reached my car, I was already sweating. The heat index was a hundred degrees and would continue awhile since it was only the middle of August.

I take it back. I'm glad I work where there's air conditioning.

Pulling out my phone, I tapped Mom's name. She picked up on the second ring. "Hey, honey, how's your day?"

"It was good. I got a lot done. How's my girl?" I unlocked the car and placed my computer bag in the backseat.

"She's great, as always. We had fun making her room real pretty today. Hold on, she wants to talk to you."

"Hi, Mama, you 'most home?"

"Well," I leaned against my car but got burned, so I quickly pushed away. "I'm getting into the car right now, so it won't be long. I've missed you *so* much." Summers off spoiled both of us.

"Me too. But I unpacked my Barbies."

"I bet they were happy to finally get out of that stuffy box."

Willow giggled. "Yeah, 'bye."

Kids.

The phone jostled around. "Hey, I'm back," Mom said.

"She's so funny on the phone." I shut the back door.

"I know. That girl's a hoot."

"Do you want me to pick up something to eat?" I got in, tossed my purse on the passenger's side and grabbed my sunglasses.

"Nope, dinner's cooking. You just come on home."

"What would I do without you?"

"You'd do just fine, same as you did for three years living almost an hour away," she said, as I tried to start my car—*tried* being the operative word. My engine wouldn't turn over, or kick in, or whatever it needed to do to ignite and actually take me home.

I pulled my lips tight, fending off annoyance. "Mom, you won't believe this, but my stinkin' car won't start."

"What? I told you to let me buy you a more reliable car. We bought that one for you in high school, and it wasn't brand new then. *Now* will you listen?"

I sighed loud enough for her to hear. "Mom, not now. Once I get my first couple of paychecks, I'll look into buying my *own* car."

Definitely, considering you won't even let me pay rent.

I glanced around the parking lot. "There's a lawn maintenance truck here. I'm going to find whoever it belongs to and see if they can jumpstart me. It's probably just the battery again."

"Okay, call me back."

"I will." I got back out into the heat and looked down at my sandals, happy for them and khaki shorts as I rounded the side of Palmer Middle School. Supposedly, an amazing football field sat behind the building, though I hadn't seen it yet since my classroom's windows faced the front. The field had to be where the lawn company guys were working.

Before I reached the back corner of the building, a machine roared, loud and obnoxious. I rounded the brick wall and stopped quick as a leaf blower blasted my legs.

I screamed as a man, a little startled himself, turned off the blower. A strange recognition washed over me as he looked up from under the bill of his baseball hat and flashed a killer smile. I froze, knowing exactly who he was.

THAD

"Eva?"

"Thad?"

Her silky hair was pulled up halfway, but strands had fallen down. Her lips still held a faint tint of lipstick, and her clothes were a bit wrinkled, but she was still beautiful.

"What are you doing here?"

The warmth of her voice flowed over me again. I shook my head to clear it. "I cut the field every Wednesday. Sorry I scared you. I figured everyone was outta here by now." I took a couple of steps closer to her. "What are *you* doing here? You're not following me, are you?" I smiled to lighten the mood.

She let out a sigh and seemed to let some tension seep out with it.

"No. Hardly." Her smile had the power to get me in trouble. "I took a teaching job here." She slowly and meticulously put her hair behind her right ear, leaving her delicate hand resting on her collarbone.

"Ah, so you're a local now."

She thought for a moment. "I guess I am." She grinned, but then a light seemed to go off. "But I came looking for the Bronco's owner, because my car won't start. Do you think you could ...?"

"C'mon. Let's check it out."

Once we got to the parking lot, I said, "I'll pull over to your car."

"Okay, great," she answered softly.

I made her nervous. I've been told my sheer bulk could be intimidating, but I wasn't sure that was the reason. I parked the Bronco nose-to-nose with her Honda and grabbed my jumper cables. She already had the hood up by the time I got to it.

"I'll admit cars aren't my thing, but we'll try this, and if it doesn't work, I'll try fiddling. If that doesn't work … well, I can at least take you home." Now I wished cars *had* been my thing, so I'd be her hero again.

"That's great. Thank you. A couple of weeks ago this happened, and it was the battery, so hopefully it's an easy start again." She peered around me as I attached the cables to the correct battery terminals.

"Okay, give it try."

Eva

Please let it start. Please let it start.

I could not have this man drive me home. The way I couldn't control my heartbeat around him was embarrassing. All I knew about him was he'd appeared out of nowhere twice. Hardly someone I needed to jump in a car with.

But he'd saved my daughter and was about to save me again three days later. Two times my hero …

I put the keys in the ignition. "Okay, ready?"

"Go for it."

It grumbled to what little life it had left.

Relief swept through me. I got out in time to see him swipe a handkerchief across his forehead, up under the bill of his cap, and down around the back of his neck. His long black hair was pulled up into a knot sticking out of the baseball cap in the back, making me wonder why I'd never liked guys with long hair before. They sure seemed sexy now. When he opened his eyes, he caught me staring.

Flushed with heat and embarrassment, I broke away from his gaze. A beat passed while I chewed the inside of my mouth.

"You should probably let the car run for a bit, to charge it up. At least, that's what I've heard you're supposed to do." He laughed. "Did I tell you I'm not a car guy?"

I finally risked looking at him. "Well, you're a car guy to me. Thank you so much, and I'm sorry for keeping you longer in this heat. I bet you've been out here a while." I leaned against the side of the car, shaded a bit from the open hood, wishing I had a handkerchief to wipe the sweat off my face too.

Maybe the sunglasses are hiding my sweat beads.

"No problem." He leaned back against the Bronco's grill, and crossed his arms over his chest. The motion revealed a four-inch cross tattoo on his forearm. The sleeves of his T-shirt strained against his tight arm muscles. "How's Willow?"

The fact he remembered her name sent a ripple over me that smoothed some of my prickly edges. No one since Alex had been able to wear down my rough places, and yet Thad was doing so with ease. Everything about him screamed safety, but safety was an illusion.

Alex's death had taught me that.

Focus, Eva. He's just making conversation, not trying to ask you out.

"She's great. My super-resilient child, as always. I, on the other hand, haven't let her go to the beach with Mom yet. Just the thought makes me terrified."

"I bet. It was pretty scary."

"I called Monday and got her swim lessons at the Y. She starts tomorrow. I told them to focus on ocean survival skills." I tried to laugh, even though my heart pounded painfully remembering the nightmare.

"They're good over there. Good job, Mom." His compliment embarrassed and delighted me. I avoided his eyes and played with free strands of my hair.

He beat out the silence. "So if you're now a local, and I saw you on Moanna, does that mean you're a new islander?"

"Um, yeah. My mom bought a house there."

How much do I tell him?

"My dad passed away five years ago, leaving her alone in a big house in Chattanooga. Willow and I were an hour away, between Chattanooga and Atlanta. We were able to visit, but not every week, and, if I'm being honest, I wanted to be closer to her … my mom, I mean … so one day last spring, she called and asked if we would move to Moanna with her. We vacationed there when I was a kid. Mostly so my dad could play golf." I let out a little chuckle at the memory.

"Every year I think that island fills up with more retirees." He held up a warning finger. "Don't go to Pop's Shrimp Hut on senior discount Thursdays. You will *not* get a seat."

"I'll try to remember that, or at least send Mom to pick up dinner-to-go and get the discount."

"Exactly what I do with my dad. Our parents seem to be a lot alike. Dad's the exact same way as yours was about golf—plays practically every day. And my mom, she passed away almost six years ago, but she's one of the reasons I love this area. She always wanted to live by the ocean."

"It *is* pretty amazing around here. And flat." I laughed. "I guess I should have remembered from when I was a kid. We'd go biking on the island or on the beach when the tide was out, and I could always do it 'cause there were no hills. Where I grew up, leisurely biking around the neighborhood was not an option. It always involved some major leg muscle work or just getting off to push."

"I grew up a couple of hours south of here, so all I know from childhood is flat. I wouldn't know what to do, riding a bike down a mountain like I've seen on TV. No thanks. I'll stick to flat and easy." It struck me as funny a man his size would be intimidated by anything, and I fought to hold in a grin. Almost as if he could tell I was about to poke fun, he smiled. "So you just up and moved here?"

"I know it's crazy, but yeah—it felt right, you know? The timing of it all?" I said those words out loud, but I only felt they were true half the time. Willow and I'd had it good in our little cottage, but the past still lurked, draining my ability to move forward. I hoped taking this big step, moving away from all the memories, would jumpstart my life again.

"I do know. Timing is everything." He held eye contact.

Not knowing what to do or how to douse the blaze I was feeling, I pushed off the car. "You think it's charged long enough?"

"Sure, it should be good." He leaned under the hood and removed the cables. "You should get that battery changed, though."

"Yeah, I know. I will."

He let the hood fall, then gave it a hard push to make sure it was secure.

"Thanks again." I walked around my door to get in.

He followed me and held it open. "No problem. I'll see you around? Since you're an islander now?"

Again with that question. "Um, sure."

Hopefully not. Please hopefully not.

He shut my door, very gentlemanly, and flashed his killer-but-sincere smile. I returned it and waved goodbye as I backed the car out, feeling like a silly schoolgirl.

This time, as I pulled away from his Bronco, I gave in to one last glance at him in my rear-view mirror. He hadn't moved, just stood there, a perfect male specimen, staring at my taillights.

Stop it, Eva. You don't date, remember? Willow is your only love, and she must always be the most important thing. It's just better that way.

CHAPTER FIVE

SATURDAY

EVA

"Okay, which one would it be in?"

I stared at the three boxes stacked in the corner of my room, one on top of the other so they blocked the sunlight peeking through the open blinds.

The middle box said "Miscellaneous Clothing," so I ripped it out, allowing the top box to tumble down on top of the bottom one labeled "Winter Clothes."

Ditching the box on the bed, I grabbed my scissors to cut through the tape, hoping to find one of the two bathing suits I owned. We'd spent almost an hour locating and preparing everything we'd need for a beach day. I felt like we'd packed enough toys, sunscreen, and food to get us through a week—we almost couldn't get our beach bags and the cooler closed, not to mention the umbrellas and chairs. It was a lot of effort, considering I didn't even want to go, at least not until Willow had had more swim lessons.

But Mom kept saying I was crazy to think Willow could live at the beach and not want to go there. She was right, but for now, the rule was she could only go when I was around.

Not that I helped any.

Thad's image as he rushed to shore carrying Willow brushed through my mind.

"Eva? You find it?" Mom yelled from down the hall.

"I found the box. So yes, hopefully." With all the beach trip packing, I overlooked the fact I hadn't unpacked my swimsuit yet. It hadn't been high on my priority list during my crazy week.

I cut through the tape and pulled the box open, tossing scarves, sports bras, a few old CDs, and a couple of dated purses on the bed as I dug through it.

C'mon, where's—

The pack of rubber-banded envelopes appeared in the pile under my fingers. The handwriting on the top envelope woke up my feisty side. As it always did.

Only ... *always* wasn't completely true, at least not since the last six or so letters—the most recent one being a year ago. Before the grapevines of guilt crawled in, I pulled out a letter from the back of the pile, an older one. I opened it slowly, as if it were a jack-in-the-box waiting to spring.

> Dear Eva,
>
> We do hope you and your baby are doing well. I am sorry we did not make it to the hospital to visit. We just thought it would be too hard to see the child and then find out it was not Alex's baby. Please reconsider having a paternity test done. We are told they can use DNA from something of Alex's or even one of us to determine this. We will pay for all of these expenses. Please understand our apprehension knowing the word going around last summer before you and Alex told us you were pregnant. We just want some confirmation—

"Mama, what's taking so long?"

Willow bopped into the room.

"Well," I said, and crumpled the letter in my hands, feeling like a teen caught sneaking out of the house. "I can't seem to find it." I dropped the ball of paper into the box.

Mom rounded the doorframe. "Here, let me help you look. At this rate, we'll never make it to the beach." She moved around Willow.

SAFE HARBOR

I lunged to get between her and the box.

"No!"

She'd ask what the deal was with the pile of letters. I had received only a few of them at Mom's house, right after Willow was born. She'd asked, and I'd avoided all questions about them—too angry to discuss them except to say Alex's parents didn't believe Willow was their grandchild.

When we moved to the cottage, I'd had my mail forwarded there. Somehow his parents figured it out, and eventually, the letters were addressed to my new house. I never knew how they learned my new address. I assumed it was through an old mutual high school friend.

Sometimes Mom brought up Robert and Pamela, Alex's parents, saying she wished they wanted to be part of Willow's life, and that I should reach out and invite them. I never told her the nasty things they'd said and assumed about me. Nor did I tell her how they now *did* want to be a part of Willow's life, but I couldn't bring myself to let them.

"Mom, I've got this. Just give me two more minutes." I squinted at Willow and baited her. "Can you even count to sixty?"

She scoffed. "Yeah." She was already excellent at math, which was assuredly from Alex's genes.

"Well, you both go count to sixty *two* times, and I'll be ready."

Mom eyed me carefully, but said to Willow, "Okay, Little Bit, let's go." She guided her out, pulling the door almost closed.

"Start counting," I yelled as I dove into the box again, grabbing the letters. I threw them in my PJ's drawer and slammed it shut hard. Too hard. I needed to release some negative energy after reading Pamela's words.

I scrambled through the box.

"C'mon …" I whispered, searching for a speck of coral or purple. Finally my fingers touched on something silky, and

I jerked it upward. "Yes." I threw my blue suit on the bed, already stripping down before it hit the mattress.

THAD

"All right, ladies and gents, welcome to our Beginner's Basics Surf Class. I've had a chance to meet all of you and hand out your foamies, otherwise known as your softboards. These are much safer for learning how to surf, because they are buoyant, not as heavy, and of course softer."

All six kids and the one adult laughed at my little joke as they stood in a line, some full of nerves, others eager to get in the water. This was always the dynamic of my beginner's classes.

"Show of hands, who here lives on Moanna?" One boy, Caden, eight years old, raised his hand, noticed he was the only one, and put it down quickly.

"Okay, I'm guessing the rest of you are visitors, getting one last beach trip in before school starts back." The kids and the adult nodded. "Well, you picked a great beach to learn. Moanna has mostly small waves every day. We call them ankle busters, but they're terrific for learning. They're easier to stand up on and you can ride them all the way 'til your board hits the sand."

"Yeah, Coach, you gonna teach us how to duck dive?" Jack, eleven, asked.

"Been reading up on some surf terms?" I responded, genuinely impressed.

"Nah, just YouTube." He smiled.

"Nice. Well, we may not get to that today, but it is very important. First though, are you guys ready to get dirty?" The kids shouted, the adult not so much. "Great, we start with the art of paddling ..."

Noticing movement, I scanned the beach walk behind the line of students, just like I'd done every day, more so since I'd seen her Wednesday at the school. It took me only a second to recognize Eva.

The class before me blurred as I lingered on her, my hearing tuning in only to my accelerating heartbeat. Eva and Willow both wore baseball caps, and Willow carried a float ring sized for her age. Eva looked prepared for a lengthy beach stay, with a huge beach bag over one shoulder, a small cooler over the other, and a chair strapped on her back. A woman whose frame mirrored Eva's accompanied them—same height, same lean body, same olive skin. She could be Eva's older twin if it weren't for the gray streaks through her short brown hair. She carried her own chair on her back, a small beach bag, and an umbrella. They stepped off the beach walk and walked north, away from me. I couldn't be sure, but I think Eva saw me before she moved away.

My students turned to follow my gaze. One of them asked, "Are you gonna teach us to paddle?"

"Yeah, sorry. Everyone, bellies on the board, feet hanging just off the back with your toes in the sand." I got down on my board to demonstrate, trying to control the overwhelming desire to watch where she finally set up camp.

EVA

"Oooh-wee, I'm sweating buckets after just walking down here and putting the umbrella up." Mom collapsed into her teal beach chair.

I followed her into my purple one. "Ah, yes, but now we can relax. At least until Willow has to go to the bathroom."

"Good thing the ocean is close."

"True." We both chuckled. How was I going to tell a four-year-old to pee as inconspicuously as possible in the shallow water?

"How are you feeling about school starting Monday? You ready for a new batch of seventh graders?" She sized me up with her stare.

"Yeah, actually. It's not the job I'm anxious about. I'm worried about Willow. She's starting a new preschool, and I can't even drop her off her first day." The thought was pure misery.

"Honey, that child's as resilient as they come."

"I know. She's had to be that way. It's just … I guess I was used to her old school. They knew my situation, and once the conversation about her father was over, it never surfaced again. I know the time will come when I'll have to tell the teachers here. Plus, now she's older, I think this might be the year she starts asking questions."

"Well, you're probably right, and we'll figure out exactly how to tell her then. In fact, that's one reason I'm glad she'll be going to a Christian preschool now that will teach her about Jesus. Then, when we discuss heaven, she may gain some comfort from knowing her father's there."

I didn't respond. I'd learned over the years it was better not to say anything instead of risking a fight between us. But what was left unsaid didn't make it any less real in its power to upset me to the point of flat-out angry.

Mom pushed further. "You know, Rick Warren says, 'Bitterness is the greatest barrier to a friendship with God.'" She always had a way of reading my mind. It was supernatural. She said it was God through her.

"You're assuming God *wants* to have a friendship with me."

"Eva, you need to learn how God works. He desires to have us close to him with an intensity we can't even fathom."

I stared at the endless ocean, a vivid example of why I

believed in God. His existence was the only way I could justify why we were here, especially after giving birth to Willow and witnessing such a miracle. What I couldn't justify was a God who would allow such a tragedy to happen to my beautiful daughter. And even if I did try to seek his understanding, try to make sense of it all, why would he want me?

Willow was enrolled in a Christian preschool out of proximity and reputation. Instead of allowing my blood temperature to rise, I looked to where Thad was giving a group surf lesson. I'd spotted him right away and tried in vain not to steal glances his way ever since. He was smiling, his bright white teeth standing out against his beautiful dark skin. He lived much of his life outdoors, and it suited him just fine. I'd never seen a more attractive man.

My gut tensed. I hadn't found any guy since Alex actually good-looking. Did that mean I was somehow losing sight of him—or my love for him?

Mom tapped my forearm. "Are you going to go over and at least say hi?"

"What? Who?"

"You know who. The guy you've been staring at since we stepped onto the sand."

"I have *not* been staring."

Maybe just a little.

"Yes, you have. It seems to me a guy who saves your daughter's life, then saves you from being stranded in a parking lot, deserves at least a hello."

"How'd you know he was Thad?"

"C'mon. Kind smile. Tall, dark, full of muscles. Who else could it be? Though I would have added *gorgeous* to that description. You need to ask him out on a date."

"Mom!" I slapped at her playfully. "You know I don't date."

"I know you don't date. Yet."

"Ah, Mom, please. Not now." This topic was a recurring battleground. "For all I know, he's a beach bum. Literally. He could live in a tent on the beach, teach kids to surf, and cut grass occasionally for the school."

Mom's laugh pierced the air. "Yeah, I'm sure Moanna would allow a bum to sleep here all night every night."

She was right. At the very least he'd have to keep moving if he was an *actual* bum, but he seemed to like this particular spot. "Ok, maybe he lives inland somewhere … why are we even having this conversation? I don't date."

Mom smiled. "*Yet.*"

I stood up fast, shaking my head, fighting to keep a grin off my face. It was hard being upset with a mother who devoted her whole life to her daughter's and granddaughter's happiness.

"Willow," I said loudly above the wind, "want to go look for shells? This time it should be okay to get your feet in the water."

She looked up from her buckets and shovels out to the ocean, likely debating how rough the surf was. "Yeah, let's go." She came to me. "Here, you hold my bucket."

"Please?" I prompted.

"Please." She nodded, as if that was going to talk me into holding it.

"Sure." I took the bright yellow bucket. "Which way do you want to go?"

I shouldn't have given her the option, because she set out in Thad's direction. He and his surf students were in the water, practicing paddling over the waves.

Willow and I walked, keeping a slow pace since she picked up anything even slightly resembling a seashell. All the while, a nervous energy built inside me. We'd be upon him soon.

Once we got within range, his voice rose above the commotion. "Good job, Jack. Paddle hard!"

SAFE HARBOR

Willow heard him too. Her head shot up and found him. She wiggled her finger his direction. "Mama, it's Thad."

I risked looking over as Willow took off running.

He stared straight at me.

Yeah, that'll really calm my nerves.

As if reading my mind, his cheeks gave way to a dimpled smile. I called to Willow too late, "Don't bother him—" Then I lowered my voice. No use yelling. "He's busy."

Willow reached him and said something sounding like, "Hey, Thad. Are you playing at the ocean again?"

He laughed.

"Yes, I am, Miss Willow." He turned to his students. "Okay, everyone take five and get some water. You younger ones, go ask your parents for something to drink and come right back." He turned to Willow. "I see you're wearing your bathing suit. Planning on getting in the ocean?" His eyes flicked up to mine. "Well, hello again, Eva."

My voice was stuck in my throat. "Hi. Sorry to bother you."

He shook his head, as if that was a funny statement. "You're not bothering me. They needed a break anyway."

"What are you doing?" Willow asked.

"I give surfing lessons. Today is my last Beginner Basics Class of the summer since school is starting, but if you want, I can teach you in a private lesson one day."

Willow cried out, "Yeah!" just as I said, "Oh, I don't think we're ready for that."

He squinted his gorgeous light brown eyes. "I give lessons to the littles with life jackets on. It's easier that way. And they develop a love and respect for the water. But," he looked at Willow, "when your mom says you're ready, it's a deal."

"Okay." Willow's cheeks balled tight from her smile. "I'm gonna go tell Gramma I'm taking surf lessons." She took off to our beach chairs. Mom sat up in hers, seeing Willow running toward her, anticipation vivid and obvious in her approach.

I turned back to him, and his eyebrow arched ever so slightly. It had a scar on its left side.

Why do I want to touch it? Get it together, Eva.

"I'm sorry for that. I should have asked," he said.

"It's fine. She'll hold you to it now, though. Be careful." I smiled, knowing how persistent she could be.

"That's okay by me. Maybe after she's had a few swim lessons."

My lips pulled into a tight line as I half-nodded, half-threw up in my mouth.

He let out a puff of air, like a chuckle without sound, making it clear he was teasing.

"So Monday's the big day. You feel ready?" He put his hands on his hips in a relaxed, laid-back kind of way. It seemed to pump up the black-and-blue ocean wave tattoo on his chest.

I brought the sand bucket in front of my body and gripped it with both hands, trying to look natural and carefree. "Yes. We start Monday. I'm looking forward to it. I get excited at seeing what kind of new dynamic my class is going to have."

"How long have you been teaching?"

"This will be my fourth year, and since all my teaching time has been in Georgia, the curriculum is much the same. I teach English."

"Oh, nice. What grade?"

"Seventh." I waited for the reaction. Everyone always reacted the same.

Ew, you teach middle schoolers? Seventh graders? Ick. I feel sorry for you.

Truth was, I loved that age and didn't want to teach anything different.

SAFE HARBOR

Thad didn't have the standard reaction. "Cool. I probably know some of your students. If any of the boys give you trouble, let me know." He smiled a cute but cocky smile, a smile that sent the good kind of chills through me.

"Oh, okay," was all I could say.

Does he teach surf lessons to the kids inland as well?

"You know, we seem to keep running into each other. Why don't we *plan* to run into each other?"

"What do you mean? Like you and me? Go somewhere?" I sounded like an idiot.

He grinned and squinted a little more as the sun reflected off the sand. "Yeah, like you and me going somewhere. Like a date."

He was confident, and I'd be lying if I said my knees didn't knock a little. The knee knock turned into panic, and I focused on the ripple formation left in the sand because of the tides.

"No. I don't date." An image of Alex's blue eyes, cropped blond hair, lean jock frame, and sideways smile that always pulled on my heartstrings formed in my mind.

"You don't date ever? Or you don't date guys like me?" His words drew my gaze up to his. Everything about him was the opposite of Alex.

I scrunched my face up and bit my lip. "Um ... maybe both." That didn't come out right. "I mean—"

"It's fine."

The boy, Jack, I think, walked up. "Coach, what we doing now?" I was grateful for the interruption.

Thad turned and squeezed his shoulder. "Well, Jack, we're gonna surf." Jack pumped his fist in the air as he ran to the ocean. Thad looked back to me. "Well, good luck on Monday."

"Thanks." I gave an awkward wave as he turned toward his students, bringing me face-to-face with the black outline of another wave tattooed across the width of his shoulders.

I was like an ocean wave, relentless, damaging to fragile sand. He met up with the kids and gave instructions, and all the while I fought the urge to run after him and apologize for being ... me.

I took a deep breath and did an about-face to walk back to my chair, realizing my heart was beginning not to feel the same way as my head.

CHAPTER SIX

THURSDAY

EVA

I looked up as the door to the hospital room closed softly, dreading the nurse's interruption telling me it was time to leave. Instead a beautiful woman entered, a woman at least eight feet tall with long, jet-black hair. Immense dark wings exposed themselves above her shoulders, and cascaded down the sides of her body.

I was stuck in a nightmare. It was like an out-of-body experience where I couldn't break free and wake up. I had to watch it play out, as I had done hundreds of nights since Alex left me and the nightmares began.

She floated to me as I sat by Alex's bed, and she smiled a sincere, joyful smile. I heeded her voiceless call to stand and move away. She needed to get to him, needed to take him home. She gave me one soft slow nod as I backed away. I took a last look at Alex, then closed my eyes, knowing I would wake, and he would already be gone.

I shot up in bed and grabbed hold of my shirt as my chest heaved. Panic like an old friend slid up my spine as I whipped my head back and forth, trying to figure out where I was. The four walls of my new bedroom came into focus in the faint light. A drop of sweat fell down my cheek, and with it some relief. My heart rate eased as I dropped back to the bed.

It was always the same course of events, in the same order. The nightmare was like a replay—a reimagining of what might have happened during Alex's accident.

It started with Alex stopped at a red light, singing along with his favorite country singer, blasting his twangy voice through the car's speakers. His right thumb pounded the beat on the steering wheel as the song came to an end, and he reached to skip to the next one. The light turned green, and without looking around the intersection, he hit the gas, pulling forward as he turned the sound up, oblivious to the eighteen-wheeler barreling through the intersection.

The truck T-boned his black Ford Mustang at full speed.

In a flash, Alex would be in a hospital bed in the trauma unit at Grady in Atlanta.

These trauma unit images stemmed from real life. Alex was barely recognizable after the accident. His face was grossly swollen, black and blue from bruising, and a tube came out of his mouth. His body was mostly covered with a sheet, but wires seemed to poke out all around him, connecting him to machines making strange beeps and thumps.

Also true to life, in the nightmare I cried violently by his body, my flood of tears falling hard onto the fabric covering him. I hoped he'd hear me through the sounds of the machines. I couldn't accept the doctor's diagnosis that said his brain no longer showed any activity.

And then, the angel would come for him.

I threw off my comforter and went to my dresser, needing to see Alex as he *was*, not the image from the hospital. I picked up the picture of us from the last Christmas we'd shared together, tilting it into the glimmer of moonlight seeping in through the blinds. My pregnant belly had yet

SAFE HARBOR

to show, but his hand was fixed to it in the picture, ready for it to pop out and be known. We were both excited at the thought of our new addition. The shock had worn off, and the happy expectancy of starting a new adventure had begun.

I'm sorry we never got to enjoy our new adventure together.

The first time the angel visited my dreams happened the night he died. The car crash had put him in a coma. After five days, his parents decided to take him off life support. Since Alex's parents and I never could seem to see eye-to-eye, my disagreement in this gigantic decision came as no surprise. It didn't matter. I was nine months pregnant with his baby, but we weren't married yet, so I had no say.

I went back to the hotel for a few hours of sleep. I planned to be at the hospital for his last moments early the next morning. I dreamed of the angel coming for him, and woke to my cell phone ringing. I knew what the caller would tell me.

Alex was already gone.

The angel had shown me what happened, and she gave me peace. Now, after hundreds of nights where she entered my nightmare, I didn't feel much peace anymore.

The day Alex died was the worst of my life, but it had given his family and me some relief to know God took him before we pulled the plug. He took his last breath on his terms. In the weeks after his death, I didn't know how I would survive, how I would be a parent without him. But then Willow arrived, and with her came joy again.

The quiet comfort came slowly, bits and pieces at first, in between spells of grief so thick I couldn't get out of bed, when Mom had to be the parent to my baby because I couldn't. During the first four months of Willow's life, Mom undoubtedly changed more diapers than I did.

Mom's coaching and pushing—and according to her, praying—finally worked. Those bits and pieces of joy grew bigger and stronger, until one day, my heart seemed full again ... because of my baby girl.

I put the picture back, behind the other ones of Mom and Dad, Willow, and the one of Mom, Willow, and me together. I always kept Alex's in the back, still not sure how to answer if Willow asked who he was. But the question would come eventually, and I knew I'd be caught totally off guard. I'd destroy Willow's life in yet again another bad decision.

I threw myself back on the bed.

Why now, God? Two nightmares in two weeks? Have I not been punished enough?

The dream became sporadic as my heart mended. Then it grew almost nonexistent. Nightmares had completely stopped eight months ago—until tonight.

I took a deep breath, preparing for the day, and grabbed my cell phone off my side table. The home screen said 6:11 a.m. *Might as well get up.* I turned off the alarm set to 6:15 a.m. and headed to the bathroom, careful not to wake the late sleepers in the house. Willow didn't have to be at preschool until nine. I started the water for a shower and stared at my reflection, my nerves still tingling.

For reasons unknown, Thad crossed my mind.

Yesterday, as I left school, I'd seen his Bronco with the trailer in the parking lot. He'd be on the field, and I was tempted to try and catch a glimpse of him. I didn't want to actually come face-to-face with him, just stare from a distance. I decided that was too risky and got in my car to speed away. But his image had implanted itself, returning in frequent—and unwilling—flashes of memory.

My defenses, once on high alert, were crumbling. And with that admission, I knew exactly why the nightmares had returned.

SAFE HARBOR

Thad threatened the space in my heart, the space I'd dedicated solely to Willow. No one since Alex had swept across my mind the way Thad was beginning to, and I was scared to death.

How is it possible for someone to do this, especially someone I don't know?

I turned on the little radio I kept in the bathroom, a habit since my high school days.

A song about regret and messy life choices, ringing with truth, played through the tiny speakers. I could have written the song. They were not words I wanted to carry into the new day, but a good reminder of my history of hurting and damaging everything in my path. They reinstated my resolve to hold tightly to the walls I'd erected around my heart.

CHAPTER SEVEN

SATURDAY, THREE WEEKS LATER

EVA

"The new field is past this old one?" Mom pointed to the fencing surrounding the top part of the new bleachers.

I chuckled at the disbelief in her voice. "Yes. I haven't made it out here yet. But supposedly they left this dingy sparse green patch of dirt for the Phys. Ed. coaches to use for games like kickball." I squeezed Willow's hand as we walked along with other fans toward Palmer's first scrimmage of the year.

I *was* curious as to what the hype was all about. The newly developed football program was the talk of every lunch in our teachers' lounge, and it was torture to not make disgusted or annoyed faces at them every two minutes.

I'd loved football, even waited for it with anticipation every year. Cheering for Alex with my sideline squad were the best parts of high school. I could never get enough of the screaming fans. Emotions ran buck wild at football games. And I reveled in the chill in the air—how every year, fall would sneak its way in and cause us to layer clothes under our uniforms. Usually by about the fifth game of the season, nature was signaling autumn really *was* on its way.

Once Alex and I got to the University of Georgia, I wasn't good enough to make the University's cheer squad, but

Alex was plenty good enough for college ball. His football career took off at full speed as he quickly earned a starting slotback position by his sophomore year on our sacred SEC team. Sports agents were calling him by his senior year. My love for football went on because of him, though my viewpoint had changed to that of a fan in the stands, watching Alex and our Dawgs play.

We entered through the gates, skirted Palmer's concessions area so Willow wouldn't beg for candy, and stopped at the top of the stands. Concrete bleachers were built into the side of the hill, all cascading down to the ...

"Wow."

"Wow is right." Mom fluttered her hand in front of her, indicating the field. "This is better than most high school stadiums. Certainly the grass is greener."

"It is." We started down the stairs. Willow inched down with me.

Mom got behind us. "I haven't watched football in forever. When's the last time you saw a game—"

Mom couldn't stop her word fast enough because her observation alerted me to mine. This was the first time I'd set foot in a football stadium since I'd lost him. For a moment, my breath was lost, trapped somewhere past my lungs, not making it out of my throat.

The only one who could ever pull me from my instantaneous and overwhelming grief snapped me out of it with her little excited cry.

"Mama, here. Let's sit here."

I jerked my head down to meet her perfect, almond-shaped, blue eyes, grateful for her ability to flood me with joy.

"This is the perfect spot."

Alex, you'd think this place was awesome.

The sports complex was massive. The school's colors of royal blue and black were painted everywhere, along with the Falcon mascot making an appearance on the buildings and even in the middle of the field.

We got settled, and Mom said, "That field is the prettiest green I've ever seen. It almost looks fake. And these bleachers! Way better than those old aluminum things. I just can't believe an anonymous donor paid for this."

"Yeah, I know. Someone is extremely generous. I heard the person bought this land, built the field, and deeded it to the county's school system. Hard to believe. But this school sure needed one, since these kids come from the poorest neighborhoods around."

"Well, I think it's wonderful. Look how many people are filing in to watch the game. How exciting!" Clearly, Mom still loved football.

"Yeah, these boys have something to keep them busy."

"I just wish they had a better mascot. The Palmer Falcons? Who came up with that?"

"Well, it's tougher than some mascots I've heard of. They could have been the Palmer Pelicans." Mom and Willow giggled as I picked through my purse, looking for the sucker I'd promised Willow if she was good. "You know, their coaches are supposed to be phenomenal. The boys in my class pretty much only talk about football right now. Here, Willow." I gave her the sugar-filled treat.

"Ooo, this one has bubble gum. Can I just bite it?"

I wrinkled my nose as she just chuckled. "No, honey, lick it. It'll last longer that way. See if you can lick all the hard part off the sucker before you chew the gum." That would keep her busy for a while.

A female voice yelled out, "Eva!"

I found Stacy in the crowd below where we sat. "Hey, how's it going?" I waved her over.

Stacy navigated through the people and plopped her purse in the row directly below us. "It'd be going great if it weren't so hot." She fanned her face and smiled. "Is this your family?"

"Yes, my mom, Ellen, and my daughter, Willow. Guys, this is Stacy, the math teacher on our team. Her room is right next to mine."

"I've heard so much about y'all." She held out her hand to Mom, her blonde, perfectly curled long hair falling around her shoulders.

Mom took her hand eagerly. "Same here. Thank you for making Eva feel right at home."

"Well, we're just glad she's here. We've had a great first month with our new students, and we've all worked well together."

"Thanks, I agree," I said. "So did you make a promise to our boys you'd come watch them today too?" I'd promised my students I'd come to their first game, their 'Jamboree,' if they made B's or better on their first test. I gave the test the day before the game, so they all went home not knowing their grades. I hoped to be able to catch their eyes on the field. Then, they'd know how well they'd done, and how proud I was of their hard work.

"Oh no. I come to all the home games, no matter what." Stacy answered with a wave of her hand.

"That's really nice of you. Way to make me feel bad," I teased.

"Oh, please. I've got nothing better to do. You've got your hands full." She nodded toward Willow.

"True."

"Though I can't stay long today. I've got some showings set up with a realtor to see some houses."

Mom threw her hands up. "How fun. I love looking at houses. Do you want something to fix up or something move-in ready?"

While Mom continued to talk Stacy's head off, I looked out onto the field, finally taking a moment to look at all the players, searching for any students I recognized with their gear on. They all huddled around a coach on the sidelines, and when they dispersed, he stood up to his full height. My breath hitched, and all rational thought left me as Thad smiled and walked over to another coach, an older black man with his back to us. Thad's long, nearly-black hair hung down underneath a black ball cap, brushing his shoulders. With a Palmer coach's polo tucked into black shorts, he almost looked like a professional. Definitely *not* a beach bum.

Stacy and Mom must have heard my intake of air, because they stopped talking. Stacy turned to follow my gaze. "Oh yeah, girl, he's the real reason I come to the game, if you know what I mean. He's some ex-pro—"

"Eva," Mom said, catching sight of him, "that's Thad."

Willow looked around at all of us, then at the field.

"Wait. Eva, you know him?" Stacy said. "The hottie coach all of us drool over?"

He faced our direction, talking to the other coach. He looked up directly at our little place in the stands as if he could hear us, though I couldn't be sure because his eyes were behind mirrored aviator sunglasses. But I was sure I witnessed a small grin break through his words.

I was still speechless, but Stacy yelled, "Oh my gosh, Eva, he's staring at you."

Around the same time, Mom said, "Yeah, we know him."

I finally broke the stare that was paralyzing me. "Uh, we've met a couple times since we've moved here, but I haven't seen him since school started."

Mom gave me a sideways glance and spoke directly to Stacy. "He saved my granddaughter's life the first day we moved here. He just came out of nowhere. She would've drowned in the ocean if it weren't for him." I almost shushed Mom, but then stopped because she *was* telling the truth. She continued. "And a couple of days later, he jump-started Eva's car. She would've been stranded if he hadn't shown up when he did."

"Oh my gosh, seriously? On top of him being a mentor to these boys, that gorgeous, kind-of- mysterious man is a hero, too? I'm havin' a hot flash." Stacy's southern drawl and face-fanning made an appearance.

I was extremely embarrassed. "Well, we don't know him too well. We're more like acquaintances."

"Oh, no one knows him *well*." Stacy shook her head. "He just showed up in our little town a couple of years ago, around the time the school began the football program. He's been coaching ever since. It's his third season now."

The announcer came over the loudspeaker to signal the start of the game.

"More on this later," Stacy said, wiggling her eyebrows in a gesture reminiscent of Groucho Marx. Then she turned around to take her seat.

Mom nudged me and wiggled hers too.

Willow spoke up. "Mama, I made it to the gum!"

THAD

I pushed the door open from what I called 'the shack,' but what the boys called our field house. People milled around everywhere. Sleepy small southern towns always seemed to show up for things no one else cares about, and I loved it. Even the middle-school practice football games, where we didn't keep score, brought a crowd.

I hiked my bag higher on my shoulder and peered through the slew of people, hoping to see her. She hadn't come to the game for me, but even so, I'd been a jittery mess trying *not* to look back at her during the game.

SAFE HARBOR

"You guys were awesome. I'm proud of all of you."

Her voice sounded just ahead of me, rising above the mob. Folks seemed to part, and there she was, decked out in the school's colors with a black V-neck shirt and bright blue shorts which showed off tan legs. Her hair was pulled into a messy ponytail, and her eyes hid behind sunglasses. I nearly had a heart attack.

She held Willow's hand while she talked to my boys Darren and Joey by the fence. I walked straight over to them.

"Well ... you must've had some of my boys in your class."

Willow yelled, "Thad!"

I put my fist out so she could give me a bump. Eva looked up, shock on her face.

"Hi, yes, I guess I do have some of your players."

Darren and Joey fist-bumped me, and said in unison, "Hey, Coach."

Eva's shock turned to amusement. "They did ... I mean *you all* did terrific."

She put some wisps of hair that had fallen out of her ponytail behind her ear, letting her hand rest on her collarbone like she'd done when I jump-started her battery. I tried not to let my stare last too long on her neck.

"Thank you."

God, why do I love words of affirmation from her so much? She clearly said she didn't want to go on a date.

A female voice called from the concession stand. "Come on, Darren."—his mom. "We gotta be gettin' home."

"Thanks, Coach. 'Bye, Miz Elliott." Both boys trotted off to their families.

And now I knew her last name.

Elliott. Eva Elliott.

"We meet unexpectedly again," I said.

Eva pursed her lips, trying not to laugh. "I guess we do."

The woman, Eva's older twin, seemed to come out of nowhere and said, "Hi, Thad, it's nice to finally meet you. I'm Ellen. Eva's mom."

We shook. "It's very nice to meet you."

She blushed, but said, "Do you teach here too?"

"No, ma'am. For the middle school teams, you just have to pass a background check and get the principal's approval to coach. I guess I'm an unofficial staff member." She nodded, and I found Eva's gaze. "You said you don't date, but is it okay for two, say, *colleagues* employed by the school to get an early dinner? I don't see you being a hot-dog-from-the-concession-stand kind of girl."

"I have a four-year-old. We practically live off hot dogs." She stalled as we got a good laugh, including Willow, who still beamed at me.

Dang, she's adorable.

Finally, Eva said, "Um, I can't, really. I need to get back. We've got dinner already started at home that I need to finish. But—"

Ellen jumped in front of her. "But we'd love to have you come over for dinner."

Eva stammered, "Oh, I'm sure he doesn't want—"

"Actually, that might be—"

"Eva, you ride with Thad to show him the way to our house." Ellen grabbed Willow's hand, already backing away.

I just nodded. Eva's mom didn't seem like the type who took no for an answer.

"Great. We'll see you all in a bit."

Willow waved with excitement, leaving Eva marooned and fidgeting.

"Wow." Eva watched her mom leave. "Did that really just happen?"

"Yup." I held back a smile, running my fingers through my hair to keep it out of my face. "It really did."

SAFE HARBOR

Dad approached us from the shack. "Hey, Son, I'm heading home." He looked at Eva and bowed his head a tad. "Hello, miss."

Dad ... always the gentleman.

"This is Eva."

"Oh, Eva. Right. Nice to meet you. I'm John."

"Hi. You all coach together, correct?"

"Yes," I answered, adding, "but he's also my dad."

Eva's mouth formed an *O*. "Oh. *Oh*. Very nice to meet you, sir."

Dad didn't flinch. We were used to people being confused when they found out I was his son. We didn't exactly look alike. "Call me John, honey."

"Okay." Eva's cheeks flushed.

I gripped Dad's shoulder. "Dad volunteers to help me make these crazy adolescent boys into men. He's a glutton for punishment."

"That's right. Been one almost thirty years now, considering yours was the first team I volunteered to coach and turning you into a man was a *very* long journey."

We laughed. Eva covered her mouth to hide her grin, so shy and nervous it was almost cute, except I didn't want her to be those things around me.

"Okay, Dad. Don't scare her off by telling stories about me just yet."

"Well, Eva, I'll give you some time to get to know him. Then I'll give you the lowdown."

"That sounds fun." Eva smiled this time, showing off dimples that matched Willow's.

"Trust me. Telling stories about him will be fun for me too." Dad met my stare. "See you at home?"

"Yeah, I'll be home after a while. I've been invited to Eva's for dinner. And you know I don't pass up home-cooked meals."

"Oh? Very nice. See you later. And Eva," he looked her in the eyes, "it was nice to meet you too."

"Thanks, and great game, sir. I mean, John," she called out as Dad left.

"Are you ready to ride in my old Bronco?" I drew her attention back and gestured to the parking lot.

"I guess so." Her tiny smile turned my insides to syrup.

EVA

"No ... you didn't?" I barely got out. He was clearly gorgeous and obviously compassionate. He saved my daughter's life, jump-started my battery without hesitation, and coached a seventh-grade football team for fun. But now, I had to add hilarious. My stomach muscles would be sore from the workout they'd gotten on the twenty-five-minute drive home.

"Yes, I did. I told them the next player who yelled 'What?' to me when I called their name meant the whole team had to crabwalk from end zone to end zone."

As I convulsed in laughter, I tried to say, "What ... what made you ... you think of that punishment?"

"I don't know. I tried to come up with a consequence for disrespect that was allowable and wouldn't get me thrown in jail for child abuse. And in elementary school gym class, I always hated that stinkin' crabwalk." He laughed so hard his shoulders shook, causing his forearm muscles to flex as he gripped the steering wheel. "It was really awkward for me, 'cause I was always so big and tall and, at the time, totally uncoordinated. So crabwalking was the first thing that popped in my head." He glanced over, catching me staring. Although I was still laughing, I looked away, and he went on, "You should have seen them all, my little crabs, scurrying in the grass. The football boys only messed up twice. Two times of crabwalking the length of the field, and now all I hear is 'Yes, sir.'"

I leaned my head back on the headrest, stopping to take a deep breath and regain my composure. "I would have loved to see it. And now, I've got some ammunition to use against Darren and Joey if I need it."

"Definitely."

We approached my road. "Take the next left. We're almost there."

He cleared his throat and turned. "I, uh, know this area well. It's a great place you picked. Or I mean your mom picked."

"Thanks. We love it. Right here, fourth house on the left."

He pulled in the driveway and jumped out of the truck fast, causing me to pause for a beat, but I opened my door. He rounded the back of the Bronco and braced the edge of the door. "Wait," he said. "I would've gotten that for you."

He was so close, I was trapped with his face right in my sightline since he was so tall. Instantly nervous about how fast my heart pounded, I stuttered, "You don't have to open the door for me."

"Well, I think I *do* have to, but I also want to." He grabbed my hands, helping me jump down from the lifted Bronco.

"Thanks." I moved toward the gate quickly to put some distance between us. "I think I hear them by the pool."

He followed me through the gate on the side of the house.

"Mama, Thad, I'm swimming." Willow released her hold on the side of the pool and doggie-paddled to the stairs. Only a few feet but great progress, especially after only a few lessons. At the stairs, she rose up and beamed.

I laughed. "You're doing great. You couldn't wait until after dinner, huh?"

She grunted. "No way. It's too hot." She was right. Halfway into September, and it was still hot enough to get in the pool. "Gramma won't get in because she's got to cook, she says, but will you? Thad, will you get in?"

Mom smiled, showing all her pearly whites. She knew she was off the hook. Thad looked down at his clothes, the same outfit from the game, only now he'd left his shirt untucked and wore flip flops.

But he kicked those off. "Well, Willow, it *is* really hot out here. In fact," he ripped the belt out from its loops and tossed it in a pool chair, "I don't think I've cooled off yet since the football game, and you know"—he squinted at her as he grabbed the edges of his polo—"I can't pass up a chance to go swimming." He ripped his shirt over his head, tossing it too in the chair before he crashed with a cannonball into the deep end.

Willow screeched, "Yeah!"

Mom and I dropped our jaws before howling in laughter with Willow. He burst out from under the water roughly shaking his hair out of his face, then he treaded water to Willow.

"You're crazy." I stood at the edge of the water.

"I never pass up any opportunity to get in the water. I told you that on the day we met." He flashed his killer smile. He *did* say that right after he saved Willow's life. "Plus, my shorts are made for both swim and land." He cocked his head at Willow. "You know, in case I decide I need to cool off."

"Well, okay."

He's off his rocker.

I turned to my mother. "Mom, I know the roast is ready, but I'll go whip up some cornbread."

Thad sat down next to Willow on the pool's stairs, looking pleased at the sound of roast and cornbread. He gave a thumbs-up to her.

"No, honey. I'll finish up dinner. It won't take me long. You go swimming with these kids." She winked at Willow and Thad.

"Yeah, Mama, go get your bathing suit on."

"Yeah, come on in," Thad chimed in.

"Oh—"

Each set of eyes desperately tried to talk me into it. Mom's and Willow's stirred a sense of home and safety. Oddly, Thad's stirred up those same emotions ... home ... safety ... which was insane, but felt good. "Oh, okay. I'll be right back."

Willow gave Thad a high-five before I slipped inside through the sliding glass door.

THAD

"You moved here four years ago?" Ellen asked, as we sat around a square table by the pool—underneath an umbrella to escape the setting sun's glare.

"Yes, ma'am, it's been a little over four years now," I said, between bites of pot roast and potatoes and carrots and onions and cornbread. I savored each one, thankful I'd put my shirt back on. I would have embarrassed myself with the way my stomach poked out.

"You started coaching right after the field was done, and you've been there this whole time?"

"Yes, ma'am."

"Thad, please, *please* stop calling me ma'am." She blushed and swatted my hand. "Ellen is just fine. But I must say, I don't know how you and Eva do it. Deal with seventh graders all the time, I mean."

"See, Mom? I'm not the only one who enjoys that age. They can be really great. Right?" She looked at me straight, and her eyes seemed to brighten as I stared back across the table. I wished she were closer, but least the distance between us came with a perk. I got to watch her hair dry in the evening air, and see her makeup-free face with little bits of mascara smoking up around her eyes.

She tilted her head, widening her eyes to cue me to respond.

What was the question?

"Oh. Uh, right. In seventh grade, they're still teachable. You've still got a chance at getting through to them, changing their bad habits in ways for the better. High schoolers are the ones I couldn't handle."

"Exactly. I agree." Eva nodded like we were a team.

Ellen picked up the cornbread basket and raised it to me. "Thad, you ready for more?"

"If I tried to fit any more in my stomach, I'd explode, but thank you. Three helpings are enough. I should probably get going soon." I placed my fork on the plate and scooted it forward. "But truly, this was the best meal I've had in years."

"You've got to be kidding." Ellen slapped the table lightly with her hands. "It's a crockpot meal."

"You haven't seen the emptiness of my fridge."

Ellen stood up and gathered the plates. "Well, you're welcome to dinner here any time."

Willow said, "Yeah, come back please. You teach me how to swim way better than Mama."

Eva scoffed, pretending to be hurt as Willow giggled. She was such a cute and funny kid, already understanding how to tease her mom.

"Just kidding, Mama. You're perfect."

Eva got up to help her mom, stacking the plates and silverware. I followed her and piled on the napkins.

"Willow, you're sweet, but I don't know about that."

I couldn't help myself. "I don't know. She may be right."

Eva's eyes shot up to me, though what emotion crossed her face I couldn't decipher. Her brown irises sparkled with gold flecks for a moment. Then apprehension settled into them and extinguished the fire.

Ellen bit her lip watching Eva, and then, she broke the silence. "Willow, let's take this load inside the kitchen. We've gotta get ready for bed. I wonder what's on TV we can fall asleep to tonight?"

"Thank you, Mom. I'll clean up."

Ellen grinned while telling Willow, "Say goodnight to Thad."

Willow jumped up, threw her tiny arms around my waist, which was still wrapped in a soaking wet towel. "'Night, Thad. I had fun."

I patted her shoulder. "Me too, kid."

Willow let go just as fast as she'd latched on. Eva watched Willow grab her own little plate and follow Ellen inside.

"'Night, Thad." Ellen closed the sliding glass door.

"Good night," I called to Ellen before I gave Eva my full attention, wishing I hadn't already been here for a couple of hours, wishing I could come up with a plan to stay longer. "Here, let me help you clean up."

"No, no, it's fine. I'll do this in a bit. Let me walk you out."

It was clearly time to go.

"Okay, sure." I tossed my wet towel over the back of the chair and rushed to open the gate of the fence for her. "Thanks for this afternoon. You know, as a *colleague*, it was great getting to know your family."

Eva looked over her shoulder, squinted her eyes and pursed her lips, letting a hint of a smile poke through. "Yes, you seem to already have both of them wrapped around your finger."

"Maybe." We got to my truck, and I leaned against the door. I wasn't ready to go just yet. "So, colleague, can I see you tomorrow?"

Eva had allowed herself to get close. Her hands were clasped behind her back, and she stood in a passive stance, rocking slightly back and forth. She finally found my eyes. I leaned down a bit, afraid her neck might pop. She sighed. "I don't date, remember."

Her voice pleased me, because I could hear the hesitation to simply say yes and break her rule. "Oh, I remember you saying that. I just don't remember you telling me to quit asking."

She snorted out a little breath through her nose and gave her head a shake.

"Listen, let's pretend I'm just repaying you for a terrific afternoon and a hearty dinner. That's all."

She bit her bottom lip, obviously thinking. We were caught up in one another's eyes. I could tell she felt the pull between us, the desire vibrating the space from her to me.

I went for it. "Just meet me on the beach tomorrow evening at six-thirty." I showed my wide grin. "Please."

She inhaled. "Okay." She bobbed her head up and down gently. "Six-thirty."

I pushed off the car door and quickly brushed my thumb down her cheek. "Thank you."

She backed away as I got in and started up my Bronco. I rolled down the window.

"Oh, and wear your swimsuit." I didn't give her a chance to protest. Releasing the emergency brake and shifting into reverse, I gave her one last look before throwing my hand up to wave and back out of her drive.

All while my thumb still throbbed from where I'd touched her beautiful face.

EVA

"Did you guys find anything on TV?" I walked into Mom's room.

She put her finger to her mouth in a *shhh* gesture and pointed the remote at the TV to turn it down. Willow was passed out in her favorite position, looking like a starfish on her belly smack in the middle of Mom's king size bed.

"She didn't last long," I whispered.

"No. I think by the time I got her PJs on, she was delirious. Mumbling the cutest things about swimming and surfing and her new school."

I climbed in beside Willow, brushing her hair out of her face and away from her cheek, remembering the brush of Thad's thumb on my own face just twenty minutes before. His touch had sent a release of endorphins through me, ones dormant for so long I'd forgotten what they felt like.

Sheer will forced me out of my daydream. "Well, the kitchen's all clean."

"Thanks, honey. I'd call this afternoon a success." Mom winked. "I really like him. He's caring, funny, gorgeous, and great with Willow."

I knew this was coming.

"Mom, I know, and I ... I agree actually, but you *know* how I feel. I don't want to give anyone or anything the attention I feel Willow should be getting from me. It's unfair to her. She only has one parent, so I've got to make up for both. Plus the idea of losing someone again is not worth the risk."

Mom huffed, ready to put in her two cents for the umpteenth time. "Honey, I hear what you're saying, and I know your motives are pure, but you'll never hear of a child who didn't benefit from growing up around adults who love each other. It won't hurt Willow for you to move on, find love, get married, have more kids"—she gave me a pointed look—"which means more grandkids for me."

I crossed my arms, leaning back fully on the pillows.

"I mean, what if he's *the one*?" She turned a little more my way, as I tried to hold my ground. "Honey, I hate to even say this, but what if Alex was never the one for you? We know God's plan for you and him included having this precious one right here. But what if that was his purpose, and once it was finished, God called him home? What if Thad, or another man down the road for that matter, is *the one* you're to be with here on earth?"

I gave her a sideways glance, which only made her chuckle.

"I mean, really. Would it be so bad to spend life with someone like Thad? He's just so sweet, and oooh-*whee*, he's a fine specimen."

"Mom, stop, please. You already flirted with him all night. Now stop marrying me off to him in your head." We broke out into laughter. Willow turned her head to face the opposite direction and we froze.

When it was safe, Mom whispered, "I'm taking Willow to church tomorrow. I think we're going to try the tiny one on the island. You're welcome to come."

"Nah," I whispered back. "I've got to get ready for Monday." An excuse, and she knew it, but she didn't push more. "Um, Thad asked me to meet him at the beach tomorrow evening ... but I'm gonna find a way to back out." I'd thought through possible reasons while scrubbing dishes.

"What? No way. You need to go."

"I don't know."

"Eva, you haven't gone out to do much of anything since Willow was born. You need to get out more. At least go and make a friend."

I chewed the insides of my cheeks. "Can you keep Willow?"

"Of course. I moved us all under one roof so it's easier for you to have a life, to have more friends than just a preschooler and an AARP member."

I chuckled. "Okay." I carefully got up off the bed. "I'll take Willow to her room."

Mom yelled a bit too loud, "No. Just let her sleep with me. I still don't like sleeping all by myself."

I frowned, acknowledging even after all this time, her turmoil at living without my dad. As I turned to leave, Mom said, "You know—"

She stopped, and I looked back at her.

"I saw you laugh more tonight than I've seen in years."

CHAPTER EIGHT

SUNDAY

THAD

I was so nervous I couldn't even grip the cords of the ten-by-ten tent I'd brought down to the beach. I felt like a teenager watching his prom date come down the stairs.

I replayed the night before over and over. The stolen glances. The small, sweet smiles. The laughter during the pool time and the family dinner.

None of my exes, of which there were too many, had ever fit into my future. Not even Becca, and I'd asked her to marry me. I couldn't picture a life with any of them. Never saw far into the future, past the party lifestyle with few responsibilities. But Eva? She was already there, living the future I'd begun to long for—the family. The beauty of life in the simple moments. The legacy. The love.

God had done an overhaul on my heart in the last five years. Seeing women through God's eyes changed me. I'd never believed in love at first sight, but now, as I waited for Eva on the same spot where I first laid eyes on her, I was thinking I'd been wrong.

I saw in her everything I missed about Mom—unwavering love, devotion, satisfaction in family. I even liked her stubbornness.

Which is why the hope, the excitement, the nervousness, all made sense.

I checked the last of the cords just as Eva emerged from the grove of trees and island brush surrounding the beach walk. She threw her hand up to her face, shading her eyes against the sun, and found me. She gave me a wave and a smile, then bent to undo her sandals to walk barefoot.

I willed my nerves to retreat as she strolled over so I wouldn't be sick in the sand, and I went to meet her. She wore a deep purple halter-style cover up, but I could see a purple bathing suit strap around her neck. Her slender legs took the spotlight they deserved. Her chestnut-colored hair was pulled back into a tight bun almost on top of her head, but already the wind was tugging strands out of its hold.

When she was close enough, she said, "Hi."

"Hey."

"The beach is empty. There's not a soul in sight."

"It gets like this fast in the off-season. Especially since it's mostly residential on this end of Moanna and not packed full of hotels and condos." I caught her gaze. "I love it."

"I'm sure." She paused outside the tent. "My, my, what's all this?"

A smile touched her lips, and my jitters retreated, settling back into their caves. I moved to the opposite side of Mom's antique quilt. "Dinner."

She checked over the food I'd laid out, then she saw my tandem paddle board just off to the side. She put her hand on her hip, though she was still showing off her dimples. "Now, this looks like a date."

I scoffed. "What? No, this is just a colleague repaying a colleague for feeding him so heartily. Anyone who puts delicious food in my belly"—I gave it a little pat—"must get paid back on that debt."

"Ah ..."

SAFE HARBOR

I indicated the quilt with my hand. "Take a seat."

She tossed her sandals in the sand and sat down with her legs to one side. "So they get paid back with food in their belly too?"

"Exactly." I sat, positioning myself as close as possible to her. "The way I figure, last night's amazing dinner leaves me with three debts. So after tonight, I'll *have* to stop by sometime soon and bring dinner to your house to repay your mom."

Eva laughed. "Oh, okay."

"And then there's Willow. Doesn't seem fair to repay a four-year-old with lasagna or something equally tasty to us, but maybe not to her. I hate to say this, but I'll probably have to take her out for ice cream sometime soon. It's only fair."

"Thad, you seem to know the way to Willow's heart." I replayed the way she said my name as she continued, "All kids love ice cream."

"Then it's a plan?"

She blushed. "Yeah, it's a plan."

I wanted to pump my arm back and forth like a kid who just aced his exam. Even though she *wasn't* going to date me, she'd just agreed to see me two more times.

I sat up a little straighter. "Let's eat."

She leaned over to take a better look at everything. "It looks and smells wonderful."

"I hope it is." I opened the containers, and she helped by grabbing spoons to dish out the food. "I wasn't lying when I said my fridge is bare. Dad and I don't, or I should say *can't*, cook. I ordered it from the diner just over the bridge. All southern comfort foods—fried chicken, biscuits, mashed potatoes with gravy, green beans, and my personal favorite, apple pie."

"Awesome." Eva sounded excited as we picked up our plates.

I loved when she allowed her guard to come down just a little, like last night when she came back to join us in the pool. Willow and I were practicing swimming from the shallow end back to the stairs. For whatever reason, Willow took to me as a teacher, and she listened as I told her to kick hard and keep her belly up. When Eva came back, Willow waved me over to the stairs and whispered, "Let's get her in the pool."

I had sat down next to her. "How?"

Willow had whispered back, "Push her in."

She giggled, and I was thinking how *that* would go over when Eva said, "I know what you all are doing." Willow and I had looked at one another as if we'd been caught. Eva just laughed and yelled, "And I'm not giving you the chance!" before she did a cannon ball. The splash was huge, and Willow convulsed in laughter, so hard I thought she was going pass out from lack of oxygen.

Eva's wall had come tumbling down, just like it was doing again as she leaned back onto her hand, meaning she inched closer to me, and she picked up her fork for a bite. With effort, I stopped watching and took my own bite.

After we chewed in silence a few minutes, she said, "Your dad seems great. How cool that must be to coach with him now."

"He *is* pretty awesome. Always been the one I looked up to, so coaching with him is a dream. Really, he should be the head coach, not me."

"So he coached you when you were little?"

I swallowed a bite of mashed potatoes before I answered. "Oh, yeah. He had me running drills by the time I was four. Willow's age, I guess. Of course, I loved every minute, running around as fast as I could while I was hanging with my dad. Playing football gave me some of the best days of my life."

"I used to love football too."

"You say 'used to.' Not a fan anymore?"

She tilted her head and bit her lip. "More like football reminds me of someone who's really hard for me to think about, so I've just put distance there."

Great. She doesn't like football. Not looking good for me.

"But yesterday was the first football game I'd seen since before Willow was born, and I have to admit I did get caught up in the excitement."

Maybe there's hope.

"Yeah, nothing beats the smells and sounds of a football game." I picked up a biscuit, handed it to her, and snagged one for myself.

"Thanks." She covered her mouth as she took a bite. "And very true." After she finished chewing, she added, "I always loved the atmosphere of the games. Cheering in high school, then being a crazy fan at UGA with face paint and all."

My eyes widened. "Okay, I have to see pictures of you as a cheerleader and with full-on fan face paint. Tell your mom to break out the photo albums."

Eva shook her head in defiance. "Yeah, right. You first. You tell *your* dad to get out the photos from your peewee football days, and maybe, just *maybe*, I'll open mine."

We got caught up in each other's eyes for a beat. Eva broke it first.

"Speaking of your dad, how'd you get ... I mean, you don't really favor each other ..." She waved her hand. "Never mind, it's a silly question."

"What? My five-feet-nine-inch Denzel Washington-look-alike dad doesn't look like he's from Hawaii like me, all six feet four inches of me?" Eva's mouth dropped open, and she took a deep breath. Before she could say anything, I jumped in. "I'm joking. We're used to it. I'm adopted."

Eva let out the breath she'd been holding. "Oh, I see. That's wonderful."

"Yeah, it is. Mom and Dad always said my arrival showed God's faithfulness. They'd been trying to get pregnant for years. They were both teachers. They retired two years before Mom passed. And well, as you know, teachers don't make enough money, especially during their first years."

Eva snorted her agreement.

"Right? So after five years, they'd discussed adoption many times, but could never figure out a way to afford it. They prayed and prayed for a baby, and also prayed that if they were not going to be parents, then for God to take the desire away. Both of them felt God wanted them to be parents. And in fact, Mom's old college roommate opened an adoption agency. They had the connections, just not the money. They filled out all the paperwork, dealt with the in-home visits, everything they could do before any major money was required. They decided to wait for God to do his thing."

I watched the waves crash to the shoreline, smiling as I imagined Mom with her arms crossed over her chest in defiance and, at the same time, praying to God, telling him she'd be patient. I had seen her same "patience" stance many times growing up.

Eva leaned in farther, forgetting her food.

"Around this time, Dad's mom had gotten really sick with lung cancer and passed away pretty quickly." Eva's hand went over her heart. "Anyway, Dad was still young and hadn't paid much attention to my grandmother's finances, but he found out when his dad had passed, his life insurance paid off my grandmother's house. So, Dad, being the only child, was able to sell the house and make a profit."

Eva gasped, maybe already knowing where my story headed.

I nodded. "My parents needed thirty thousand dollars to adopt a baby. After everything was settled—the funeral, and a couple of small debts of my grandmother's—guess how much was left?" Eva just smiled. "Yup, thirty thousand dollars. With the money, along with Mom's friend moving them up the waiting list, they brought me home about five months later."

"Wow, what an amazing story. You were meant for them."

"I was. Dad used to say all the time when I was in high school sassin' him, 'Son, you're proof of God's provision and faithfulness.' Then he'd add, 'I'm gonna let that sass pass one time. But only once.' He said that phrase way more than once over the years, but I knew not to push him too far after he'd uttered those words. It would usually put me in my place. *Usually.*"

She laughed and brushed away a loose wisp of hair, leaving her hand loosely on her chest by her collarbone like she always did. She watched me with a tenderness I hadn't seen before. "You know, I can see the resemblance between you and your dad more clearly now."

I moved toward her, my heart pulling it along, the desire strumming through me so strong my muscles tensed with each inch closer to her lips. A moment before my mouth would have made it to hers, she jerked away.

I froze, hoping her walls hadn't built back up in mere seconds because I'd lost physical control.

"How long have you been surfing?"

EVA

His lips approached mine too fast. I'd looked over to see a super long board, and blurted out the question.

"Uh, I guess it's been at least ten years now." He sounded like he wasn't angry with me for completely dissing his moves.

I chanced a glance his way, and he was smiling. I asked, "That long?"

"Yeah, I've been all over—Australia, Spain, Hawaii, Fiji, El Salvador, South Africa—and every spot in California there is. I searched the top ten surf spots and went to every one. I couldn't surf some of the breaks, like Teahupo'o Tahiti. I wasn't good enough to attempt it, but I loved watching the surfers who *could* ride there."

"Oh wow, I'm jealous. How'd you afford ... I mean, how'd you get to do ...?"

Why can't I stop asking dumb questions where I put my foot in my mouth?

I resisted the urge to throw my head into my hands. Again, he saved the day, ushering me out of my ignorance and stupidity.

"Are you asking how a surf instructor and middle-school football coach gets to travel the world?"

I bit my lip and squinted one eye, internally nodding.

He chuckled. "Truth is, I'm ... I'm retired now." He sounded like he was trying out that excuse for the first time.

"Retired? How old are you?"

"Thirty-three. Turning thirty-four in December."

"Huh." Only eight years older than me. How was he already retired?

"But just so you know, that is not a surfboard."

"It isn't?"

"No, ma'am. *That*"—he pointed to the super long board—"is a paddleboard." There were paddles next to it in the sand.

"Oh yeah, a paddle board. Obviously I've never been on one."

SAFE HARBOR

"Good day for a first. Are you finished eating and ready to get wet? We can save the pie for later."

My eyes bugged, but I did manage to help pack up the food, definitely not hungry anymore. "The food was wonderful, thank you. Um, aren't we supposed to wait awhile after we eat before we get into the water?"

He scrambled up off the blanket. "I think that's an old wives' tale. C'mon." He grabbed my hand, pulled me up, and dragged me over to the board. Admittedly, I was starting to want to follow him anywhere, especially when his hand held mine. Except for maybe the water ... the ocean ... full of scary things.

He let go of my hand and reached over his head to grab the back collar of his T-shirt. As he ripped it off, he said, "It's a tandem board, wider than a normal paddleboard, and really long to give better balance." He tossed the tee on the blanket. "It's designed for more than one person. It's fun, I promise."

As he raved about paddleboarding, I sat there, stunned, with his tightly defined abs inches away, pretty much staring me in the face since he was a foot taller than me. "Um ... I'm not sure ... in the water with you ..."

He leaned down to look closer into my eyes, a smirk plastered on his face, and waited for me to spit out some coherent words.

I inhaled deeply. "I get nervous in the ocean, and not just because of what happened with Willow. It's so big."

"Well, pretend I'm your instructor, and you're my student. Trust me, I'm never going to put one of my students in a bad spot. Face your fear. Bring it under your control, so it can't debilitate you anymore."

His eyebrows went up, waiting for my answer. His caramel eyes sought out my prickly places, bringing them under *his* control.

"Okay."

Trying not to look sheepish, I dropped my cover-up onto the sand. Since Willow's birth and the pregnancy stretch marks which now lined my stomach underneath my belly button, I wore only one-piece swimsuits. Surely it would be better for paddleboarding, right?

Before I backed out, he bent down to pick up the paddles and handed them over. He heaved the ridiculously long board up, gripped it to one side of his body and put his extra hand on my shoulder softly.

"I won't let anything happen to you. Plus, you're an islander now. You've gotta see the island from the best viewpoint." He waved toward the water and his eyes stared out past the waves. "And it's right out there."

He meant what he said. He'd protect me, and I felt safe. "Let's do it."

He winked, drawing my attention to the sexy battle scar over his right eye, and we took off to the waves.

CHAPTER NINE

THAD

"I think you've finally got it."

"You're just saying that because we—well, I—haven't fallen off in, oh, probably four minutes."

"Okay, true, but it's a start. And you're having fun, aren't you? Best viewpoint around."

"Yes, I'll agree with you there." She chanced a look to her right, back at the shoreline maybe sixty yards away. We were out past the breaks of the waves, where the ocean was smoother and glistened like glass. "The sun setting over the trees is beautiful from here. You can see it better for sure."

"Yeah." I looked down at my Apple watch. "The sun sets at seven forty-nine tonight. Just about fourteen minutes from now."

"How do you know when it sets?" She tried to glimpse me from over her shoulder. Her movements were too quick, and she struggled to regain her balance. Too late. "Oh ... oh ..." As she tumbled into the water, she let out a cry. "No!"

Now I wobbled too, so I jumped in after her. Easier to get wet than to struggle in front of her.

When my head broke the surface, she was laughing. She wiped her eyes and cried, "We were doing so good."

"I know. C'mon, we'll just sit now." I snatched up the paddles floating next to us and latched them onto the board to keep them from getting away, then propelled myself onto the extra-long, no-skid surface. *I knew this specialty board would come in handy one day.* Once I'd straddled it, I held out my hand to her. "C'mon up." She slid hers into mine, and I tugged her onto the board.

"Good thing you have this—what is it? Tandem board?" I nodded, proud she remembered its name. "Maybe I won't make us fall in while we're just sitting here." She righted herself, facing me with her legs dangling in the water. For a beat, we were quiet and still. Everything about her urged me to draw closer—her hair, now fallen, draped over her shoulders and dripping saltwater down her chest, her cheeks rosy from the late afternoon sun, her delicate jawline, her full lips—they all begged to be touched, my fingers longing to make it happen.

She blinked, then studied the board. "Thank you for today. I would have never gotten on this thing if it wasn't for you. I'm not much of a risk-taker ... at least not any more."

"You're welcome." I reached out and caressed her fingers as they traced the pattern of the artwork on the board.

She took a breath, stilling her hand and allowing me to hold it.

"It's just—with Willow, I'm the only parent she's got, and it makes me crazy protective, I guess. Over me, over what I do, over who I spend time with."

Ah, so that's why you don't date.

"I understand. Willow's dad's not in the picture?"

She shook her head. "No. I mean he would be." Her eyes found the water, where the ocean met the sky. "Willow's dad passed away right before she was born."

Oh.

SAFE HARBOR

I sighed. No words of wisdom came, but I gently turned her hand over, gripping it in mine, and rubbed circles into her palm. She allowed me to for a moment, studying, watching our hands together. Mine, huge and calloused. Hers, small and delicate.

She sighed and pulled her hand away. "So isn't this where Jaws eats us, at least our feet, and we topple into the water, never to be found again?"

I let laughter escape toward the dusky sky. "I can assure you Jaws would go after my meaty leg first before he'd test out your dainty one."

She dropped her mouth. "Are you sure? Isn't it cliché to go after the damsel in distress?" She put the back of her hand up to her forehead and contorted her face into a melodramatic panic-stricken one.

"You do that face well." I applauded, and she swatted at my shoulder, causing us to teeter. She leaned forward quickly and grabbed hold of both edges of the board to regain her balance.

I saw her gaze go to my knee. She reached her fingers out to my thick three-inch scar there and traced its length. "Where'd you get this? It looks painful." Her words and touch were so gentle my insides stirred.

"I had knee surgery years ago. Twice, actually."

Seeing concern flood her features was worth every bit of torture her touch caused. She leaned in and rested her fingers over my scar. "Does it still hurt? Your knee?"

I leaned forward too, and covered her hand with mine. "Not when you're touching it."

Her breath hitched as her lips formed a tight line. Her eyes flicked about, but she inched closer instead of away.

I slowly reached up to her face, hovering my hand there, waiting for her gaze to find mine. When it did, the softness there spurred me on. I wove my fingers into her hair at the base of her neck and drew her into a kiss. She closed her eyes. She was going to let me this time.

EVA

Pleasure rushed through me when his hand touched my neck. His lips brushing mine were only a feather at first, almost tickling the tender skin. He withdrew a few centimeters. I licked my lips, tasting the salt from his, and took a long slow inhale, taking in the sweet smell of what must be his shampoo mixed with the ocean air. He was perfectly still, waiting for my cue to continue. My hand moved before my brain registered what it was doing. My fingers entwined in his hair, pulling him back to me. He took a frantic breath before our lips collided, only this time there was a fury behind them, but it only made me want to crawl up closer to him, find a way to crawl inside him. I hadn't been kissed in so long ...

And now Alex's lips aren't the last ones to have touched mine.

The one thought, swooping across my mind, brought me back out of its lust focus and into reality. A reality I didn't want to think about, but it tore through my heart anyway.

"Stop," I cried and pushed him away with a force I'd regret later. My heart accelerated on its way to a panic attack. My breathing came in quick, heavy draws. I closed my eyes, trying to calm down my heart as grief set in.

Really? Oh God, please have mercy and don't let this happen now.

My voice quivered. "This is a mistake. I need to go."

"Eva, I'm sorry. I was out of line. I ... I shouldn't have taken advantage of the moment. It's too soon."

"It will always be too soon, Thad." I sat up straight. "What was your play? Woo me out here? Get me in your bed later?"

"What?" He recoiled. "No. No way. Never."

I rambled, saying things that were likely untrue. "I mean, this nice-guy-all-the-time thing and a romantic dinner—"

"So you do think I'm romantic—"

His smile softened me a fraction. I inhaled, pulling in courage. "I just need to go home. I'm sorry you've wasted your afternoon."

Thad whispered, "This was in no way a wasted afternoon."

The sweetness in his words did bring some light to the darkness shadowing my heart. *How can he be so nice when I was so mean?*

"I'll push us to shore. You paddle with your hands to help me steer."

I nodded, averting my gaze in an effort to hide my tears.

He dove off the board in the easy way only a water baby could, and as he pushed and pulled us to shore, I stayed trapped in the memory of our kiss and in my fake anger with him. He wasn't the problem. I was. I'd never be able to move on, and didn't want to.

Tears trickled. I'd been able to faintly recall Alex's kisses, urgent and strong, but now his touch might be lost forever.

CHAPTER TEN

MONDAY

EVA

"Now we finish our conversation from this morning."

Stacy set her lunch tray on the back table of the teachers' lounge. We'd claimed the spot the first week of school. I sat picking at my sandwich as if I'd already consumed a full meal instead of just beginning one. "Let's review the highlights. He comes to dinner. You said it was amazing. Relaxing, I think you even said"—Stacy used her fingers to make quotations marks—"'it's so easy to be around him.'"

I nodded before dropping my head in my hands.

"*Then* he sets up a beach picnic at sunset, which I'm still jealous of, by the way."

"He was just being nice. Repaying me for dinner."

"Oh, please. Don't be so lame. You know good and well that's a façade."

My lips pinched hard.

She kept on. "He kisses you. You kiss back, then a rush of emotions take over, and you push him away."

"You got it. Add to that the fact I was mean to him, though he didn't deserve it. And that's the recap, *proving* I can't move on." My forehead creased almost painfully. "Which is good, because I shouldn't. It's not good for Willow. She needs and deserves all my attention."

"Whoa, girl, slow your roll. You can't be serious." Stacy's fork hung in mid-air, full of the cafeteria's version of green beans.

Over the past couple of weeks, I'd developed an unexpected fondness for Stacy. She certainly was beautiful, tossing her long blonde hair over her shoulder and batting her blue eyes to get herself into or out of any situation. Being young and single, from a wealthy family in Savannah, and happy in the gym meant she was the polar opposite of me—a plain-Jane, single mom of a four-year-old whose muscles hadn't seen a gym since college.

At first, I didn't see anything we'd have in common. Turned out it didn't matter. She was a fun and fabulous teacher who brought me out of my shell and whittled her way into my life.

"Yes, Stacy, I *am* serious. It's safer for me to be uninvolved. Alex is proof love can be ripped away in the blink of an eye. I can't allow Willow the possibility of the same pain if I were to meet someone, and she got attached, or loved them, and then they disappeared for whatever reason. She's already asked when she's going to see Thad again."

He was a superhero to her. His height and bulk did give off that vibe, and he did save her life ...

"You have to stop. You're twenty-five years old. Did you really think you wouldn't eventually find someone? Wouldn't fall in love again?"

"You sound like my mom."

"Well, good, because if we're both saying it, then there must be some truth to it. Just see what happens. Don't stress about it."

"Well, I'm not dating him. He probably doesn't even want to date me after that fiasco, so it'll be almost impossible for much to happen." Stacy gave me a stern stare that knocked into me the way Mom's always did. "But okay, we'll see what happens."

"Good." She smiled and wiped her mouth. When she set her napkin down, she was back to her old self. "I can't believe you and Mr. Pro Football Player already had your first kiss."

I dropped the chip in my hand. "What?" She cocked her head, so I repeated it. "What did you call him?"

"Uh, Mr. Pro Football Player."

"Why?" My voice came out too loud, and the three other teachers in the room turned to look at me.

"Because he used to play in the NFL." At my bulging eyes, she asked, "You didn't know? I thought I told you Saturday. Wait, I think I started to tell you—"

"He was in the NFL?" My heart pumped harder.

"Yeah, he played somewhere on the other side of the country. I don't know where. We could ask around. Or Google him."

Stacy rambled on as another panic attack threatened.

"Eva, why does that matter? I mean, it's kind of cool."

My back hit the chair hard. "Nothing. Football just reminds me of Alex."

And it hurts my heart too much.

"Alex was actually getting looked at by a couple of agents and NFL teams our senior year, but nothing ever came of it."

Which his parents blamed me for.

His senior year wasn't his best, statistically speaking, and they said my pregnant belly and I caused it by adding extra stress and ruining his chances. I'd wanted to scream a million times at them, *"It takes two to make a baby!"*

"Eva, I'm sorry I threw that on you. And true, I don't know everything about Alex, but doesn't everything have the potential to remind you of him? Maybe it's not a bad thing. It could keep his memory alive, which is great for Willow, but you have to find a way to make new memories too."

I closed my eyes and nodded with clear reluctance.

"Just see what happens, all right?"

"I make no promises." Not until I sorted out what was going on in my heart.

"Oh, Miz Elliott, if there's one thing I've already learned, it's that you are one stubborn woman."

"Thanks." I teased.

"I did *not* mean that as a compliment." She laughed. "C'mon, we got to get to class to be ready for our hoodlums."

Mom came into the kitchen in her PJs, toweling her wet hair.

"Willow's asleep?" she asked.

I sat at the bar top. With the dishwasher running and counters cleaned, I had nothing more with which to busy myself. "She's out. I promised to read two books. She was asleep before I'd made it halfway through the second."

"We're lucky she's such a good sleeper." Mom got a glass down and went to the dispenser in the fridge door.

I felt her stare but kept my focus on Google's homepage, calling to me to type in 'Thad Smith.'

Mom dropped her towel on the counter. After she took a sip and continued her stare down, I finally said, "Go ahead and ask."

"Are you going to tell me what's up, or do I have to guess?"

"I found out some interesting news about Thad." Saying his name helped me type it into the search engine. Finally. I gasped as thousands of hits came up, and plain as

SAFE HARBOR

day, there was Thad's image staring back at me. Definitely younger, and in uniform at an NFL game, showing off his killer smile, his shorter hair, wet with sweat, holding a football helmet in the air.

Mom made her way around the bar to look at my screen.

She sucked in a hard breath too. "Oh my. Click on that."

I was still unable to form words, but I tapped on the article.

Mom leaned in closer and read aloud.

"'Damien Smith, starting tight end for the San Diego Chargers, announced today he will be officially retiring at the end of the season, citing his second torn ACL. This injury happened during the Forty-Niners game last week, when Damien caught a pass and the opposing defensive end hit him low in his knees. He said, 'The injury will not leave me in a position to return ever again to the field in the kind of shape needed to play at the NFL level.' Damien was drafted from his alma mater, the University of Iowa, after his senior year, and hails six seasons in the NFL, all with the Chargers. The head coach of the Chargers said, 'I am saddened by this news. Smith has been a huge asset to the team, and he'll truly be missed.'"

"It's true. He *was* a pro football player."

Of all things.

Mom's tone did not mimic mine. "He used to go by the name Damien, but still, I can't believe we hadn't figured this out yet." Mom talked more to herself than me as she looked around the room, thinking. "If your dad were here, he'd have figured out Thad was a former pro-baller by now. Probably would've known the second he met him. He always knew those ESPN stats or whatever. Oh my gosh." She patted my forearm. "A former pro-footballer." Her gaze found the computer screen again. "When was this article published?"

I scrolled up to the top. "Looks like it's a press release from December ... what, almost six years ago?"

"Yes." Now, she tugged my arm so I would face her. "Is this what's gotten you upset?"

"Well, yeah. I feel like I've been lied to."

She put her hands up in self-defense. "Calm down. He may have his reasons for not discussing his former NFL career. We haven't known him long. Have you ever asked him what he did for a living?"

That question took the air out of me. "Well, no, not exactly. He talked about traveling around to the world's best surfing locations, and I asked how he could afford to do that. He said he was retired."

"Okay, not a lie." She pointed to the screen. Her words only irritated me more. "Give him a chance to explain."

I rubbed the bridge of my nose. "I don't know. There are too many ... factors against us."

Mom let out a very audible sigh. "Eva, ask him about it. See what happens. You don't have to make any decisions today, for goodness sakes."

Once again, Mom's words mirrored Stacy's. She didn't know how utterly disastrous my dinner with him had ended. Best to keep it that way—especially now. I slammed my laptop shut and went to my room for the night.

CHAPTER ELEVEN

THURSDAY

THAD

I left practice early, leaving Dad in charge of conditioning the boys, and rang Eva's doorbell at five-fifteen p.m. on the dot.

This could go really bad.

Worse than Sunday.

It was my fault. I was *not* out for a fling, but I'd royally given her the wrong impression.

Only now, showing up on her doorstep could make me look like a crazy stalker.

Why hadn't I thought of this before?

She might think I was like a guy on a *20/20* episode. Fake façade, true nightmare inside.

After four seconds of no movement behind the door, I put the food bags on the mat and turned to leave, but the deadbolt unlocked. I turned back as Ellen pulled open the door.

"Thad, what a surprise!" She saw the bags. "What's all this?"

I rushed to helped her pick them up. "Mrs. ... I mean, Ellen. I hope I didn't come at a bad time. It's dinner. Unless you've started something already, and then it could be tomorrow's dinner." I laughed, stumbling over my words.

"But—but why?" She looked at me like I had gone bonkers. "What? Why ..."

"I told Eva I was going to bring dinner by for all y'all sometime. For feeding me last Saturday."

"Thad, you did not need to do this."

"I wanted to. I was hoping if I stopped by early enough, I might catch you before you started cooking. Anyway ..."

Stop rambling.

"Here, you've got to take it now." I held out the handles of brown paper bags.

Ellen reached for them. "What have you got in there? It smells wonderful."

"It's Italian, from the little place just before the bridge."

"Thank you. I haven't started anything, so this is perfect." Ellen looked down the hall. "I'm thinking since Eva and Willow didn't come to the door, they must have fallen asleep. They do that sometimes after she gets home from school. You know, just cuddle up together and zonk out. Eva's always exhausted from those crazy kids."

"I'm sure. It's no problem. I can't stay," I lied.

EVA

The doorbell had jolted me out of what my dad would have called "resting his eyes." By the time I'd carefully released my arm from underneath Willow and gone into the hall, Thad's voice sounded in the foyer. I drew up short. I wasn't ready to see him. I didn't know what to say—or even how to understand my feelings.

Thad's kiss stirred longings that had been boxed neatly and put away in the basement of my heart. Finding out he played in the NFL only increased my confusion. Why would an ex-NFL player want to date me anyway?

So I just listened. A mix of sadness and relief bubbled when Thad declined to stay.

But then Mom said, "You don't have her number?"

Mom ... I rolled my eyes. She wasn't going to give up.

Thankfully, Thad said, "No, don't worry about it. I'll ask her for it next time I see her."

"Well, okay." Mom sounded defeated, her matchmaking hopes shattered.

"So, uh, yeah. You all enjoy."

His words hung in the air for a beat before Mom said, her voice perky again, "We definitely will."

"And tell Eva that now two of the debts are repaid." Mom must have questioned him with her eyes, because he added, "She'll know what I mean."

Mom laughed, probably thinking the matchmaking wasn't a total loss. She always said inside jokes are a sign of love. She and Dad had millions of them. "Well, okay, thanks again for dinner. Italian's my favorite."

"I'm glad. See you," Thad said, a second before Mom closed the door.

I pictured him walking away, his broad shoulders taking up the whole stone walkway as he went back to the Bronco.

"You're in the hall, aren't you?" Mom asked.

Busted.

I stepped around the corner to face her. "Yes ..."

"I could sense you were there, but I also knew since you hadn't made an appearance, maybe you didn't want to." She had the food bags in one hand and the other on her hip.

"Mom, I didn't know what to say."

"Eva, just try, okay? Try to allow someone other than Willow and maybe me in, someone who could possibly make you happy. Just ... try? He's so wonderful."

"Yeah. He is." I risked saying it out loud. "But I don't date, and trust me, after Sunday—I don't want to go into it—he's just being nice. Extra nice."

Mom studied me. "Hmm. Well, at least you admit he's nice."

I huffed loudly.

"And what does he mean by 'two debts have been repaid'?"

Of course she'd want to understand the inside joke.

"I thought he was joking around, but I guess he meant it. He said he owed all three of us for Saturday night's dinner." Mom started to say something, but I waved her off. "I know, I know, but he's obviously serious." I pointed to the bags. "Sunday evening, he repaid my debt—tonight was yours, and now he owes Willow ice cream." Mom laughed, and so did I. "I think it was his way to get me to agree to see him again. But that was before I ran away"—after his super-luscious kiss in the middle of the ocean—"and, uh, found out he played pro football."

Mom *tsk*ed. "Well, he has to, since you won't agree to go on a date with him. C'mon, let's warm up this food."

She turned, and I followed her into the kitchen, wondering if I had already betrayed my pledge and released the emotions from their box in the basement of my heart.

CHAPTER TWELVE

Friday

Eva

"Like, you know he'll be at the pep rally." Across the teachers' lounge table, Stacy paused, her taco hanging in midair. "And there are no bad seats in our fancy stadium, so you'll definitely get a good look at him. Maybe even come face-to-face, depending on where our students sit."

Stacy took a bite of her taco, then laughed behind her napkin at my clear annoyance.

I shrugged. "At least the pep rally takes the place of our last-period classes. That's a plus."

"*Always* a plus. Now we've got to make it through another hour and a half of them jumping off the walls."

"They're always crazy on Fridays, so this doesn't help."

"That's an understatement."

"Are you planning on talking to him? Or are you just gonna avoid him like the plague?"

"The plague has been working." She deadpanned me, so I added, "I don't know what to say, but no, I wouldn't avoid him. He's too ..."

Perfect.

"He's too sweet," I said. "I feel so stupid."

Stacy finished chewing another bite. I pushed my half-full lunch tray away. My stomach was telling me not to eat anything else, and if my nerves were already shot, they'd be ridiculous when I stepped into the football stadium.

"Hmm, you have a wonderful weekend with him, find out he played in the NFL, and then he stops by your house a couple of days later, toting dinner. What's there to feel stupid about?"

"Well, I made a fool of myself after we kissed ..."

"In the middle of the ocean at sunset," Stacy added.

"Yes," I said with a full-on sarcastic edge, "and when he shows up at my house with dinner, I can't even face him."

"Well, I'm just glad you don't seem as upset about the NFL thing."

"Yeah, but it'll never work. I'm a single mom."

"Girl, I know you like him. You can make all the excuses you want, but you *do* like him. So put on your big-girl panties and stand up tall when you walk into that stadium. *If* you get the opportunity to talk to him, all you have to do is say thank you for dinner. *Both* of them. And say, 'by the way, can you please admit you played in the NFL?' And when he does, you're golden."

"You're right." I placed my plastic fork and napkin on the tray and pushed my chair back to stand. "I should just be confident. Not date him like everyone seems to want. But be friends. A guy and a girl can be friends."

"Umm, we'll go with that for now if it gets you both talking again. And yes." Stacy stood too. "Be confident like him. If anyone wears confidence like a second skin, it's him. You do the same."

"Got it." I nodded as we turned to exit the teachers' lounge. Our kids would be arriving in the classrooms soon.

Stacy winked. "You've got this."

SAFE HARBOR

THAD

The stadium speakers blared "We Will Rock You" so loud the beat thudded along with my heart, and I couldn't help but bob my head to the music. I'd taken up my normal position on the field and watched the seventh-grade classes file into the stands. Eva would be somewhere among them.

"I see you looking for her, Hot Shot," Mike yelled over the music. He gave my shoulder a hard slap.

I hadn't seen my friend—the eighth-grade head coach—approach. I matched his volume level, thankful no one else but Dad was close by. "Are you ever going to quit with the Hot Shot stuff?" I ignored his comment about Eva.

"Nope. Too much fun. I keep wondering why more people don't give you a hard time about it. You must keep them confused with the surfer dude look you've got going now."

I crossed my arms. "Ha. Ha. At least I've got *some* kind of look going."

He crossed his arms too. "Hey, I've got a look. It's called 'smiling Jason Statham without the kick-butt capabilities.'"

I chuckled. He wasn't too far off. He did resemble Jason Statham. He *was* on the shorter side, almost bald, with tight muscles, only he smiled constantly and almost assuredly couldn't kick and punch like the action star.

"You know, Hot Shot ..." He let those words hang for a beat. "Last week when our small group came to your place for a workday on the site of the new camp, I couldn't help thinking you're eventually gonna have to come clean about ... well, everything, I guess. Your career ..." He cocked his head to one side. "And your donation of the field to the school."

"Shhh. I know."

Toward the middle of our first season, coaching what was then a mixed seventh- and eighth-grade team, Mike had asked me if I were the Damien Smith who played for the San Diego Chargers. Up until that time, no one had come out and asked. I'd guessed they either assumed the rumor was false, or it was true, and they just didn't care. A few weeks later, Mike had gotten the nerve to also ask about the very field we stood on. The fact he'd kept my secret and my past quiet for so long secured our friendship, and he was now my closest friend.

I took a deep breath. "Yeah, well, maybe it's time people knew."

I saw her then, walking in line, heading to the middle of the stands. She caught my eyes briefly and gave me a sweet smile with a tip of her head and a small wave. She was so tiny, I could have mistaken her for one of the students. I smiled and waved back.

Mike's stare was tangible. I shifted my gaze around to him. He smiled. Obnoxiously.

"Maybe it *is* time. It'd be nice to call you Hot Shot openly."

"You, my friend, are about to get put into a headlock."

He laughed as the music lowered until it was barely audible. He held up the mic in his hand. "Nope. It's showtime. You ready to get dunked?" He backed away and clicked the button on his mic.

"We'll see. Are *you* ready?"

His wicked smile teased before he faced the crowd, his voice booming over the stadium.

"All right, all right. Y'all ready to get this party started?" Any kids who weren't already standing and cheering got up and yelled. "Well, let's get our players over here."

The team had lined up on the visitors' side and now jumped up and down, pumping themselves up, while the cheerleaders made their way to the middle of the field to form a tunnel with their pom-poms for the players to run through.

"Let's hear it for our team's starters ... Darrrrrennnn Johnson ..." The students clapped and screamed as Mike ran through the players' names.

SAFE HARBOR

My gaze wandered away from the rowdy boys and found Eva. She'd parked herself on the front row next to a blonde I'd seen at almost all the home games, along with a couple of other teachers. Eva shone in a royal blue Falcons school spirit T-shirt and denim capris, which showed off her now deeply tanned olive skin. She was both simple and strikingly beautiful, her honey hair falling around her shoulders straight and silky.

All the players had made it over and scattered amongst the sidelines. The cheerleaders wasted no time and went into their performance.

After they finished, Mike announced, "And now for the show that's sure to get everyone on their feet!"

By that, he meant the comedic performance.

Mike, our coaching staff's obvious wingman on the mic, called out, "We have a special treat for you all. Look at it as our effort to keep you pumped up and ready to play our biggest rival, the Panthers, tomorrow. What do ya say? Y'all ready to get pumped?"

The crowd went wild.

"Coaches, will you do the honors?" Mike gestured at the huge tarp we had near the fifty-yard line. Dad and I, along with Mike's assistant coach Joey, pulled the tarp away to reveal the dunk tank.

"Now, now, calm down. Coach Thad and I have placed a little bet. Each of us thinks *our* grade is superior, and we need your help to prove it. We've decided each of our team's three captains will choose one teacher from their grade level to throw the ball and hit the bull's eye to dunk us. Each teacher gets three tries. The coach who gets dunked the most times has to wear a pink tutu tomorrow during their team's entire game."

Dad pointed at me, laughing hysterically.

I nudged him. "You better watch it. If I lose, I'll figure out a way to get you into a tutu at the next pep rally."

"Forget it," he said, though the students were so loud I could only read his lips.

Mike called up my team captains. The boys picked the only two male teachers in seventh grade. One of their picks, Mr. Murdock, a social studies teacher, had been sitting right behind Eva, and she high-fived him as he passed. And Mrs. Watson, who taught science and coached the girls' basketball team, was chosen. "Good choices, boys," I called out as Mike handed me the mic and got into the dunk tank.

By the time Mrs. Watson got up to make her throws, Mike had been dunked one time by Mr. Murdock.

"Okay, Mrs. Watson, you can do this." I tested my skills on the mic, and my whole team chimed in, hooting and hollering.

Her first shot was a dud. Missed by at least eight inches.

She let the second one go and ... *bam.* Mike went into the water. Dad and I, along with the whole team, jumped up and down like we'd scored a touchdown. I stole a glance at Eva. She was on her feet too, laughing and clapping.

Then the magic of the moment wore off as I realized it was my turn. Mike got out and toweled off before grabbing the mic again.

His eighth-grade captains chose two female math teachers and a male science teacher, whose kid I'd coached my first year here. I figured he'd be a great shot.

A few minutes later, I had gone down twice already with the two female teachers. I found Eva in the crowd and shook my head. *This doesn't look good.* The tutu was calling my name. She brought her hand up to cover her mouth, but I could see her shoulders shake with laughter.

Next up was Mr. Downing. He winked at me right before rearing back with the natural ease of a former baseball pitcher, and I knew it was over.

CHAPTER THIRTEEN

Saturday

Eva

"'Bye, Miz Elliott. I gotta find my parents and watch the eighth-grade game." Darren seemed to be one of the last of the seventh-grade team to exit the field house.

"'Bye. You did great. I'm proud of you," I called as he waved and turned the corner to the stands, leaving me all alone.

I could kill Stacy for talking me into this. I couldn't resist seeing Thad in a pink tutu, so I'd left Willow with Mom to meet up with Stacy and watch the second half of the game.

But Stacy was long gone now.

Leaving me all alone.

Well, not exactly.

A horde of students and parents stood ten yards away at the concession shack, and tons more sat in the stands watching the game. But they seemed really far away.

I wrapped my black cardigan tighter around my Palmer Falcons blue T-shirt, grateful I'd worn my Keds again. Mom-ish, but practical and comfy meant more than fashionable nowadays.

The second week of September had ushered in the autumn weather. The temperatures in the past week had consistently hit the high seventies, but the wind tore through the trees with a force that brought even the green leaves to the ground. The wind brought with it a chill at dusk, which inched earlier and earlier every day. It was only six-thirty p.m., and the sun already lingered just above the pine forest behind the field.

The announcer's voice boomed. "First and ten. Palmer on the twenty-five-yard line." The game had begun just fifteen minutes ago, and Palmer was already up by a touchdown.

I glanced around the vacant concrete section where I stood waiting on a guy whose feelings I'd likely hurt more than a few times. He *had* avoided telling me he was a pro football player, but I'd almost talked myself out of that being a big deal. The fact it reminded me of Alex had been more of a problem.

This is silly. What if he doesn't even come out this door? And what if he doesn't want to see me?

The door burst open, and Thad's dad John came out. He drew up quick. "Oh, hey, Eva."

"Hi, John." I pretended I wasn't waiting on his son, but instead just casually standing outside a middle-school field house.

"How are you this evening, young lady?" He let go of the door so it could close on its own.

"I'm good, thank you." My smile for him set off a soothing feeling inside. Something sweet about his soul called to me. "Congrats on your win."

He bowed his head. "Why, thank you." He slapped his thighs. "Thad will be out shortly. He'll be glad to see you."

I stiffened and forced my smile to hold, knowing his statement might not be true.

John backed away toward the parking lot. "See you 'round ..."

SAFE HARBOR

Like father, like son. "Yeah, sure."

And I was alone again.

Before I could talk myself out of waiting any longer, Thad pushed the door open. He stopped short when he saw me. A look of sheer surprise—and what I hoped was excitement—washed over his manly features. It extinguished at least half of my on-edge nerves.

"Eva. I saw you in the stands but didn't expect you'd still be here. I would've hurried—"

"You're fine," I said. "I haven't been waiting long." *Not true.* "I just wanted to ... uh ... congratulate you on your win." I was bumbling. Miserably.

He was gracious. "So you witnessed the tutu." He scratched the base of his neck near the knot of his long, tied-up hair. "Go ahead and laugh."

His ease loosened me up. "Oh, I laughed plenty. Mostly, I thought about how you're a good sport, and how happy you make those kids."

And how you're the only man who could wear a tutu and still be drop-dead gorgeous.

"Thanks."

For the first time, I witnessed a slight blush color Thad's cheeks. He adjusted the strap of the gym bag resting across his chest, and I caught a whiff of soap and his "something really studly" cologne. He looked sporty tonight in his athletic tee, stretched to the max against his muscles, with basketball-style shorts and tennis shoes. Somehow they seemed to fit his aura just as easily as flip-flops and swim trunks. "And thank you for dinner Wednesday. It was delicious for all of us. Willow's plain-spaghetti-noodles-and-sauce kid's meal was extra thoughtful."

"You're welcome." His light brown eyes flirted for a beat, treasuring me like a prize possession.

I took a deep breath, gearing up. Gratitude was easier than apologies.

"I also wanted to apologize."

He squinted.

"For last Sunday, when I shut down on you. I said things I really didn't mean, and I'm sorry. You didn't do anything wrong. I just wanted you to know."

He stepped closer and bent his head down toward my face. "It's okay."

I closed my eyes, needing to break the contact, break the power he had to make me want to reach out and throw my arms around his neck. When I opened them, I stood a little straighter. "Okay, great. Well, I guess I'll be going."

He grabbed my hand. "Wait." He looked at the watch he always wore. "I was gonna go sit and watch Mike's game. But come with me somewhere. I think we have plenty of time to make it."

"Uh—" The heat coming from his hand burned my insides. "Where?"

"It's a surprise." He tightened his grip. "C'mon. You'll always wonder where I was gonna take you if you don't say yes."

I wanted to say yes. I just didn't fully trust myself around him. But my sense of reason left when he leaned down and whispered, "Please."

"Okay, sure. Let's go."

He jumped back. "Yes. Hey, are you hungry?"

"No. I ate earlier." I laughed at his boyish excitement.

"At the concession stand?"

"Yup. A hot dog."

"Man, you are something, Eva Elliott." He gestured for me to walk with him to the concession stand.

"What? I told you we practically live off hot dogs."

"Yes, you did. Well, I'm gonna grab a couple, and we'll be on our way. You're gonna love it."

SAFE HARBOR

Thad, if you only knew—even though I'm fighting it, I'm beginning to love anywhere you are.

THAD

Eva leaned closer to her window to peer into the woods as we turned down the gravel and packed sand road. We'd only been driving about ten minutes, but I didn't mention my property backed up to Palmer's field. Since we were heading in the opposite direction to the west side of my acreage, I didn't think it would come up.

Though Mike might be right. My anonymous donation might not be anonymous for much longer.

"We're not going on some ghost ride, are we?" I felt her eyes on me. "Where we drive through spooky woods that are supposed to be haunted, and see if we spot any ghosts rumored to make their appearance every night at dusk?" She made those last words come out with an Addams Family kind of spooky tone.

"Have you been on one of those ghost rides before? That ruins everything. I wanted this to be your first." I couldn't help myself. I pointed to the woods. "Look! What was that?"

She didn't scream, but she did pop her head around. She knew within a second of me laughing I wasn't serious. "You—! I was only joking, but when you said that I thought, maybe? You're terrible."

"I couldn't help it. Too easy." I leaned over the armrest, stealing a glance away from the road. "I'm sorry."

She pressed her lips together. "You're forgiven. But seriously, where are we?"

"This is my property. I call it the farm."

"Is this where you live?"

"No, all this is pretty much raw land. I own a thousand acres of beautiful Georgia swampland," I said with full-bore sarcasm. "Well, about half of it is considered swamp and flood plain, anyway. But the rest is pretty great. I've got a fifteen-acre lake too, perfect to paddleboard on if you're interested."

"Are there any waves on your pond? 'Cause if not, then maybe." She grinned at me, turning my insides to slush, before sitting up more in her seat to get a better look. "But for real? A thousand acres?"

"It's the perfect amount to roam free and get a little dirty." I turned as the dusty road opened up into pastureland. "You can see the beginnings of the lake in the distance. That way." The trail opened up to a view of my barn as we approached.

"Wow. That's a really nice ... barn."

"Thanks. I built a lot of it myself. I call it the barn loft." I stopped in front of it and killed the engine. "It started as a barn, but then there was all this awesome space up top. You'd normally put hay up there, but I don't anticipate having animals, at least not any time soon, so I made it a livable space. Now I can stay here whenever I want." I looked at her as she admired my craftsmanship. "You ready?"

"I guess so."

"Good. And don't you dare open that door. Hold on."

I jumped out and made it to her side at warp speed. Opening the door and reaching for her hand, I said in my best English knight imitation, "M'lady."

She blushed. "Your dad called me 'lady' tonight too."

"You saw him?"

"Uh-huh." She jumped down to the gravel.

"Yeah, he was always the perfect gentleman to my mom. Taught me well."

Though I lost sight of that part of me for a while.

She followed me to the barn's big double door, and I put the key into the lock. "What are you thinking right now?"

"I'm thinking how beautiful this place is. The lake with those big oaks scattered in the pasture. And this barn is gorgeous." She chuckled. "And I never thought I'd hear myself say that about a barn."

"Thank you." I yanked one of the doors and slid it aside. "It took me quite a while to build"—*years*—"but it was kind of fun."

She walked inside, and I flicked the switch to light it up. They went on in a wave through the barn, illuminating all its nooks, its structure, and its character—the farming equipment neatly organized on the bottom, with a set of chunky wooden stairs leading to a small kitchen, bed, and couch area above. The loft seemed to float over half the barn. She spun around the space, taking it in.

"Wow, I've got to add farmer and builder to your list of job skills." Her voice held a lightness.

"Well, I'm a man of many trades. You can't grow up in South Georgia and not have a little farmer in your soul." Her gaze settled on the bulky, tarp-covered lumps off to the right. I grabbed her hand and pulled her in their direction. "Don't be scared."

She drew her lips into a nervous thin line. "I don't know. Last time I agreed to do something with you, I ended up on a paddleboard in the middle of the ocean."

"And you saw the very best view of the sunset."

"True."

I let her go to pull one of the tarps off. She grimaced.

"Are those four-wheelers?"

I tried to hold back a laugh. "At least you know what they are. That's a good sign. These are my big boy toys."

She smiled now. "Big boy toys?"

"*Oh* yeah." I climbed on, turned the little key I always left in the ignition, and cranked the red Honda Rancher. She backed out of the way as I reversed out of the barn and spun around to point in the direction we were heading. I left it to idle and went back to her. "I can tell you're apprehensive, but I promise we're traveling on mostly flat ground."

"Mostly?"

"I'll take it easy."

She took a deep breath and whooshed it out. "Okay."

"Come help me grab a couple of things out of my truck." She followed me to the back hatch. "You're probably freezing already, and it'll only get worse once the wind hits you." I started searching through my stash of gym bags. "We won't go through any high brush or grass, so your clothes won't get messed up or anything." I found what I was looking for, and held out the brown hoodie. "Here, put this on."

"Thanks." Once it was on, it swallowed her whole body. She saw my amusement and held her hands out as if on display. "Not only will it keep my torso warm, it'll keep my legs warm too."

"That looks really good on you."

Maybe it'll smell like her later.

She broke eye contact, tucking herself further into the material, and I turned back to the Bronco. I found a hoodie for myself buried underneath another gym bag, along with two old tie-dyed beach towels and my old stadium blanket with the Chargers colors of gold and powder blue. At least all of them could be considered clean.

She held the blanket and towels while I put on the hoodie, and then I took them back from her.

"We're gonna latch these on the back rack of the four-wheeler." I went to work, then swung my leg over it. "Let's go." I nodded behind me. "Hop on. Unless you wanna drive?"

SAFE HARBOR

"Oh, no." She put her tiny foot in the groove behind mine and swung her leg around, gripping my shoulders as she did. Settling in, she slowly put her arms around my waist.

"Is this okay?" she asked.

"Definitely."

She hesitated, then interlocked her fingers and tightened her grip.

I put my hand over hers for a beat and said, "Just hold on tight. I promise not to scare you."

Her breath was warm in my ear. "I'm more excited than scared. You bring out the risk-taker in me."

Energy radiated off her, like a lit firecracker about to blow. The calculated, careful Eva had moved into the background, allowing space for carefree Eva to enjoy the limelight. I smiled to myself, kicked the Rancher into first gear, and we took off through the pasture.

Eva

The wind whipping around us ignited my adrenaline, and I could almost feel my blood swirling. We roared through the woods, leaving the pasture and getting back onto a gravel road. It was a struggle to see over Thad's incredibly huge shoulders, but seeing didn't matter. I was content to catch glimpses of the immense clear sky, whenever I could see it through the breaks in the trees. Mostly pines, they stood tall with thick trunks and sturdy branches extending to meet the stars. Soon the moon's light would dominate the sky.

I closed my eyes to the display above and rested my cheek on Thad's back, envisioning his tight muscles underneath his shirt, strong and sturdy like the trees around me. I relished his smell, a scent that triggered a longing in my heart. His blend of oak and hickory mixed with lavender—probably his laundry detergent—combined and encouraged tendrils of serenity that began in my heart and were carried out to my veins all over.

We're just friends.

He kicked the Rancher into a higher gear as we hit a straightaway. The trees whipped by faster, and he again placed his hand and arm over both of mine to draw me tighter in a protective fashion. Though I didn't need his reassurance, because I already felt secure with him.

He released my arms as he shifted gears down and slowed, then pulled just off the path.

"Okay, now we're really going off-roading. I'll take it easy, but we'll be pretty much making our own path the rest of the way. Not much further."

I pushed up to get closer to his ear to hear me over the engine. "It's fine. This is awesome. I'm beginning to enjoy trying new things."

"Good." He hit the gas, propelling us into the trees.

He navigated the bumpy terrain as I gasped and even giggled over the humps that knocked us side to side. "You're doing this on purpose, aren't you?"

He leaned back and spoke over his shoulder. "You know it."

We slowed to a stop, and he killed the engine. I got off first and looked around. The headlights shot through the pines and shrubs. Why was this the mysterious place?

"I know what you're thinking." He stood in front of the headlights, wearing a grin the size of Alaska. "Where in the world are we?" He walked to the back and got the blanket and beach towels. "Well, do you happen to listen to country music?"

"Um, yeah, actually." *Just not Alex's favorite artists.* "I grew up in Tennessee and went to the University of Georgia, after all."

SAFE HARBOR

"Right. So, have you ever heard that old song about listening to a train? At night?"

"Uh, I think ..."

He started making a pallet on the forest floor with the blanket and towels, in front of the headlights. "Well, you're about to have a little night train experience in"—he lit up his watch— "twelve minutes, give or take a few."

My forehead scrunched, but my cheeks slid up into a smile. "I'm not sure what that means, but you're excited, so it must be good."

"C'mon." He gestured to the pallet. "This is the best way to experience this."

I went over to it and sat down.

"I'm going to turn off the headlights," he said. "Your eyes'll take a minute to adjust, but then I think we'll be able to see pretty good."

"As long as you're not leaving, I'm good." In the few seconds after the lights went out, I could more sense than see him get close to me.

As my eyes adjusted, he grabbed my shoulders. "Lie back, so you're ready."

I did what he said, and his back hit the blankets too, our shoulders rubbing up against one another as we lay still, staring up at the night sky. After a while, he spoke.

"Right after I bought the property, I was out here walking around one evening, getting my bearings. I had some general ideas about what I wanted to do here." He exhaled. "They're kind of crazy ideas. Things I could never do on my own."

"I think you can achieve anything you put your mind to, Thad."

"I assure you, any success I've had in life is not because of anything I've done. It's God who's allowed it and showed me the way. Anyway, back then I wasn't sure if my ideas were coming from my own ambitions or God's ambitions for me. I wanted to seek him here, see what he needed from me. Basically, I was doing a little soul-searching. And like every other time I've been out here, away from the noise, I found him so easily. The ideas poured out, complete and satisfying. They were way bigger than I'd originally dreamed, and I knew they weren't my ideas. I wasn't smart enough to come up with them, that's for sure."

His shoulders rocked with his laugh. "And just as I was thinking, 'How? How, God, can I make all this happen?' a night train sounded off in the distance, loud and proud, shaking my body. It appeared out of nowhere. I hadn't even noticed I was near the train tracks. I wasn't aware they lined a small area of this property."

I felt his stare and turned, seeking his eyes. "I'd always loved trains as a kid. I don't know why. Some kids like trucks or dinosaurs. I liked trains. They're the wise old grandpa of the transportation industry. Some people say they're outdated because of their tracks, but I see it differently. They can never make a wrong turn, never get off their intended path." He turned back to the night sky. "When I heard that train at the very moment I was calling out to God, I knew he was trying to get my attention, to let me know he was in control. Reminding me to stay on his track, and I wouldn't go the wrong way."

"Wow." I turned to him and propped up on my elbow. "Your words, the way you speak about God as your close friend. How does that happen? How do you get close enough to him to know, like, if you're on his track?" His words had worked over my insides, instilling them with a strange feeling of hope.

He moved onto his side too. "Well ..." He hesitated. "Years ago, I found myself in a desolate place. I felt like everything had been ripped away from me."

SAFE HARBOR

His words could have been my words. They also gave me the space to shape my question. "Thad, I'm just going to come out and ask you. Are you talking about your knee injury when you played for the Chargers?"

He fell to his back with a sigh. "You found out?"

"Yes."

"Please say you didn't Google me."

"I did. But I only read one article. One about your retirement."

He exhaled a sharp breath. "That's a relief. I'm not proud of a lot of things I did back then. Truth is, I don't talk much about it. Haven't had anyone I felt an urge to talk about it with." He nudged me softly, and it was more than just physically. It penetrated my heart, because again, his words could be mine.

"God ripped quite a few things away from me in the blink of an eye," he said. "My career was only one of those things. I'm sorry I didn't come out and say it. People here know and don't care, or don't know and don't care. I've grown to like the anonymity in Moanna. You're not mad?"

I rolled back over. "I was, for about twelve hours. Then I realized I couldn't be, because I hadn't let you explain."

"When you said football reminded you of someone, and that reminder brought pain—" I could feel his shoulders flinch, "—I thought I'd save the NFL tidbit until you'd fallen head over heels for me." We both laughed. Surely he was joking. Right?

"It seems neither of us talk about how football was part of our past. The game reminds me of Willow's father. He played at UGA for four years. He was looked at by a couple of teams too, getting calls from sports agents ... that is, until we found out we were having a baby. His priorities changed."

My mind spun, but it was almost freeing to talk about Alex. As long as I didn't have to discuss his death.

"I think that's wonderful, his priorities changing."

"It is. It was." Chills doused me. "We were really excited. Young and naïve, but excited."

Thad elbowed me lightly. "Look at us, both talking about our past."

I elbowed him back. "Yeah, you've caught me in a rare moment." And now it was over. "Enough about me. What happened with your career?"

"When I was in college, late in the season of my sophomore year, I tore my ACL."

"Huh?"

"Anterior cruciate ligament. My knee. You know, the nasty scar?"

"Oh."

"I had surgery, missed the last two games, but had the off season to recover. By the time training camp came around, I was running at almost optimal force again. I worked hard at therapy, and it paid off. I knew if I hurt the knee again, I was done. But I just kept on going.

"A couple of years later, I was drafted, and six seasons after that, I caught a pass right near the sideline. I was ten yards from the end zone, so even though two linemen were heading right at me, I went for it, thinking I could push through their tackle and maybe even score. So instead of rushing out of bounds, choosing to be safe, I ended up receiving two hard tackles—one at my waist, and the other at my knees. And that was it. That one choice, made in a split second, ended my career. I knew instantly I'd torn my ACL again, and my knee was done." He sat up and rubbed his knee like he'd just noticed its ache.

I followed him up. "I'm sorry. You really loved it, didn't you? Playing football?"

He shrugged.

"You know, yeah, I thought I did. I thought it was God's plan for my life, to play pro ball. But really, how does that glorify him? If I play pro, but don't lead people to him in the way I live my everyday life, that's not glorifying him at all. It's glorifying me." He inhaled deeply before saying, "Anyway, with the injury plus some other circumstances, I was a complete mess."

"So how'd you move forward?" I whispered, not even sure if he heard me.

He leaned back on his hand and moved closer. "God used my circumstances and my dad's words to call me back. Dad said, 'Son, I don't even know who you are anymore, but God does. He's the only one who sees your heart and can save it. You better get on your knees and cry out to him.' Those words felt like a punch to the gut, because I knew they were true. So I did. I got down on my knees and cried out to Jesus for forgiveness and restoration."

Though I couldn't make out every detail of his face, his breath brushed my skin as his words flowed over and past me like a stream. I wished I could snatch them up and make them mine.

I sighed. "What if it's been a long time, you know, since everything was ripped from you?" I said. "And what if since then, even though you've tried to make good decisions and be a good person, you've still kept making mistakes?"

He reached out and caressed my cheek, letting his fingers linger for a beat on my chin. "Eva, it's never too late to get down your knees before God."

I leaned into his fingers, wanting to believe his words. But he had no idea the things I'd done, the bad decisions I'd made before and after Willow. I still harbored resentment and unforgiveness, leading to a never-ending circle of anger and regret.

He must have sensed I was done talking, because he took a deep breath and lay back down. "You know, a few days after I first witnessed the train, that song came on the radio. Of course, he's singing about him and his girl. They disappear into the night to listen to the train go by. It's all romantic and exhilarating. I remember laughing, realizing I'd had my own night train experience, only with God."

Grateful for his subject change, I relaxed back onto the pallet and stared into the darkness as the song's chorus ran through my mind.

Just as the last few words of the tune escaped, the ground moved, shaking just little at first. Then the wheels' rhythmic sounds came, and the gears' turning got louder and louder. The train didn't blow its whistle and wasn't traveling fast, but I could see over Thad's chest a headlight shining from the engine, about to pass not far from our position.

Then its passing was upon us. Loud, really loud, vibrating my skin, making my heart pump faster and faster. I held my breath and was suddenly aware of how close Thad's hand was to my own. He must have felt the pull too, because he interlocked a few of his fingers with mine. They fit together so perfectly, so comfortably, so naturally, that my eyes welled up with tears.

Why does his touch have to feel so perfect—perfect enough to make me want to cry?

After what felt like far more than a couple of minutes, the train had moved on into the night, leaving us silent in the quiet woods. I breathed in, released his hand, and willed my heart to slow.

"That was amazing. My whole body is still trembling."

He pushed out a happy sigh. "Yeah. I love the power you can feel coming off it."

I sat up all the way and turned to him, invigorated and wanting to know exactly what ideas God had placed in his heart. "So finish your story. What are you going to do here?"

THAD

I had to tread delicately, not lying, but not revealing every detail of the plan God had placed on my heart years ago. I wasn't ready to admit I'd funded and donated the football stadium.

"Okay, well, just know I'm counting on God to open the doors."

"Would you stop?" The whites of her eyes glistened, revealing anticipation instead of the sadness from minutes before. "I won't think you're crazy. Remember, you're talking to someone who just moved herself and her daughter along with her mom into a house we'd never even seen before she bought it. That's crazy. Now tell me."

"Okay, okay. I think I'm going to open a summer camp here."

"Really? Cool." Her excited reaction made my adrenaline pump. "This place would make an amazing summer camp." She scrambled up to sit on her knees, fully facing me. My hoodie draped over her knees like a skirt. "Is it going to be a specific kind of camp? You could have water sports on the lake, and maybe even get a few horses." She clapped her hands softly by her chin, obvious remnants of her cheerleading days. "And campfires. Oh, wait, is it going to be an overnight camp?"

Eva's joy overcame the doubtfulness I'd allowed to creep in. I stuttered, trying to figure out what question to answer first. "Um ... yeah, it'll be an overnight camp. I've got to build bunk cabins, another barn to store all the water sports equipment, a mess hall with a kitchen, and an extra big rec room."

"Absolutely a rec room. You never want to get stuck without a place for the kids to go if it rains."

"Exactly."

"You've got to have games in there like ping pong and air-hockey—no darts or pool—and maybe a little stage area." Her eyes shimmered. "There'd be all sorts of possibilities. The kids could do karaoke or come up with little skits."

"Those are great ideas. I'll have to show you the building plans and see what you think. Of course, I have to build practical things like an office building, a nurse's station, and a couple of free-standing restrooms too. But I've already started work on a couple of the fun things."

"What?"

"I'm about to put in a fire pit area overlooking the lake. I've also started clearing brush to make more functional hiking and biking trails. This past summer, I worked the pasture, leveling it out in spots, so I can get it to be more of a sports field for games. I'm actually planning on holding football camps here too, at least a couple of weeks in summer."

I ran through the list I'd just rambled off and realized I'd left out the most important part. "Oh yeah, and I'm going to build some type of worship center. I can't decide if it's going to be a traditional space or a more contemporary setting, but something."

She knitted her forehead and shivered a little. I ran my hands up and down her thighs, trying to warm her up. She watched my hands as I said, "I've got a million things to do, including getting another couple of permits from the state. My plan has been to get the football program up and running—"

Oh crap, I let that slip.

"I mean, get in the swing of coaching, and then focus on starting here. My first meeting with the planning and zoning folks went well. They've told me the things I need in order for them to review my plans. The camp won't be ready by next summer, but with God's help, maybe by the following one.

"I'm hoping it will be a blessing in the community. Most of the kids in this county could never afford to go to an overnight camp, so we'll offer full scholarships to any kids who go a whole school year keeping a B average and staying out of trouble."

What better way to use God's money that's just sitting there earning interest than to give it to his children?

I stopped rubbing her quads. "You're really quiet. Are you thinking how to gently tell me how nuts I am?"

That got a smile out of her. "No. No way. Honestly, I don't even know what say, except ... I think it's amazing. I think you're amazing, and I can't wait to see it happen here for you."

"Oh, you'll see it. In fact, I could use someone with your knowledge of adolescent kids to help with fresh ideas. Your teacher expertise would be appreciated."

"Okay," she said, her voice warm with pride.

"I have a workday planned here next month with a group of friends from my church. Coach Mike will be here. I'd love for you to come."

"I'd like that."

"I'll give you a firsthand look at everything." The color in her cheeks wasn't visible in the darkness, but I knew she was blushing. I pushed a little further. "You know, not dates, just you and me hanging together and discussing our lives, our families, careers, futures. But not a date, definitely not a date. *Never* a date."

Her laughter spilled out like a melody. "No, never a date. But time spent with you sounds pretty okay with me."

"Well, that settles it. We'd better go ahead and exchange numbers. You know, so we can find time to discuss the things going on in our lives." I grabbed her hands and helped her up, pulling her into a hug.

She chuckled into my chest at my ingenuity.

"Thanks for listening to my dreams tonight," I whispered into the side of her head. Her hair smelled like Skittles.

"Thanks for telling them to me," she whispered back, holding me tight, the electricity between our bodies palpable.

It took me a while to let go, but finally I released her and reached for the blanket. I gave it a couple of hard shakes. "C'mon, let's see if we can find a way to keep this around you while we ride back to the truck and get some heat blasting on you."

CHAPTER FOURTEEN

Sunday

Thad

I went to the door when Ellen and Willow came into view, approaching from the parking lot. No Eva. But I'd not gotten my hopes up when I invited her. She'd said she wasn't ready for church. I was unsure exactly what she meant by that, but she was quick to add that Ellen was actively looking for a church. I'd texted the address, and here they were. Willow looked as cute as ever. And by the look on Ellen's face, she wasn't taken aback by my little church that met in an old drug store building at the end of a small shopping center.

The church had initially leased only the former drug store, but as it grew, we kept leasing and occupying adjacent spaces as they became available. We now had four additional spaces to house the church offices, a fellowship hall, the children's ministry, and even a space for middle schoolers to meet on Sunday mornings.

I opened the door for them.

"Morning, ladies." I bent down to Willow's eye level as she clung to Ellen, her gaze scoping out the place. "You are going to love kid's church. I hear they sing and dance a *lot*."

"Will you be there?" she asked with a bit of apprehension.

"No, they don't let me back there. I'd mess everything up. I don't fit very well in the kids' chairs either. I'd probably break 'em." I stole a glance at Ellen, who covered her smile. "But Gramma and I will drop you off, go to the boring adult service, and pick you right up afterward. That okay?"

Willow pursed her lips a second. "Yeah, that's okay."

"Great." I stood and withheld my urge to rub my throbbing knee after being down like that for a time. "C'mon. I'll show you the way."

Ellen mouthed *thank you* as we walked toward the entrance to the kid's ministry area. By the time we got Willow registered and signed in, she ran into the room on her own. The place was way too cool to be scared. The murals on the wall alone allowed the kids to feel they were entering a magical place, which they were, since it was God's house.

"That was super easy, though I'm not surprised since she's not at all shy. She definitely didn't care we were leaving," Ellen said as we walked back to the lobby.

"I've heard they do a great job. She'll have fun and learn about Jesus, so it's a win-win." I nodded toward the worship center doors. "You ready?"

"Oh, yes. Lead the way."

We meandered around the slew of people who lingered and chatted in the lobby. I waved at Mike, who was about to take a sip of his steaming cup of joe from the free coffee bar. At the entry doors, one greeter handed us both a bulletin, while the others gave us multiple hellos and welcomes and good mornings. I gestured for Ellen to go first through the doors into our quaint worship center. She paused and looked around, probably taking in the contemporary feel. We had soft chairs rather than pews, more of a stage than a pulpit, and a hipster band with skinny jeans, flannel, and full beards in place of choir robes. She turned back to me with acceptance in her eyes, and I led her to where Dad sat. When we entered the aisle, he stood to greet her.

"Good morning—Ellen, is it?"

"Yes, good morning. John?" she asked.

"Yes, ma'am. I've heard a lot about—"

"I've heard a lot about you—" They ended at the same time and laughed, turning to look at me. I shrugged, secretly giddy to know Eva had been talking about me.

Ellen and Dad jabbered about everything and nothing as we settled in.

The church was packed. My friend Ryan—she ran the general store on Moanna—passed by with her dad. She saw me too, as she entered the aisle two rows in front of ours, and she gave me a chin tip nod. Her dad looked to see who she greeted, and he waved, smiling. I'd have to introduce Eva to them one day.

Strange. After only meeting her a month ago, and despite her insistence on *not* dating me, I kept inserting her into my life.

The room quieted down as the band fiddled with putting on guitars and getting into the drum cage. The female worship leader spoke into her mic.

"Welcome everyone. Y'all ready to sing praise to God this morning?"

Anyone not already standing rose to their feet, including us, as the band hit their first notes and the worship leader sang.

You are the rolling thunder,
the powerful force that beckons me.
Draw me ever closer Jesus,
I'm waiting here for you.
You fight for me when I am weak.
You hold my head up high.

*You whisper to me through the wind.
I've never felt so alive.
And oh, your love, it clings to me.
My brokenness heals with your touch.
And oh, your love, it clings to me.
I didn't know I could love this much."*

In the break after the chorus, I looked at Ellen. She swayed to the music, her eyes closed, her face lit with joy. I decided she'd be returning next week before Pastor Andrew even spoke a word of his message.

EVA

"Hey, Mom. How was it?" I asked into my phone as I put the last dish from the dishwasher into the cabinet. I'd tried to keep busy around the house and not regret *not* going to church. I hadn't attended church since before Willow was born, since before Alex's accident, and it hadn't bothered me until recently, until Moanna, until Thad ...

"Eva, it was so fun." *Fun?* "Truly, truly great. Amazing music and children's church for Willow, and their young pastor—Andrew was his name—is terrific. He was hilarious and engaging, but still biblical. We're definitely going back for sure."

"That's great, Mom. Are you guys heading home?"

And did you see Thad?

I wanted to ask, but I couldn't get the words out of my mouth.

"Yes, that's why I'm calling. We're stopping by the house to change clothes, but then, we're meeting Thad and John to go fishing on the bay somewhere."

She paused, and Willow yelled out, "Fishing on the bay."

SAFE HARBOR

"And by we, I mean all of us. You, me, and Willow. Can you make us all some sandwiches for lunch?" Again, she paused, then spoke away from the phone. "Thad, John, are turkey sandwiches okay?" I heard some mumbles, then Mom again.

"Thad and John are going home to grab their fishing gear, and I told them we'd bring a picnic lunch. We've got to hurry and meet them in forty-five minutes. That's when the tide's coming in, and it makes for good fishing. John explained it to me." Away from the phone, she called out, "'Bye, guys. See you soon." She chattered on her end. "What a great man, that John. C'mon, Little Bit, let's get you into the car. Honey, are you listening?"

I was still caught up on the fact we were all going fishing, like all of us ... my family and Thad's ... together. It felt too intimate, too real.

A pang of guilt threatened my heart. I was getting overly attached to Thad, becoming predictably happy when my longing to see him came true and ended with a night like last night.

But Mom and Willow getting attached, getting predictably happy to see him, put me on edge. So far it felt like they'd stayed at a safe distance. What would they do when I put an end to Thad being around? When he was threatening the space in my heart where only Willow should be, and I had to break ties? Or worse, when Thad realized *he* didn't have time to waste on a single mom who lived with *her* mom?

"Honey, are you there?"

"Yeah, Mom, I'm listening. Make lunches, check." She must have been able to hear the resistance in my voice.

"Eva?"

"Yeah?"

"It's okay. It's just lunch and fishing."

"I know." I opened the pantry, secretly hoping we were out of bread. We weren't. "I'll change and then start on the lunches." I tossed the bread onto the counter. "See you when you get here."

I hung up, still torn, always wanting to shield Willow from any foreseeable pain. But life couldn't be lived like that. And if I was honest, who else was going to take Willow fishing? I sure wouldn't, or more like *couldn't* since I couldn't kill a worm to put it on a hook. My dad would have, but that was impossible for Willow too.

My heart eventually beat out my head, because internally I couldn't pass on an opportunity to see him.

It's just fishing, right?

I rushed to my room to figure out what someone wears to go fish.

THAD

The wooden boards of the whole dock rattled when Eva stepped on its top stair. In jeans, tennis shoes, and a light gray UGA T-shirt with a big red G on the front, she looked sporty and spunky. Her hair was pulled back into a loose ponytail swinging behind her head. Except for when she wore a swimsuit, I had seen only the preppy teacher-appropriate side of Eva Elliott. I liked this one, this laid-back, effortless version.

"Hey," I called out as all three of them descended the stairs. "You found us."

Willow zipped past her mom and ran to Dad and me.

"Willow, please be careful," Eva cried, though her face lit up when she met my eyes.

The satisfaction of being near her again swept over me.

SAFE HARBOR

Willow high-fived me as she passed by and went straight to Dad. He was stringing a new line on one of the poles, and he paused to smile and look Willow in the eyes from underneath his faded Chargers hat. "Hey there, Willow. You ready to catch some fish?"

"Yeah!" she screamed. "Whatcha doing?" she asked, as I went to meet Eva and Ellen halfway down the dock.

Eva had a life jacket in one hand, and with the other, she held up what looked like a picnic basket, but turned out to be a bag constructed out of navy chevron fabric. "We come bearing gifts."

"Awesome. Here, let me help you." I grabbed the basket, and Eva leaned in. Her perfume rushed into my nose, replacing the fishy smell surrounding us.

"Thanks. Willow's mad at me for making her wear a life jacket."

We both looked over at Willow, who clearly heard her mom. "I told you I can swim. I don't need it."

"Well, I know you can swim, but this water is different from a pool. It moves in and out, back and forth all day, from here to the big ocean." Eva looked at me. "I don't know why I'm trying to explain it when I don't even understand."

Dad saved us. "Willow, you see out there?" He pointed to where the bay opened to the sea. "Out there is the ocean. It's huge. And full of all kinds of fish and sea creatures. Do you know some of them?"

Willow nodded, intently watching Dad.

"Well, some of them—certain fish, crabs, conches, starfish—don't get all their food out there." He pointed again at the bay, and then at the water below the dock. "They get their food right here. God made them that way. There are specific plants and little fish they can find better here. So, God makes the water from the ocean pour into areas like these twice a day, so all the creatures can eat. Isn't that amazing?"

"They come here to catch food to eat, and we catch *them* to eat?" Willow tilted her head down, lacking confidence in her statement.

"What a smart girl you are, Willow." Dad's compliment made Willow stand straight again, proud. He leaned closer to her. "That's what makes this the perfect time to fish, 'cause they're all here, distracted by getting their own food, and bam! They get caught on our hooks. Make sense?"

"Yeah ..."

I touched Willow's shoulder to draw her attention. "If you'll watch while we're here, you'll see the water start to rise higher and higher." I moved my hand to demonstrate. "That's why we call it *high* tide. And with the high tide, and all those creatures and fish out there we just talked about, you better wear your life jacket. That way if you fall in, you'll just float right on the top, and we can pull you out of the water in a snap. Okay?"

"Okay."

A wave of visible relief washed over Eva as Ellen said, "Possible tantrum avoided."

Eva stepped over to Willow and embraced her little chin. "Thank you, baby." Eva had the life jacket strapped on her in seconds. "Still, be careful. We're not dressed to get in the water." Eva's shoulders flinched. I knew what memory crossed her mind because it crossed mine too. "Everyone be on guard." She cast glances at each of us, and we all nodded yes to the mission. "Do you guys want to eat now, or fish a while?"

"Fish," Willow said quickly.

"I knew she was going to say that," Ellen mumbled. "Can't wait to get her hands dirty."

Dad stood. "This pole and that one are ready. I'll take her." He looked down at Willow. "Let's go to the bank over there and see what we can catch."

SAFE HARBOR

Willow cried, "Yeah!"

Dad winked at Eva as he passed. The bank above the three-foot seawall was not near as scary as the dock when it came to Willow and her swimming skills. She fell in line behind Dad as they tramped down the dock.

"Thanks for that," Eva said, still watching Willow. "She'd probably do anything you ask. She thinks you're a superhero."

"What?"

She shrugged. "I can see it. You're super tall with lots of muscles, and"—she looked into my eyes, sincerity filling hers—"you *did* save her life."

My stomach rolled over at her tenderness. She turned back to Dad and Willow, whose voice pulled my gaze to the seawall. "Mama, will you come fish too?"

Eva didn't hesitate. "Of course I will."

"Great," Dad called to us. "Snatch up that minnow bucket and bring it over."

"Minnow bucket?" Eva peered into the contraption.

"Hey, Dad, make sure you let Eva bait a hook. She says she wants to try." He nodded as Eva shot me a look of fear while Ellen clamped down on her lip, trying not to laugh. "Don't worry. If you don't like the look of a mud minnow, there's finger mullet in there too."

Eva narrowed her eyes at me as she picked up the bucket full of tiny fish and lugged it down the dock. Ellen and I watched her turn to meet Willow and Dad. He'd walked to a spot where the cattails were sparse, and the water was wide open.

I looked at Ellen. "Sit and eat?"

"Yes. I'm starving."

We both sat down on the weathered boards, and she pulled two sandwiches from the basket, handing one to me.

"Thanks." Turkey and cheese with the perfect amount

of mayo and mustard. "Just the way I like it. How'd you know?"

"Eva made all the sandwiches. She must be attuned to you."

Ellen teased, but she'd never know how true I felt those words *were*.

"Say, it's Sunday afternoon. Don't you have some football to watch?"

"She told you?"

"Sort of. I came in at the right time to see what her Google search pulled up about you."

"I'm sorry she felt I wasn't open with her from the start. I'm still not good at talking about that time in my life."

"We all have something we're still recovering from."

"True."

"I'll never get over losing Eva's father, but I can tell you it does get better as you open up about things." We both fell silent and took a few bites of our sandwiches, content to watch them in the distance as they messed with the minnows and practiced the motion of casting a line.

"You know," Ellen said, "she laughs and smiles a lot around you." She paused, and I looked at her, finding warmth there. "I mean, I'm not saying she's a Debbie-Downer, 'cause she's not that at all."

She put her sandwich down so she could talk with her hands, her short brown bob dancing around her face.

"It's just ... she carries this seriousness, this desire to keep everything in order, moving efficiently. She leaves nothing to chance—well, except maybe agreeing with me to move here. And that doesn't really count, because she wouldn't move before she got a job here and researched the area schools and preschools, household incomes, and sex-offender lists for the county. You name it, she probably researched it before fully agreeing to jump ship from her cozy little North Georgia set up.

"She's afraid any misstep may lead to something she can't fix or handle. It's a protective mechanism. The problem is, she's denying the One who *is* in control. 'In your heart you plan your life, but the Lord decides where your steps will take you.'"

I nodded in agreement. "Proverbs sixteen, verse nine."

Ellen's surprise of my Bible verse knowledge showed in her features.

"Indeed." She smiled. "You know, her guard is down when she's around you. She's happy. She's more my old Eva with you, and for that, I'm grateful."

I shook my head this time. "I haven't done anything."

"Yes, you have. And the more I get to know you, the more I see Jesus working in your life. I think that's another reason she's drawn to you. She longs for Jesus, for the relationship she had with him once, but some days I'm not sure if she knows it. With you, she gets him, his little pieces of joy that flow through you."

EVA

In a smooth motion, John cast the line out into deeper water. It was a long cast, landing exactly where he'd told us the fish were hiding. In the ten minutes it took to get the mud minnows baited on the hook, the water had risen on the seawall a couple of inches. According to John, as it got higher, we'd be able to cast closer to where we stood and still have some luck.

"Great cast, John." Excitement spilled into my words, an anticipation of the unknown.

John reeled in the line a few feet. "Thank you. It landed just where I wanted it. Probably won't get that lucky again, though." He laughed. "Eva, you want to hold this one? And Willow and I can cast the other one out together."

"Ooo, yeah." Willow jumped up and down. John handed me the pole as Willow asked, "And then can I hold the pole?"

"Sure. It's kind of heavy, but if we sit down and prop it on the bank, you should be just fine."

Willow nodded. John picked up the other pole, already baited, and guided Willow to place her tiny hands over his big ones as they drew back and cast it into the bay.

"Perfect spot." John freed one of his hands to give Willow a high five. I wasn't sure if he was lying or not, but either way, Willow couldn't be prouder of herself. "All right, ladies, let's sit down. We've got to rest up for when we get a fish and have to reel it in."

"Yeah, we'll need to rest now." Willow acted as if she knew exactly what John was talking about.

We all sat. The ground felt a little damp underneath me, but I'd take a wet rump any day if it meant sitting here staring out over the bay of Moanna, with the wind rattling the leaves of the water oaks and poplars. It was the perfect autumn day in Georgia.

It's never too late to get on your knees before God.

Thad's words from last night came on the wind, swirling around me.

My eyes drifted to him. I was glad I hadn't talked myself out of coming. As always, things felt easy and right when he was around. Not to mention this was the first time I'd seen him in jeans and a tan, short sleeved button-down with the Carhartt logo on the pocket. He didn't have his usual flip-flops or tennis shoes on. This time, he wore dark brown heavy boots, and with his hair pulled back, and a few days' worth of scruff on his face, he looked like a man who could easily wield a chainsaw. He looked tough and strong and ... sexy. If he'd been wearing a flannel, I'd have called him a lumberjack.

He and Mom looked to be conversing nicely. Well, Mom looked like she was doing the conversing, but it seemed to suit him just fine. He must have felt my stare because he looked over, and I cut my eyes away, hating *and* loving that he could give me butterflies with just a look.

Willow piped up. "So, what do we do now?"

John nudged her with his elbow. "We wait."

Willow deflated a bit, already needing something more active to do. I was about to say something, anything to try to get Willow's mind back into waiting for the fish to come, when John started to sing. I immediately recognized it as "Sittin' on the Dock of the Bay," a classic which suited his deep voice with its low and hearty texture.

Both our mouths dropped, amazed at the beautiful sound coming from his lips.

John's rendition changed the word *sittin'* to *fishin'* and continued to weave new words into the verses to reflect Moanna's landscape.

The words were hilarious. I began to snap my fingers to the imaginary rhythm as he made up new lines without skipping a beat.

When John started whistling at the end of the song, Willow and I were in a groove with him, swaying and snapping and clapping in time. Once he faded his whistle out, we both erupted in cheers.

"Sing it again." Willow jumped to her feet and nodded to urge him on.

"That was wonderful, John."

"Thank you." He grinned, only now a bit embarrassed.

"Did you just make that up?"

"Yeah, but it's one of my favorite songs, so the real words I know pretty well. It was easy to swap 'em around."

Willow said, "Teach me."

"Okay, but first we've got to get the beat down."

She sat down again right next to him, getting serious. "Okay." He laid the pole on the bank and tucked her up under his arm. It was beautiful to watch. Willow was so happy her cheeks would hurt soon.

"Let me help you feel the rhythm." He took her wrists and made her hands clap to the slow beat.

My line jerked as he was about to start the first line of the song.

"Oh ..." Willow and John looked over as I yanked the rod hard to me, trying to get the hook set good in the fish's mouth. *Wasn't that how you did it?* Before I could second-guess myself, there was another jerk. "Oh, yes, definitely something on there!" I scrambled to my feet. "Do I reel it in?"

"Yeah." John stood, stepped over his pole and rushed to my side. "Now reel it in slow." I did what he said, and we could both see my line was pulled taut. "Do you feel something tug or maybe feel like it's heavier?"

"Oh, yeah, we've definitely got something." I bit my lip, concentrating hard.

Willow watched the action as John knelt by the seawall, ready to grab the line and pull the fish up.

"There it is. I can see it." Willow bent over her knees to peer around John. Before long, with John's help, it was on the grass next to us. "It's huge!" Willow screamed.

Yikes, it was large.

"Yeah, it is. What kind of fish is it?"

John leaned down to pick up the line and let the fish dangle in front of Willow's face. "This is a redfish. You can tell by the spot right here on the tail. It's probably a good nineteen inches." He looked over at me with a wide grin and nodded. "Good catch, Eva."

On the dock, Thad yelled, "Way to go, Eva."

We looked over to see Mom and him standing and clapping, full of smiles. Willow gave Thad a thumbs-up sign, and he returned it.

Mom yelled, "Bring it over so we can get a closer look."

"Okay." I turned to John just as the fish jerked under his grip. "Um, how about you hold the pole with the big fish, and I'll reel the other one in."

He laughed. "Of course. Willow, let's start walking. We've got to get this fish in some water."

THAD

"So, what do you men do with the fish you catch? Do you have a fish fry? I've never had one of those, but I always wanted to throw one." Ellen's voice faded as if she processed that thought.

Dad chuckled and rearranged his legs to prop his elbows on his knees.

"No, ma'am, I wish. We end up tallying who won for the day in inches of fish caught. Loser usually has to buy dinner or something. And then we let the fish go. Truth is, Thad and I are pretty inept in the kitchen. Before my wife passed, she used to take care of us real nice, but now if something doesn't involve warming in the microwave or the oven, it doesn't make it into the grocery cart."

I grimaced and nodded at Eva in shame. She covered her mouth because she was chewing, but I could see her laugh lines leaving the cutest crevices in her face.

Dad continued, "Well, except Thad's healthy foods. He eats a ton of fresh vegetables and fruits. You should see how much he tries to cram in the fridge drawers each week."

Eva said, "Can you teach a four-year-old to love healthy foods?"

"Yuck, like carrots?"

"Yes, baby, like carrots. Maybe one day."

Everyone quieted, all taking bites of their sandwiches, chips, apple slices—and carrots, of all things—from the picnic Eva had packed. I had Willow's fishing pole, under instructions to not let anything get away while she ate. Little Willow already showed signs of being competitive. She couldn't allow her mom to beat her.

"Eva, did Thad tell you his mom and I were teachers? We taught in rural South Georgia until retirement. Thad said you taught a couple of years in North Georgia before y'all moved here?" Dad popped the last bite of sandwich in his mouth.

Eva sat up straighter. "Yes, Thad told me you two were teachers. I graduated from UGA in May and had Willow in June."

"June seventh," Willow said proudly.

Eva reached to tug her closer. "Yes, June seventh. And ... I didn't get a teaching job right away." She paused, contemplating what to say. "I didn't even apply for one, actually. I had just moved back in with Mom."

"Gramma," Willow filled in for us.

Eva smiled. "Yes. We both moved to Chattanooga, my hometown, and when Willow was about to turn seven months old, I took a long-term sub position. I'm sure you know what those are, John."

"Oh, yes, my wife had to have one while she was on maternity leave when Thad came to us. And I had to have one when I had back surgery about ten years ago. Just old injuries acting up."

"Well," I said, "*I* don't know what a long-term sub is. A substitute, obviously ..."

SAFE HARBOR

"Yes," Eva turned to me. "A sub that knows they're going to be in the same classroom for an extended period of time. In Georgia, if it's anything over two weeks, that sub has to be a certified teacher in the state."

"Got it." I put my finger to my temple and tapped. "And you were the certified teacher hired for the job opening."

"Yup, I came in when the teacher was put on bed rest and later, maternity leave once the baby arrived. I basically taught the kids, seventh graders, from January until the end of the school year. The same school offered me a teaching position that summer. So, I took it, and Willow and I got a little cottage close to both the school and her daycare. I taught there for three years, and here I am."

Ellen jumped in, "Yes, she loved that school, but I hated the fact she and Willow were an hour away. Her doing the parenting thing on her own, you know?"

"Mom," Eva threatened.

"Anyway, I finally decided it was time to sell the big old house in Chattanooga. James and I had always talked about buying a house on Moanna, so it just felt right to move here with my girls."

"Well, we're glad." Dad winked at Willow. "So, no other brothers and sisters in Chattanooga? No other grandparents?"

I shot my eyes to Eva. Dad asked the question I had been wondering. *Where are Willow's other grandparents?* Eva bit her lip, hesitating, and Willow blurted out, "No, Mama says she's an only child, like me." Willow beamed at her mom. "And I just have Gramma."

Dad nodded sincerely at Willow. "Ah, I see."

Ellen sighed with clear frustration. "Yes, I'm the only one. We do *not* want to go there."

Eva clapped her hands, snapping my gaze back to her, a look of panic touching her eyes.

"No, we do not." She stood. "Okay, I'm ready to fish again. Thad, Willow, and Mom on a team. John and I on the other. My guess is y'all are going down, especially since we're already one ahead because of my catch earlier. And since you"—she pointed at me—"haven't had a nibble on your line yet."

I stood up, pole still in hand and a glint in my eyes as I stared her down. "You're on."

CHAPTER FIFTEEN

TUESDAY

THAD

Bo, my running back, and I jumped off the railing from where we sat as his mom pulled into the parking lot in her older model maroon Toyota Corolla. She stopped in front of us and waved through the window, her apron from the café where she worked still tied around her neck.

She rolled the passenger window down as Bo tossed his gear and school backpack into the back seat. "I'm so sorry I'm late."

"It's fine, no problem," I said as my phone sounded in my back pocket. I pulled the phone out and said to her, "You all drive safe. 'Bye, Bo."

He shut the door as he got in. "Thanks, Coach. See you tomorrow."

I waved and looked down at my caller ID.

California?

I slid my finger across the screen. "Hello, this is Thad."

"Thad? You're going by your first name now, I see." Becca's voice tumbled out of the phone into my ear.

"Becca?"

"Yes! Man, Damien, it took me a while to track down your new number. But I finally got Matt Robinson to give it to me."

Matt, my old Charger teammate, and one of the only guys I still kept in touch with on that side of the country. Why'd he *do* that? He knew what she'd done to me.

I tried to hide the betrayal I felt.

"Oh. Okay." I picked up my bag and started to my truck.

"So, did you really move to Georgia? Back to your roots? I can't believe it. I can't imagine my Damien anywhere near the country. I mean, I know you've always had a hint of twang, but seriously?" She rambled, and since I didn't know what to say, I let her. "Are you ready to come back to San Diego yet? I'm sure you are."

"Uh, no. I'm doing really good here. I coach a middle school football team. Just got done with practice. We're pretty good." Now I rambled. What was I supposed to say? Flat-out asking why she'd called after all this time seemed rude.

"For real? Oh gosh, well that's, um, shocking. I mean, I always thought you were great with kids, always were a sucker to give the kids in the stands autographs or high-fives, and even go to those appearances at the children's hospital, but coaching? Like, Little League? It's just too much." She laughed loudly, and I pulled the phone away from my ear.

I opened the back hatch window and checked my pocket to confirm my keys were there before throwing my bag in. "Well, it's true."

"So where in Georgia are you living?"

What would it hurt to tell her? It's not like I set out *not* to be found. It happened by coincidence, and I'd just kept it that way. I leaned back against my bumper. "I live on Moanna Island. Not too far from Savannah."

"Ah, that sounds more like the Damien I know, living on the beach. I might have to give you a surprise visit soon."

I laughed like she was joking. I saw movement out of the corner of my eye and turned to see Eva walking to her car.

SAFE HARBOR

She'd been watching me, and when our eyes met, fireworks exploded inside my heart. The intense pleasure I received every time I saw her was addicting. "It was nice catching up, but I've got to run. Sorry," I said as I approached Eva at her car.

Becca called out, "Wait, Damien," just before I tapped the red button. She'd have to call back if it was important.

"Well, hey." Eva smiled as she hiked her purse and computer bag higher up on her shoulder.

"Hey to you too. Let me grab those." I reached for her bags, and to my surprise, she let me.

She unlocked her car and reached around me to open her back door. "You can just toss them in there."

"You're here way too late, Miz Elliott." I laid the bags down and shut the door.

"I know. We're getting ready for Open House tomorrow." She motioned back toward the front door. "I keep running through my list of to-dos and hoping I haven't forgotten anything. This is my first impression with these parents."

"I'm sure they'll love you."

Her breath hitched, and she looked at the ground. "I hope so. I'm still the new kid on the block."

"Who everyone falls for immediately." Now she really blushed. "I was hoping to catch you. I remembered last night that I owe Willow some ice cream."

Her teeth slowly dragged across her lip, stirring the embers always smoldering when she was around.

"Are you ladies free Friday evening? The best place for ice cream is by the lighthouse in the harbor, so we could check out the lighthouse too."

She perked up. "I *have* been wanting to take Willow there. She'd really love that."

I opened her door for her. "So can I pick you both up at six thirty?"

"Sure," she said before she climbed in.

"Okay, then, it's a da—it's on the schedule."

She laughed and put her hair behind her ear, leaving her hand on her collarbone. "Yes, it's on the schedule."

"'Bye." I closed her door as she started the car. She reversed out of the parking spot and waved, smiling the whole time, all the while stoking those embers inside.

As I watched Eva's car disappear, Becca's voice shook its way into my mind.

Damien, it took me a while to track down your new number.

Even my name, the one I didn't go by anymore, got under my skin. I thought I was over the anger and guilt from when Becca was my fiancée. My irritated attitude told me different.

God, I've moved forward. Please don't allow my past to mess up my future.

CHAPTER SIXTEEN

FRIDAY

EVA

"Mama, come on."

"I'm here, I'm here." I found Willow in the foyer staring out the window, waiting for Thad's Bronco to appear. She didn't turn away when she said, "I'm so excited. This is gonna be the best day ever!"

Regret, a feeling as common as my daily coffee, bubbled inside me. The risks were too high. I'd decided to tell Thad that whatever was happening between us couldn't happen anymore. It was clear Willow's heart was already in play.

"Is the lighthouse big?"

"Yes, it's really tall and skinny. We'll have to walk up a bunch of stairs. Are you sure you can handle it?"

"Yeah, I'm big."

"I know, baby." Willow's black fancy Sunday shoes shined up at me. "We've got to change shoes. Here, let's put your boots on." I grabbed them by the door. "These will be more comfortable."

"But I wanted to dress up for our date."

I froze, half of me wanting to laugh, half of me wanting to cry.

Where'd she hear that? I don't even date.

"Willow, no fussing. Boots it is."

Mom walked in from the kitchen, drying her hands on a towel as I put the second boot on and zipped up the side. "Don't you look adorable?"

"Thanks." I turned to the mirror to adjust my light brown and crème silk scarf. It lay on my lightweight brown sweater paired with dark blue skinny jeans and brown ankle boots.

Mom cocked her head and whipped Willow lightly on the behind with the towel. "I meant this little four-year-old." Willow caught onto the joke. She curtsied in her blue ruffle skirt, matching blue and purple top, and black leggings.

Mom winked. "But you look good too, my dear."

"Well, thanks," I said sarcastically.

"Don't forget to put on lipstick."

"Does lip gloss count?" I pulled out my favorite subtle color of lip gloss from my purse. Mom always wanted me to wear bolder colors of lipstick than what I was comfortable with.

Mom mumbled, "Sure, sure."

"I want some too."

"Okay." I applied a tiny layer to her lips and turned to the mirror to apply mine when the doorbell rang. Faster than I thought was possible, I applied, capped, and threw the lip gloss in my purse in time to see Mom pull open the door and Willow jump into Thad's arms.

THAD

"Whoa." My reflexes caught Willow in midair.

"Hi, Thad." Her hair bounced into her light blue eyes.

"Hey to you," I said as she locked her skinny arms around my neck, her tiny fingers linked together. I looked past Ellen to see Eva's own deep brown eyes.

SAFE HARBOR

I put Willow down onto the porch. "Wow, Eva, you're just ... gorgeous."

"Oh, please." Eva reached behind her, snatching up her purse. "You mostly see me at the school with day-old makeup on or soaking wet from the ocean or pool." I started to say something, but she added, "Y'all ready to climb those lighthouse steps?"

"*And* get ice cream."

I nodded to Willow. "Definitely get ice cream."

"'Bye, Mom. Don't wait up." She winked at Ellen, who laughed and waved. We made our way to the driveway, and Willow slipped her tiny hand into mine, sending a jolt of lightning to my brain. Not only was I falling in love with Eva Elliott, but I was falling in love with Willow too.

EVA

"Why do I feel like I'm negotiating with *two* kids right now?" I stopped and put my hands on my hips as both Willow and Thad showed off their best puppy dog eyes.

"You could give in to the kid inside you too." Thad broke the word "too" into two syllables and said it to the tune of a song. "Just say yes." He begged with his light brown, velvety eyes.

I blew out a hard breath and threw my hands in the air. "Okay, I give in. Dessert before dinner."

"Yes!" Both Thad and Willow high-fived as we proceeded to the ice cream truck parked along the boardwalk. To our right, the lighthouse towered over us, casting shadows into the ocean. To the left, storefronts with condos above them faced the bay. The condos' balconies overlooked a harbor packed full of gigantic yachts and charter fishing boats that rocked back and forth in the shallow wake. The smell of saltwater and decaying fish was rampant, yet the views outweighed any offense to the nose.

"All right, girls, what will you have?" Thad pointed to the menu above the head of the teen behind the window.

"Ooh, Willow, they have mint chocolate chip."

"Yeah. That one." Willow licked her lips.

"Okay. And the peanut butter for me," Thad said.

"That's the one I was thinking. You *cannot* go wrong with peanut butter anything."

"Agreed. I'll get them. You guys go find us a table."

"Okay."

Before the word was even out of my mouth, Willow ran toward the picnic tables set along the boardwalk, butting up close to the stone barrier railing.

"Willow," I called out, "this one's empty." In reality, they all were. People walked in all directions, but no one stayed still enough to enjoy the scenery. I patted the bench next to me and leaned back against the edge of the table to look out at the water. "Come sit by me, girlie."

Willow sat crisscross next to me. In the distance, a golf course stretched to meet massive rocks lining the shoreline. They jutted out at sharp angles into the ocean. Waves beat against them over and over, spraying mist up into the air. I was mesmerized by the rhythm of the waves, and their power as they crashed into the rocks and wore them down over time.

"Whatcha thinking about?" Thad knocked me out of my daydream as he followed my stare to the rocks.

"Oh, nothing. Goodness, those are huge." He balanced two cones in one hand and handed Willow hers with the other. The double scoop was nearly the size of her face. Her face took on a look of pure indulgence as she went to work. Thad pulled a big wad of napkins out from his back pocket and held them over her head.

SAFE HARBOR

I acknowledged the huge mass with my own wide eyes.

Willow mumbled, "Thanks, Thad." She didn't even look up, couldn't break her eyes away from the light green cream about to drip onto her fingers.

"You're welcome." Thad handed me my cone before sitting down next to me.

"Thank you."

"Of course. Are you going to tell me where your mind was?"

"Um." I bit the inside of my cheek. "I was just thinking how the waves wear down the rocks over time, hitting them like that. How the rocks may not want to be changed, but the waves wear them down anyway." I couldn't risk a look into Thad's eyes, couldn't find the courage to see if he realized I was thinking about him.

"Huh." Thad reached out and pulled me to him, leaving his arm around my shoulders, holding me close. He brought his mouth close to my head. "Maybe the rocks secretly want to be changed. Maybe they're stubborn and like the idea of being sturdy and strong, but what they don't realize is they can be that way and still give in to the waves' persistence."

I sighed, loving the feeling of his big arm securing me to him. We both worked on our ice creams for a moment. Willow remained in her own little world of sugar and stickiness.

Thad squeezed my shoulders once more, then released me. "You know, that's how God works." He used the cone in his hand to point to the crashing waves. "He's like the big ocean using the waves to shape us, molding us to be like Christ. We can resist him, but like those waves, he's never going to stop."

How did he manage to turn this conversation to God?

His stare was like a force. "You see how those rocks reach right up to the railing?"

I could only nod. My throat had closed up at the mention of God and his persistence to draw us to him.

"Well, I come out here sometimes. At night. And jump the railing. Only when the tide is out, of course, which it is definitely *not* right now. But when it is, you can sneak down to the rocks and go out there where the big waves are right now. I sit there, and it's like you can hear his whispers in the wind and feel his power so strong out there in the elements. But still, it's a safe place, tucked into the harbor. Being there makes you feel like ... like you can almost touch him."

The wind rushed our spot, and I swept my hair back out of my face in time to see Thad shake his head and run his hand through his own hair.

When the wind died, he said, "Remember, Eva." The peacefulness I felt flowing from him on the beach after he saved Willow's life continued to make its way into my soul, navigating the twists and turns into the ocean of my heart. "I've been there at the crossroads between turning toward him or continuing down the same old path. Trust me when I say turning toward him— turning back to him—was the best decision I ever made."

THAD

Eva sat with her forehead scrunched up, hopefully allowing my words to penetrate down to her heart. God had urged me to be bold, but before the silence could loom over us for long, Willow cried, "Uh-oh, it's drippin.'"

Eva went into mom mode and reached for the stack of napkins. "Here, let me grab it." She traded Willow's cone for a napkin. Through her laughter, she said, "Well, you got pretty far with this huge ice cream, didn't you?" Willow had almost made it to the actual cone.

"Yeah, it was *so* good."

Holding the cones upright in her hands, Eva propelled herself off the bench. She licked one last time around her own cone's rim.

"Okay, I'm going to throw these away. You freeze, Missy. I'll be right back to wipe your sticky face." Eva made a face at Willow, who returned one.

I loved watching the ease of their relationship. Eva was a wonderful mother, but I'd learned that the first day we met. I'd always imagined my birth mother as a single mom, and being so, she gave me up thinking she couldn't raise me alone. But Eva was faced with the same scenario, yet she pushed on. My birth mother's decision was brave and admirable. So was Eva's.

She hustled back and rubbed Willow's face delicately, which was almost impossible due to all the green and brown on Willow's chin. She licked her thumb and ran it along the edges of Willow's lips.

She felt me watching her. "Thad, do you need a spit bath too?" Willow laughed and tried to look over her mom's fingers at me.

"Yes, please."

Eva scoffed, looked over with playfulness in her eyes. "Seriously, though. What?"

"Nothing, I just love to watch you with her."

Eva gulped—hands frozen on Willow's cheeks. A beat of intense eye contact passed between us before Willow shook herself free. "Mama, you done?"

She turned from me and kissed Willow's nose. "I guess so."

I popped the last of my cone in my mouth. "All right. Lighthouse, then dinner."

"Yes," Willow said, so loud passersby looked over. Then she jumped up from the bench. I followed.

"Hey, Willow, I've got a bad knee. You think you could carry me up all those stairs?"

Her eyes got really big before the joke clicked home. "I can try."

Eva chuckled as she sidled between us.

"Awesome," I said. "Maybe we'll catch the sunset from up there." We craned our necks to see the landing at the peak of the lighthouse. Willow grabbed her mom's hand, and I gently tugged Eva close.

EVA

"Gramma, you up?" Willow burst through the front door and ran to the family room, where the glow from a lamp showed.

Mom got up from the couch. "I am." She rounded the couch as Willow crashed into her legs and wrapped them up in a hug. "Did you all have fun?"

"Oh, yeah. The lighthouse was so high. Thad had to carry me up some. My legs were tired."

"Really? He had to use those superhero muscles?" Mom patted Willow softly on the head and winked at Thad.

He found his voice. "She did really good." He bent to look Willow in the eyes. "It was only a couple of stairs. You pretty much did it all on your own."

I lay my purse in the foyer chair and unraveled my scarf to place it on the small table, preparing myself for what had to come.

My plan had wavered the whole evening. *Maybe the rocks secretly want to change ...*

SAFE HARBOR

Did I? Should I?

Part of me relished Thad's presence, with his sweet, funny calmness and his adorable way with Willow, and how Willow adored him. But those same feelings had the other part of me reeling. Those very things were the reasons I should just tell Thad whatever was going on between us needed to end. Who was I kidding anyway, to think he'd want a future with someone as tainted and messed up as me?

And Willow? The risk of Willow falling in love with him—already happening—only to lose him one day when he saw I wasn't good enough, was too much. The remote chance Willow might one day feel that pain was enough to knock the breath out of me.

Mom's voice intruded, "Eva? Earth to Eva."

I shook out of my daze to find them all grinning.

"Uh, sorry. Thad, I have to get Willow's car seat from your truck. I'll go through the garage and open it so we can put it in my car." With the colder weather, I'd started parking inside on occasion. "That okay?"

"Sure thing." Thad nodded to Mom and Willow. "Good night, ladies."

"'Night, Thad." Willow hugged his legs.

"Good night," he said as he ran his hand over her hair.

"Good night, Thad." Mom waved as he opened the front door.

"I'll meet you there." I turned before my emotions showed and went through the kitchen and mudroom into the garage. Shutting the door behind me left me in the darkness of the garage, with only the light from the opener button shining. I took a deep breath, gaining courage for the conversation I was about to have.

Pushing the breath out, I clicked the button, and turned to see Thad's feet, already on the other side waiting as the door went up.

THAD

I could sense a shift when we got back. Just a slight coldness radiating off Eva. Not anger, just ...

Distance.

The garage door opened, and Eva's feet moved to her car. By the time it was all the way up, she had the back seat's door open. "You can just toss it in there. I'll strap it in later." She wouldn't look at me.

I shut the door and took in a long breath. "Eva." I faced her. "What's wrong?"

She fidgeted. "How do you read me so easily?"

Because I think I love you.

Those words surfaced, but I shook my head and shrugged.

She flinched behind closed eyes. "I hate how you make my mind spin round and round."

"What do you mean?"

She huffed. "I mean, what are we doing? This? C'mon, how could this ever work out between us?"

"What?" It came out sounding a little too harsh, and I softened my tone. "Why would you say something like that?"

"I've got—let's just call it baggage. Lots and lots of baggage. I'm damaged goods, Thad." She threw her hands up. "Damaged goods trying to protect the one thing I got right."

I stood there dumbfounded. "Eva, you don't see yourself the way you should. You are *not* damaged. You may have some broken pieces needing mending, but don't we all? You're amazing. How could you think those things about yourself?"

"You don't know me."

"I know what I need to know. You are an amazing mother, amazing daughter, amazing teacher …" Her eyes glistened a little. "You have a tendency to seem a little standoffish, but only at first." I took a step closer. "You try really hard not to laugh sometimes, but usually you fail miserably." I risked another step closer. She held her ground. "You're also trying really hard not to fall for me, but you're failing miserably there too."

She tried not to smile. Realizing what she was doing, she smiled anyway, a soft curve of her lips. I braced my hand on the hood of her car and leaned in, effectively pushing her back against it. I was close enough to see her long lashes behind the fallen strands of her hair on her cheeks. She moved them behind her ear, leaving her hand resting on her collarbone. Her exposed neck so close to my lips made them tingle with want.

I drew close to her ear and inhaled, allowing her mix of perfume and Skittles shampoo to fill my lungs. My voice came out barely above a whisper. "You also have this insanely sensuous habit of resting your hand on your collarbone, not intentionally trying to draw attention there, but again failing miserably."

I brushed her cheek with mine, then kissed the bone next to her fingers. She arched her back and rose to meet me. Her hands embraced my face, and her thumb swiped my bottom lip. Both lost in the moment, bodies tight against one another, my heart raged with lust and desire to kiss her, but I held back. Waiting.

Her teeth tugged on her bottom lip.

"And now I know you're really cute when you're frustrated."

She shook her head, slid her hands to my chest, and rested her forehead there.

"See? Round and round I go again. Why do you have to make this so hard?" Her shoulders rocked, and the sadness in her voice ripped my heart out. "Willow has to be my only focus. I can't bring in anyone else who could be taken from her. The risks are too high. Even your football background is a red flag."

The football background remark threw me. But she pushed on.

"When Willow learns about her dad, it will be a permanent reminder of what she's lost forever, a reminder of the tragedy that left an unfillable hole in her heart. I have to protect her."

Oh.

I forced her chin up to look at me. "What if my past proves we're meant to make a go at this? What if I can help her make a connection with her dad that would've been lost otherwise? And Eva," I said sternly, "my whole life has been an example of how God can make something beautiful out of tragedy. You forget I was adopted. It was tragic my birth mother felt she had no other choice but to give me up. But my parents, my adoptive parents, were capable of filling my heart to capacity with love." I let that soak in. "And just so we're clear, I'm not only falling for you, I'm falling for Willow too."

"You are?" Tears trickled down her face.

I chuckled. It came out sounding like pure joy. "Yes, I can't even explain it, but it's true. And I *know* having more love in your life can never be wrong."

Her closed eyes tried to hide tears, but her sob took my already ripped-out heart and threw it to the ground, fragmenting it beyond repair. I pulled her to me.

"Shh," I whispered, my lips touching her hair. "Don't say anything else. Just let it be. Let *us* be." I braced her face in my hands. "For what it's worth, you don't know me either, Eva. There are tons of things about me, about my past, that I want to tell you, and I *will* tell you. But for now, let's accept we both have broken pieces that need mending. And know who you see before you *is* the real me, just like I see the real you—a wonderful woman allowing me to tread carefully into her life." She moved her hands to my wrist and squeezed, which I took as a good sign. "Let's just ... see what happens."

I took in every inch of her features from close up, pleading with her internal force to be responsive to my call. She bobbed her head slightly in my hands. "Okay."

"Okay?"

"Okay." She nodded with more firmness.

"Okay. I'll call you tomorrow." I brushed my fingers over her cheeks quickly, backed away and turned to leave before she could say anything else.

By the time I was in my truck, she'd made her way to the door leading into the house. She watched me crank the engine, my headlights lighting up her smile even more, a smile so big it only confirmed what I already knew. Her heart hadn't wanted to turn me away. She was used to controlling every situation, but the heart can't be controlled like the mind.

She waved and hit the garage door button as I put the truck in reverse. I watched her fade away, my body still strumming with a subtle hum that left me feeling like I'd had the most intense make-out session ever.

Yet I hadn't even kissed her lips.

CHAPTER SEVENTEEN

SATURDAY

EVA

"Okay, girlie. You're dressed for our adventure. Try to go to the bathroom, and then, find your hairbrush and a hair tie. I'm going to put on some better bike-riding clothes."

I heard Willow mumble, "Okay," as I went into my room and flipped through my closet for a long sleeved T-shirt and sweatshirt to match the black yoga pants with the hot pink stripes down the sides I already wore.

What a difference a day makes. I hadn't gone through with my plan, and I was happy about it. He was falling for Willow *and* me, and I was pushing away the feeling that one day he'd regret being with us. Now I was determined to wait and see what happened.

God, we haven't talked in a really long while, and I know I've done wrong by you, but I do want to do the right thing when it comes to anything or anyone who might affect Willow, so please guide me.

My phone dinged from my dresser, signaling a voicemail. I grabbed a turquoise sweatshirt and an old staff T-shirt from my former school. Definitely didn't match. But who would see us? I snatched up my phone. Giddiness flowed when I saw the message was from Thad.

I clicked the voicemail. "Hi, Eva. Sorry I'm just now calling. We just finished our game against Cedar Hill—you may not know where that is—anyway, we won. Still undefeated." Pride laced his words as well as the noise of the rowdy boys in the background. "Now we're on the bus again, so we'll be back in about thirty minutes. I'll call again then. 'Bye."

"Honey?" Mom called from the hall.

"I'm in here." I tossed the phone on my bed and ripped off my older T-shirt to exchange it with the newer old one.

She poked her head in the doorway. "I'm heading to the store. You need anything?"

"Nope, I'm good."

"Why are you grinning like that?"

"Like what?"

"Like you just opened a birthday present." She saw me glance at my cell. "Did Thad just call?"

"He left a voicemail. How'd you guess?"

"Please. The only one you smile like that for, besides Willow, is Thad." She smiled a satisfied look.

"Well, he's funny.

"Uh-huh, he's funny." Mom nodded sarcastically. "Anyway, so you and Willow are going to bike ride to the marina, then come home on the beach to look for shells again."

"That's the plan."

"That girl will find enough shells to fill every dish or bowl in the whole house by next year at this rate." We both laughed. True, all too true. "Are we cooking dinner tonight? Or do you have plans?"

"No, he's getting back from the away game soon, but we hadn't made any plans. Maybe I'll ask him to eat with us here tonight." I looked in the mirror and pulled my hair into a low ponytail with my hands.

SAFE HARBOR

"Definitely. I like the Eva I see when you hang with Thad. You've got to keep your streak running."

I cocked an eyebrow at her. "What are you talking about?"

"Well, you've seen Thad at least twice for two weekends in a row. Why not go for three weekends in a row?"

"You're ridiculous." I turned as Willow came into the room with a brush. "You got the hair tie too?"

"Yeah." She handed it to me and turned around, knowing the drill.

"All righty, I'll be back later. Have fun on the bikes." Mom left.

"'Bye."

"'Bye, Gramma."

I finished with Willow's hair, braiding the low ponytail in hopes it would stay out of her eyes better. "Okay, let's see. We need a sand bucket to put in my bike basket for when we get to the beach and helmets. What else?" I asked, not really expecting an answer. "Oh, don't let me forget my wallet for ice cream at the marina's General Store."

"Yeah." Willow bounced out of the room with me close behind, ready to load up for our adventure, forgetting my phone on the bed.

THAD

"You're still here?" Dad asked as he came out of his room into the kitchen. "Finding anything?"

I peeked around the open fridge door. "Not much. We've got bread, so I was hoping for some lunch meat, but nope." I closed the door. "I was trying to talk myself into a plain cheese sandwich."

Dad flinched. "I know there's peanut butter. But maybe no jelly."

"Well, that's better, I guess. I might just order pizza."

"You're not seeing Eva and maybe Willow tonight?" I liked how Dad fit them into my world already.

"I'm not sure. I called her before I jumped into the shower, and she didn't answer. She'll call back soon."

"Okay, well, I'm going to Joe's to watch the Iowa game." He still watched every game from my alma mater, even listened to it streaming online if they weren't on TV. He'd forever be a University of Iowa Hawkeyes fan. "He has all those ESPN channels." Dad's eyes got wide.

"Okay, have fun."

He started down the hall toward the garage. "You sure you don't want to come?"

"Yeah, I'll be fine. Might even fall asleep on the couch."

"Okay. 'Bye."

I collapsed on the sofa. My hunger pains must have been more out of boredom than actual hunger, because they vanished as the cushy couch called my name. I got comfortable, and just as my muscles released their tension and my body was feeling weighted down along with my eyelids, the doorbell rang.

I swung my feet to the floor, hoping I wasn't about to open the door to a solicitor selling vacuums. I pulled it open, ready to say "Thanks but no thanks" when Becca's voice blasted my ears.

"Damien?"

No.

She looked exactly the same—perfectly put together, prim and proper. Well, except for the tight leather jacket and too-short skirt. "Surprise!"

She shuffled to me, her usual heels clicking, and jumped into my arms. Literally. Her feet left the ground and I fell back into the foyer, off-balance in so many ways. I put her down fast and put some distance between us.

"Uh ..." I forced a smile. "Hey. What are you doing here? How'd you find me?"

"It wasn't that hard. Once you said you lived on Moanna, I searched the property records over the last five years, and here I am."

"Oh." I swallowed hard.

"I can't believe Damien Smith of the Chargers moved from San Diego to this tiny island. But I have to admit this house is gorgeous."

"Thanks. Come on in." I couldn't leave her standing there. She walked in and immediately started down the hall to the back of the house, her steps loud on the hardwood floors, rattling my brain and triggering the start of a headache. I shut the door and followed her.

God, calm me down. I am not hothead Damien anymore. She's here for a reason. Help me help her.

She looked around my kitchen. "Oh my. Good job choosing this house."

"Dad actually picked it out. I told him we could live on the beach anywhere, and he chose Moanna. Though it wasn't much of a surprise. He's really into golf now, so it was a no-brainer for him."

"Well, I guess I see the appeal. I wasn't too sure about this area before I crossed over the bridge. It looked really run down. But the island is awesome. Lots of money here."

I fought the urge to cringe. Her words were true on statistics, but I didn't like hearing them out loud. It made me feel like I was cheating on my boys, giving in to the idea that if you lived on the island, you were somehow better than they were. I tried not to let my irritation build.

"It's nice here, but Palmer's great too. Lots of hard-working families. And the community really rallies around our football program. Before it got started, these boys didn't have any kind of organized football league in the area. These kids were trying out for high school football, having never actually played." Crazy, but true.

"That's great." Her blue eyes caught mine. "You seem really ... proud."

I smiled and shrugged. "I guess I am."

She set her purse on the counter and sat on one of the barstools.

"Would you like something to drink? All I have is Gatorade and water."

"Sure. A water is fine." I grabbed two bottles from the fridge and slid one over the counter to her, opening the other for myself.

"What have you been up to?" I leaned against the sink and watched her take a slow sip, so calculated, so careful not to smear any lipstick. She was the Becca I remembered—even after five years still caught up in so many things that didn't matter, like makeup and manicures and fancy clothes. Priorities I hadn't noticed she had until God ripped my legs out from under me.

"Well, I'm doing some modeling again, which means traveling. My shoots are always everywhere in California *except* San Diego. But I still love it there. Still home, I guess."

"That's good. San Diego is a beautiful place to call home."

She smiled and tossed her long wavy blonde locks over her shoulder. She went to the wall of windows and stared silently out at the ocean, brooding over something.

I followed her. "Would you like to go outside to talk? The ocean does wonders to clear my head."

And to remind me who's really in charge.

"Sure."

SAFE HARBOR

As if the sea called, she strolled past the porch and down the stairs to the pool, stopping by the small gate that closed off my short ramp to the beach. "Wow, your condo on the beach in San Diego was nice, but it's so crowded there compared to here."

"Yeah, Moanna is a wonderful place."

Silence loomed until she sighed.

"There's a lot I want to say." She caressed my elbow and faced me. "I didn't realize how hard this would be." She moved both hands to my chest. "And how much I've missed you."

I covered her hands in mine and smiled, trying to be sensitive to her vulnerability. "Let it out, Becca. Tell me why you're here." Movement behind her stole my attention.

The blur dissipated, and Eva came into focus, frozen in the sand, staring at me.

"Eva," I said softly. I brushed away Becca's hands and moved her direction, practically tripping over the gate before recovering and yanking it open.

"Damien," Becca called. "Where are you going?"

I didn't answer. I was moving away from my past, running toward my future.

EVA

"Eva!"

I saw them together and froze. My feet, my mouth, my heart—all turned to ice.

Thad and a woman—a gorgeous woman—embraced behind the gate of a stately beach house next to *our* beach walk. His eyes landed on me and when he called out my name, his voice jolted me from my immobile state. I pushed my bike over the hard-packed sand to get away.

"Willow, this is it." I tried to utter the words calmly as she stopped with her training bike a few yards ahead of me. "C'mon, we've got to go in."

She responded, but I didn't hear what she said. All I heard was Thad.

"Eva, stop!"

Willow's head followed his voice. Exactly what I didn't want. "Mama, it's Thad."

"I know, baby, but we can't talk right now. We've got to get home." I gestured for her to keep going even though she looked at me like I had sipped crazy juice.

Too late.

"Hey," he said, breathless from his run. His hand wrapped around my arm and spun me to him. "I didn't expect to see you here."

"I can see that." I willed an awkward smile as I pulled away. He let his hand drop back to his side.

The woman came up behind Thad, her fingers latched through the straps of her high heels. She eyed me carefully, as I did her.

"Damien, are you going to introduce us?" She scooted Thad out of the way. "Hi, I'm Becca." She stuck out her hand. She was at least four inches taller than me *without* the heels.

"Hi. I'm Eva." Our handshake was a bit contrived.

Get it together, Eva. You have no right to be jealous.

I felt Thad's eyes but couldn't look at him. After a beat, Thad said, "Uh, Becca, Eva is a teacher where I coach."

She mumbled an "Oh, how nice."

"And that's her daughter, Willow." Willow just waved, oblivious to the weirdness.

"Becca is an ... old friend."

She swatted at Thad. "Don't be so drab. We were going to get married." She said the word "married" looking straight at me, and linked arms with him.

He removed her arm from his but seemed perplexed as to what to do or say next. I took it as my cue to flee from the awkwardness.

I stood up straighter, pushing a lightness into my words. "Well, you guys probably have a lot to talk about." I turned to Becca. "Nice to meet you." I tried really hard to sound sincere. It wasn't her fault she was special to Thad. "See ya."

I did a one-eighty and moved as fast as possible to the beach walk. Willow fell in step with me, and Thad followed.

"Wait. You don't have to go. Stay. Let me explain."

I didn't even turn.

"Please." His tone was softer, apologetic.

I made it to the beach walk and waved Willow onward.

"Go on, baby. Gramma's probably wondering where we are by now. I'm right behind you."

I could sense his closeness behind me and turned. Becca still lingered in the sand.

"Don't follow me, Thad."

"Then I'm coming over later."

"Don't." I shook my head. "Just ... don't." I allowed ice into my words, then turned and fled before he could see the coming tears.

THAD

With Becca on my tail, I stalked back to the house full of adrenaline, fueled by guilt and irritation. I crumpled—that's what it felt like—to the couch.

"Becca, why are you here?"

She breathed deep and kept her distance, still hovering by the back door. "This isn't going how I planned. I came here because I'm turning over a new leaf, and part of that means righting my wrongs."

She paused. I didn't respond.

"We didn't break up on good terms," she said.

"Right. Because you cheated on me with a teammate. Right after my mom died. And while I was still recovering from the knee injury that ended my career."

She turned, and I sensed black mascara was about paint her cheeks. "I know." She looked at the floor. "I know, and I'm so sorry."

God, what would you have me say?

I leaned back and crossed my arms. No godly words magically came. "So you came to right that wrong? To tell me you're sorry for cheating on me? It seems like an awful long way to travel, considering you've already apologized a thousand times years ago. Especially after you realized he'd never commit to you."

My ex-teammate was known for his playboy ways, yet she'd been fooled into thinking he might be able to give her something I couldn't. She was lured by a player still in action, still a celebrity, and still making tons of money. Instead of me, the guy who was old news before the bandage came off.

Becca pursed her lips. "I deserved that." She gestured to my couch. "Can I sit?"

"Sure. Whatever."

She struggled to regain her composure.

"So what you don't know," she finally said, "is after you moved away and changed your number, I went to a really bad place. It's not your fault, obviously—I mean, I made my own bed so I had to lie in it. But I became really depressed. I started drinking. A lot. And it got worse and worse. At first, I drank because I was sad and then because it made me feel happy for a little while. Then, I drank because I needed it to function after work, and then I needed it to function throughout the day."

I maneuvered to see her better, resting my arm on the back of the couch. Her words stirred an emotion I couldn't quite place. Maybe empathy. Maybe something else.

She nervously fiddled with the hem of her skirt. "Anyway, I did some stupid things. I was really lost for a while."

Her words brought Thad back and left Damien behind. We weren't so different. I reached out and patted her forearm. "Hey, we all do stupid things when we're lost. I know I did."

"Yeah, well, I'm turning over a new leaf. I came here to apologize again for hurting you, but also for something else."

I cocked my head, waiting.

"Before I went into rehab, I was low on money. My agency knew I was having issues, so they weren't sending me to many auditions. I wasn't getting many jobs."

"And?"

"And I'm so sorry, but I sold the engagement ring you gave me." Her look was one of deep shame and self-reproach.

I chuckled.

"Why are you laughing?"

I threw my hands up. "I don't know. I just thought what you had to tell me was a bigger deal than that."

"Really?"

"Really. I'm kind of relieved."

She smiled, the tears retreating.

"It's fine, really," I said, waving a dismissive hand. "I gave that ring to you."

"I know, but when we broke up, I should have given it back. I just couldn't."

"I wouldn't have taken it. It was yours to do with it what you wanted, and if it helped you out of a tight money situation, then good."

Relief washed over her features.

I paused, finding the words, and found her eyes. "Becca, you know how before I left, I'd begun attending church every Sunday and doing my own Bible study every morning." I didn't need to mention those new habits were a major reason we'd grown apart.

"Yeah, I remember."

"Well, you know with Mom's death and blowing out my knee for the *last* time, I was in a bad place too. And those habits—returning to those habits I'd had in my youth—were what got me out of my own sadness. They continue to provide me strength every day."

She nodded. "I knew you'd say something like that. And I welcome those words now."

"Well, good. You hungry?"

"Maybe."

"How about ordering a pizza?"

"Sounds good." The old Becca would have laughed in my face. Maybe she had changed over the years.

"C'mon," I stood and headed to my phone in the kitchen. "I'll tell you how I beat my own issues. Maybe help you out if you're open to him." I pointed to the ceiling.

"Okay." She stood to follow, but I halted mid step.

"Oh, and I forgive you. For everything. And please forgive me for all the millions of things I did wrong over the two years we were together."

"Sure." She grinned, and I started for the kitchen again. "And Thad?"

I glanced at her over my shoulder.

"I'm sorry for earlier."

I frowned, confused.

"For when I met Eva. She's really, *really* cute, and she seems sweet. I can tell you both are totally into each other, and I'm sorry I did what I did. I guess a possessive urge came over me, even after all this time."

SAFE HARBOR

"It's okay."

I hope.

I grabbed my phone, resisting the urge to call Eva. God needed me with Becca now, though I was surprised he'd chosen me to help her.

God, speak for me this afternoon. What do you need Becca to know to get her on your track?

I scrolled to the pizza joint's number and tapped. "You're gonna love this stuff. Best, *and only*, pizza joint on the island that delivers."

"Cool," she said, just as the clerk said hello through the phone.

Eva

"He's at the beach with this beautiful woman, like seriously gorgeous, Mom. She's the polar opposite of me—high heels, long, bleached-blonde hair, huge blue eyes, perfect legs. Which were easy to notice because she was wearing a short skirt."

"High heels and a skirt? It's too cold for that outfit."

"That's not the point." I dropped my voice, afraid Willow would wake up. "He sees me and rushes over. She follows him. So he introduces us, which is mortifying enough. Then it turns out they were going to get married."

Mom crossed her arms and sat on my bed. Willow had told her we saw Thad, but I told Mom not to ask. She'd waited until Willow was asleep to confront me.

"And that's not even the worst part. I think it was *his* beach house, because why would he be there with Becca who's from San Diego if it wasn't? It makes sense now, why he was always on that part of the beach—but why didn't he tell me he lived a block away? The next street over, Mom. The next street over! This whole time I've assumed he lived in Palmer." I ran my hands down my face, begging the tears to stay behind my eyes.

Mom's face didn't wear the shock and disgust I expected it to. *Wanted* it to. I threw my hands up in a gesture of frustration. "You're already on his side, aren't you?"

"No, he should have told you he lived down the street. But did you *ask* him where he lived?"

"No, but—"

"He still should have told you, I agree. But as for marrying this girl, whether she's pretty or not, remember he *didn't* go through with it."

My phone rang. Mom was closer to where it was on my dresser and snatched it up. "It's Thad."

She handed it over. I denied the call.

"Eva, don't do that. Talk to him. Give him a chance to explain."

"Mom, I let him in. I went against what my head told me to do and listened to my heart. I can't deal with any more pain there. I can't. It hurts too much." I needed to erect my prickly places again, to protect my heart and Willow's too.

Mom pulled me into her arms. "I know, baby."

I allowed myself to finally break, to be a child again in my mother's comforting embrace. She rocked me as she spoke. "Love is always a risk. Always. I didn't get to have your father as long as I wanted to, but loving him completely was the best decision I ever made. I believe in love, Eva, but we learn *how* to love through God. He's the first lover of our souls, and he understands it fully. I wish you'd let him in and pray for his guidance in this, instead of pushing someone away who just might be the salve you need to heal your heart once and for all."

SAFE HARBOR

Her words sank in and mimicked a longing that had developed in my heart since Moanna. Since Thad. A longing to be restored to God. But I could never shake the guilt over my endless sin. He wouldn't want me in my stained condition.

I was a lost cause.

CHAPTER EIGHTEEN

SUNDAY

THAD

"Can I squeeze in, boys?"

Ellen's voice caused Dad and me to look up. He stood quickly and allowed Ellen into our row as the worship team made its way onto the stage. The church service countdown clock read under two minutes.

"Ellen, you came." I stood to greet her.

"I loved last week's service, and so did Willow. We couldn't wait to come back." We sat. She put her purse in her lap and looked over the bulletin.

"So it's just Willow here with you?" Kind of obvious, but I asked anyway.

Ellen patted my knee. "Yes, just Willow and me. Eva gets more stubborn by the day, but God's doing something. I can see it in her eyes."

I nodded.

Does she know about yesterday? About the three times I called Eva last night?

We rose to our feet as the music started. Ellen reached to pat my shoulder, giving me a warm smile.

I returned her smile, then slid my eyes away.

Ellen's verse from a week ago washed though me. *In your heart you plan your life, but the Lord decides where your steps will take you.*

Becca had needed me. I tried to be on guard, always listening, whether it was an ex who did me wrong or a single mom trying to figure out a life with broken pieces.

Oddly, helping others draw close to God had healed my own wounds. Becca's visit gave me peace and closure. I hadn't even realized I'd needed it until we'd finished talking. And Eva ... Eva filled the loneliness no one had ever been able to and completed my joy in my new life. Only now, I might have messed it up before it even really began.

All because I was too ashamed and dumb to be open with her right from the start.

God, help please...

After the service concluded, Dad allowed Ellen out of the aisle. I followed and said, "I'll walk you to the children's area."

The crowd thinned in the wide hallway, and I fell in step next to her. "Enjoy the service again?"

"Of course. It's wonderful here. Everyone is so welcoming, the music is great, and the pastor's messages are spot on. It surprises me"—she sent me a look—"that I like it so much, because I've only been to traditional worship services. But this feels like a breath of fresh air. I know Eva would enjoy it."

"She mentioned the other night she's 'not ready for that' when I invited her, but I take it she grew up attending church?"

"Oh, yes. her father was adamant about our family attending every Sunday, and I taught Sunday school classes back in the day."

We got into the line to retrieve kids by the door to Willow's group.

"What happened? Did she fall out of the habit?" I backtracked. "I mean, I'm just wondering. I strayed away for a long time too. Too long, in fact."

"Thad, many of us have a backstory. Eva covered her sadness with anger toward God over her and Willow's situation for a long time." She looked up at the ceiling and closed her eyes. "It was easier that way. And I truly think she doesn't know how to get back to him. She won't talk about it with me."

At the door, Ellen gave the teacher Willow's security tag. She saw us and jumped up from the table to run to us.

"Gramma, I made art." She hugged Ellen's legs.

The young teacher said, "Yes, you did a good job. Don't forget your pages." She handed me a few papers, including a picture of Joseph wearing his coat of many colors. The colors of the coat were done in different fabrics the kids had glued onto the paper. She smiled, and a strange warmth spread out from my heart.

She thinks I'm Willow's dad.

We walked back to the front. Ellen took the papers. Willow grabbed Ellen's other hand and looked around her at me. "Thad, are we going fishing today?"

Ellen cringed.

"Um, I don't think so. Maybe some other time."

Willow shrugged. "Okay."

In the lobby, Willow caught sight of Dad. "John!"

She took off in his direction. The light showing in his eyes when he saw her made me think he felt the same warmth and happiness spread through him that I'd felt minutes ago.

God, how can I fix what I've messed up?

CHAPTER NINETEEN

THURSDAY

EVA

Before I even turned off the engine, Willow ran down the steps into the garage.

"Hey, baby." She flew around the door and rushed me for a hug before my feet touched the concrete. "This is the best part of my day, getting to see you right when I get home. Scoot over and let me get out."

"Mama, when do I get to get my costume?"

"Well, Halloween is still weeks away, but maybe we can go looking for one this weekend." She didn't know what a weekend was. "You know, when Mommy's off work for a couple of days?"

"Okay, I want to be a princess, but I don't know which one. I need to watch all the Disney princess movies over again to know."

"Oh, I see." I opened the backseat door to grab my bags. "That might take longer than a day, but maybe we can narrow it down." I shut the door. "Have you and Gramma gotten the mail today?"

"Nope." She immediately skipped to the mailbox at the end of the driveway.

"Don't you dare step into that road, young lady! You *wait* for me!"

She halted just in time. It took major effort on her part to hold on for the few seconds it took me to get to the end of the drive.

"Okay, let's look both ways." We did. "Since no cars are coming, you may get the mail."

I took an extra glance down the street. I'd been on the lookout for Thad's Bronco ever since Saturday. How could God orchestrate so many chance encounters, and yet never one on Ocean Oaks's main road?

Willow could barely reach into the mailbox, so I helped her out. "Good job. Thank you for helping."

"Welcome." She gave me a thumbs-up and ran back to the house.

I mindlessly flipped through the mail, mostly junk. "Tell Gramma we've got to start a princess movie so—"

"Okay!" Her response was front-porch distant as she went back inside the house.

My body came to an emergency stop. My heart, brain, hands, fingers—all quit working. The bag fell off my shoulder, crashing into the crook of my arm, and I dropped all the papers except one.

One envelope with familiar handwriting crinkled between my fingers.

"No, no, no, no, please ..."

My own words echoed in my head and knocked me out of my trance. I put the letter into my bag quickly and picked up the fallen mail, forcing my feet to move.

"Hey, dear," Mom said as I brushed past her in the kitchen.

"Hey. I'm going to change." I forced out joy. "Be out in a minute. Then it's princess time."

In my room, after locking the door behind me, I slumped to the ground. My bag tumbled open, and I scrambled to find the letter. I sat back against the door, opening it quickly, ripping the envelope to pieces.

SAFE HARBOR

Dear Eva,

Robert and I are hopeful this letter reaches you, that you have had your mail forwarded to your new address, and we don't find it returned to our home, address undeliverable. The other day, we drove by the cottage you rented, as we sometimes do, hoping to get a glimpse of Willow... of both of you. But we were met with a new family playing in the front yard. With building anxiety, we traveled to your childhood home, only to find much the same—different cars in the driveway and new porch furniture. Clearly, the only conclusion is Ellen and you have both moved.

Eva, we know it has been a while since we wrote to you, knowing you needed more time, more space to figure out your future. We hope the timing is right now. We want to reiterate how sorry we are for the way we treated you after Willow was born. Please give us a chance to make amends, give Willow the chance to know her father's family, a family who loves her. We don't want to interfere, just be given the opportunity to give love to Willow, to love both of you. We should have done this right from the start. Please forgive us and tell us where you are located now. We would love to visit.

Until then, we remain in our home, Alex's home, waiting for you.

With sincere love,
Robert and Pamela

Tears smacked onto the paper.

"Mama, let me in." Willow wiggled the doorknob.

I wiped the wetness off my cheeks, floundering as I stood. *Weak in the knees* was a term I could use for this moment when all else blurred, and grief and regret loomed like a hot air balloon overhead, threatening to drag me away.

"Mama," Willow whined on the other side of the wall.

"Just a minute."

"Open up." Willow's tone said she knew something was wrong. The girl knew me better than anyone on the planet.

"Coming," I said with counterfeit brightness. I raced to my dresser and yanked open the bottom drawer. I scooted old pajamas pants over and threw the letter on top of the others. Once the drawer was slammed shut, I opened the door.

"Mama?"

"Hey, I couldn't find anything to wear. Would you like to pick me out something?"

Willow squinted, contemplating something behind her perfect bright blue eyes. I swiped strands of her hair away.

"Sure," she finally said, and stalked past me to the closet. "Your favorite sweatshirt?"

"Baby, you know me so well." She pulled the sleeves of my faded—once red, now more of a pink—UGA sweatshirt out from the clumps of hanging clothes. "That's just what I was looking for, and you found it." I winked and tapped the tip of her nose.

White lies told to protect someone are okay, right?

Willow smiled. "Let's go. I picked Sleeping Beauty. I like those fairy ladies. Wait, are they fairies?"

I laughed, pulling off the sweater I'd worn all day, leaving my camisole on. "I don't remember. Good thing we're watching it."

"Yeah. I'm gonna go ask Gramma." She bounded out of the room.

I took a deep breath and tugged the sweatshirt off its hanger, holding it out to relish in the memories of fall semester on campus, strolling hand and hand with Alex. I hugged it to my chest.

Oh, Alex, I wish you were here to tell me what to do ... how to make things right.

CHAPTER TWENTY

SATURDAY—A WEEK AND A HALF LATER
EVA

A soft knock rapped on the front door. I opened it to see Thad, his hair pulled and knotted high on the back of his head, rain dripping onto his navy jacket. His hands were tucked into his jean pockets. With the sun gone for the day, an icy chill had infused the air as a cold front moved in. I slipped outside onto the small covered porch, pulling the door closed behind me.

"What are you doing here?"

The overwhelming desire to throw my arms around his neck hadn't diminished after two weeks of avoiding his calls. The feeling was only amplified by our close proximity.

Thad took his hands out of his pockets and leaned toward me.

"I've been really off balance for two weeks, and I couldn't take it any longer. But now that I'm next to you, all is right again."

I narrowed my eyes, determined not to give in to his power, letting the sarcasm fly. "Nice, Romeo."

He laughed. "Come with me." He was always saying those words, and they always pulled me in. "Let me explain. Afterward, if you still don't want me around, then fine. At least I tried. Please?"

The wind whipped past us, and I crossed my arms. Thad went to grab my elbows, realized what he was doing, and pulled back, stuffing his hands in his pockets again. We engaged in a stare-down. All I could think was that I desperately wanted his hands on me.

Stop it, Eva.

"And if I don't agree to come?"

"I'll just come by tomorrow and ask again. Two weeks of voicemails and texts haven't been working. This way you have to say, like, twelve words to me face-to-face, so I'm moving in the right direction."

I analyzed every line on his face, mostly the laugh lines I knew all too well. He brought his head down, placing his eyes directly in line with mine. "You don't have anything to lose. You're already mad at me, so you'll either stay mad, or ... you won't."

I sighed because I wanted to go. I wanted to hear what he had to say. I'd wanted to give in and return his call for two weeks but wouldn't allow myself to. Now he was here.

"Give me a minute."

He nodded, and his face lit up. I slipped back inside and tiptoed to the library where Mom was curled up reading on the comfy chaise lounge we'd found last weekend. It completed my favorite room in the house. "Mom."

She looked up and pulled her reading glasses from her nose.

"Can you watch Willow? She's in my room watching a movie. I know it's only seven o'clock, but she was already about to fall asleep."

Mom studied me for a beat. "Everything okay?"

"Yeah, um, Thad stopped by and wants to talk."

Mom's eyes perked up. "Oh. Well, by all means go. Of course I can watch her." She rose from her chair. "I'll go on into your room."

"Thanks." I went to the mudroom to grab my purse, wishing there was a mirror to see what I looked like. I combed through my hair with my fingers and straightened my coral Moanna Island hoodie over loose and ripped mom jeans.

Ugh.

I slipped on a pair of coral flats sitting by the garage door. At least they matched.

I remembered Becca, the image of gorgeous according to about every man in the world, and felt a pang of sickness.

This is what jealousy feels like. Get it together, Eva.

I straightened up and went to Thad.

THAD

She pulled her hood up and ran through the persistent rain to the Bronco while I hustled behind her to open the passenger door. I dashed to my side and started the truck quickly, reversing just as fast. Eva didn't say anything as I turned down the next street over from hers.

Whistling Pine Drive, a road built before Ocean Oaks was even developed, looked mostly like all the others until you got to the elongated cul-de-sac at its end. My house was positioned to the far left, right next to the beach walk Eva strolled so often. To the right was a newer home similar to mine, and on the far right sat two of the oldest homes in all of Moanna, pieces of island history. One was in pristine condition, the other in dire need of restoration, but both were worthy of an awestruck gaze.

I didn't think my house could compete against them, but when I pulled into my drive, Eva's face paled. She peered out the windshield as the wipers sloshed back and forth.

My stomach rolled, knowing I was the reason her skin had gone white and her forehead furrowed with tension.

I killed the engine, leaving the headlights on to create a pathway of light to the front porch while I talked.

Here goes...

"Welcome to my house."

Her eyes, big as saucers, looked around at my colonial-style home with its gray siding, deep navy shutters, dark-stained, ten-foot-high, double front door, and the carriage-style doors on the three garage bays.

Her voice was cold. "I figured as much."

The sound of the raindrops on my hood pinged, waiting for one of us to break their rhythmic volley. Eva rubbed circles into the palm of her hand.

I sighed.

"After I retired, which I'll tell you about later, I moved back to my childhood home with Dad. Being in it without Mom felt wrong. No smells coming from the kitchen, no endless jazz music being played, no decorations coming and going with the seasons. So not long after I'd moved home, we began searching for a new place. Dad wanted golf, golf, and more golf, and I wanted an ocean view, so Moanna was an easy choice. Even the word Moanna means 'ocean.' Dad fell in love with this house, because it's the one my mom would have loved."

A tenderness warmed her gaze at the mention of my mom.

"C'mon, let's go inside."

On the front porch, we had to shake and stomp. I pushed open the door and flicked on the light.

"Wow," she said, crossing the threshold. "It's beautiful."

"Thanks." I shut the door. "It had been recently renovated when we bought it, and I had someone decorate. Dad and I could care less, but it seemed a shame to have this beautiful house and only put an old couch, a couple of beds, and two or three TVs in it." I shrugged off my jacket and threw it over the chair. She wouldn't make eye contact. Instead, her gaze traveled down my curved wrought iron banister. She shivered.

"C'mon, let's get you warm." I led her to the back and grabbed a light cotton throw off the couch. "Here. You may want to take your sweatshirt off, since it's pretty much dripping now."

She looked down at herself. "Yeah, I could wring it out." She let a smile slip.

There's my Eva.

She shook her head. "But I'm not sure what condition my T-shirt is in underneath this. It could be one I've had since high school. You sure you want to risk seeing something your eyes may never forget?"

Yup, there she is.

I let out a rumble of laughter that started deep in my core. "Yes, definitely worth the risk if it gets you warm."

"Okay, you asked for it." She tugged off her top layer, revealing a paper-thin, faded maroon tee.

"Raiders, huh?"

"Yup, a Walker Raider through and through." She tossed her sweatshirt on the bar countertop, accepted the blanket, and pulled it tight around her. "Though I wasn't always the biggest fan of our maroon and gold color scheme."

"Yuck. Florida State colors."

"Exactly." She went to the side table and picked up a picture of Mom, Dad, and me on my high school football field. Her fingers caressed the glass.

"That's us from senior night. Clearly a *long* time ago."

Her lips twitched into a smile. "You look exactly the same, only skinny."

"That was before I found protein shakes."

She laughed softly. I bit my lip, not wanting to get too excited over her light mood before she actually heard what I had to say.

"Where's your dad?"

"He's got a better social life than I do. He's doing what he always does on Saturdays in the fall—watching football at a buddy's house."

Eva raised one eyebrow and gave a nod. "I see."

I moved to the French doors and pushed them open. "This is our favorite part of the house."

Even in the rain, the view could take your breath away. The line on the horizon where the ocean met the sky was almost invisible in the fading light and clouds, but its utter vastness was enough.

"I can see why." She put the picture down and stepped onto the porch, watching the waves hit the shore in the distance. The wind picked up and whipped her hair in crazy directions. She pulled the blanket up around her neck.

I followed and gripped the railing, grounding myself for the talk.

"I was sitting right there in the dunes at the bottom of my ramp when you and Willow showed up that first day." She didn't say a word, just nodded her head. "It's hard to explain, but I felt compelled to get up and follow you. I remember thinking, what will I do when I reach them? Stick out my hand and introduce myself? And then—"

"Willow got trapped in the waves."

"Yeah. Right before she went under, I sensed it was about to happen. I think I was running to her before her face even went under."

"You were her angel."

I moved closer, and she faced me.

"I think I was just a good listener. After that day, I thought maybe God needed me to be there at that exact moment for Willow's sake, and my quick obsession with you was just a by-product."

"Your quick obsession?"

I shrugged. "Yeah." I got down to her eye level. *She's so tiny.* "But I knew it wasn't a by-product when I saw you again in the parking lot of Palmer, then here on the beach again, then at the game. There was no denying God wanted *you* in my life."

She backed away. "But why'd you ..."

"Why'd I not tell you where I lived?"

She nodded firmly, her shoulders drawing upward and squaring off. "Yes."

I dragged my hand down my face. "Honestly? You're the first woman I've *wanted* to invite over since I moved here." I cast my eyes to the ceiling to avoid her penetrating stare. "When you play ball, everyone's your friend just to see what they can get out of you. It's always about how you can benefit them. You become hardened. You don't let people get close, like a defense mechanism. If they don't know what you've got, they can't manipulate you, so I got used to keeping people at a distance. Keeping my home *mine*." I watched the waves. "It did get harder and harder not to tell you I was your neighbor. I wanted to, but I didn't know how."

I looked in her dark brown eyes, noticing the intensity had diminished.

"Thad, you should have just told me when—oh, I don't know, the night you came to dinner when we drove to my house. Or the next day when we had dinner right over there." She pointed to the beach.

"I know. Please forgive me? I promise to come clean about more of my life."

Still holding the blanket, she used her index finger to put her hair behind her ears, leaving it resting on her collarbone. My eyes locked on that spot.

"You know," she said, "I told Mom it was very possible you were a true-to-life beach bum."

I almost snorted. "Why?"

She shrugged. "Because we saw you here on this speck of beach a couple of times in a row. I thought maybe you just liked it here, not that you *lived* here." She gestured to the house.

"Easy assumption." We laughed. I felt compelled to take her face in my hands. "Eva, to hear your voice again makes my world right."

"I feel the same way," she whispered. "You spin me round and round."

The movement of her head against my fingers was like a calming touch. I pulled her to me, putting my lips to her hairline.

"Let's get out of this cold. Will you come upstairs? I want to show you something—well, let you hear something. And I'll tell you a story. My story."

She nodded beneath my lips, then breathed me in the same way I did her before she pulled away.

Eva

We were both silent as I followed his lead up a second set of stairs coming off his fancy kitchen. They led to a long, cream-carpeted hall. I hated treading on it in my wet shoes. He turned at the last set of double doors on the right. I stopped in my tracks at the threshold. The room was clearly his master bedroom.

"Um ..."

He turned and saw my gaze locked on his huge bed, with sheets a twisted mess and no comforter to be found.

"Oh no. I brought you up here to come over this way." He pointed and took exaggerated steps to the other side of the room where a large plush ivory lounging couch faced the ocean.

Oh.

He jumped off the ground and fell back into the big cushions like a kid. The couch was more like an extra-large chaise, but his Nikes still hung over the edge. He patted a spot next to him. "C'mon."

I tossed the blanket on the armrest. My body heat had risen about ten notches since I'd set foot into his intimate domain. I kicked off my shoes and crawled to him, lying back in the fluffiness.

"Okay, now close your eyes and listen."

Only when I closed my eyes did I hear the melody of the rain beating on the roof, almost leaving me in a trance. "The rain is so loud and clear."

"You may not have noticed, but we have a tin roof. It's not easy to keep up in this ocean air, but it's worth it." He took a soft breath. "My mom lived in this little farmhouse with a tin roof when she was growing up. She always told me she wanted one again, that one day she'd have a house with one because it made the rain and storms beautiful. I'd asked what she meant. She'd said the pitter-patter on a tin roof would lull you to sleep faster than anything else, that it was God's lullaby to us."

A warmth spread through me that had nothing to do with being in his master bedroom. I felt his eyes but kept mine closed. In the silence, I found the melody of the rain again.

"You hear it, don't you?"

I nodded. "Yes. It's wonderful."

He shifted in the pillows, grabbed my hand, squeezed it once, and laid it back by my side. When I opened my eyes, the room had darkened, the moonlight scarce over the ocean, leaving just slivers of reflection through the windows. An aqua glow from the pool shone into the house.

I waited for him to begin, pretending he was still stuck in the doghouse, but he'd already loosened some stones in my wall.

Okay, quite a few stones.

Being with him felt right. No surprise there. When it came to Thad, I'd proven many times I was incapable of saying no, incapable of standing my ground.

"Let me tell you my story, really my testimony."

I'd heard the word from my youth group past. *Testimony*, a story of God's grace and redemptive powers. "Okay."

"I grew up a couple of hours from here. Got a scholarship out of high school to play football at the University of Iowa. I was there four years and got drafted at twenty-two to the San Diego Chargers. I think you know this already."

"Yes."

"Well, let's just say I didn't make tons of great decisions while I was in the NFL. I was the starting tight end almost immediately. I was good. Really good." His pride let loose a little. "But I was still a kid when I was given all this money and fame, and they began to rule me. I'd moved to a college halfway across the country. Started then to retreat from Jesus. By the time I was drafted and moved over two thousand miles away from my parents and old Christian friends, I'd completely backtracked on God. I left him on the back burner for years.

"I partied way too much on the off season, even some during the season. I was quick to get hot-tempered when things didn't go my way. I drove a fancy sports car around town, used people—women." He hesitated. "I can see now my relationship with Becca was superficial. We both met each other's needs in a twisted way—she looked good on my arm, and I looked good on hers." He turned on his side to face me, propping up on his hand. "I know how bad this must sound to you."

"No, it's okay. I was mad at first when I saw you two, which I know wasn't my right, so it's fine. I have a story too. We all do." I couldn't control the impulse and reached over to squeeze his free hand. "What happened?"

"Well, I used to think it was a course of unfortunate events, but later I realized they weren't necessarily *all* bad, because they changed me."

He found my eyes in the glow of the room. "I flew Mom and Dad out a couple of times to San Diego, and they came to as many games as they could on *this* side of the country." He sighed and shook his head. "I'll never forget this one time they were in San Diego. After a game, I wanted to go out on the town to celebrate our win, leaving them by themselves at my condo, instead of spending time with them the way I should have. My dad looked me straight in the eyes that night and said, 'Who are you? Certainly not the son I raised.'

"The sad thing is, I went out anyway. Not long after, I found out Mom had cervical cancer. I was probably dealing with denial on some level—I didn't even fly home to see her. Dad took her to radiation and chemotherapy for months. He spent every day going to some kind of doctor's appointment or caring for her while she fought the effects of all those nasty aggressive treatments. All the while, I partied, worked out, and relaxed by the pool."

He rolled onto his back and stared at the ceiling. Pain and regret shadowed his voice.

"By the time I took a long weekend to fly out, she was so weak, so frail, I barely recognized her. And I couldn't handle it. I avoided any serious discussion and couldn't wait to leave, to go back to my untroubled life. I told her I loved her, and I'd visit again soon. That was the last time I saw her."

The memory of the last time I saw Alex flashed before me. His peck on the cheek as he put his wallet in his back pocket and grabbed his phone. The slap on the backside as he left our apartment, making me jump, thrilled he still wanted me with such a huge belly.

Tears flowed. Thad had gone quiet. Both of us lay there, caught up in memories. I whispered, "I know what it's like to have a last memory."

He grabbed my hand. "I know you do." He brought my hand up to his lips, kissed it, and held onto it, resting it in between us.

"A few weeks later, Dad called to say she was in the hospital, and things didn't look good. Her immune system was so weak that she couldn't fight off pneumonia. I should have left California right then." The sadness in Thad's voice brought out my mothering, and I wished I could cradle him to me and take the sadness away. "It was a Friday, and we had a home game on Sunday. I told Dad I would fly out Monday morning. She died Sunday afternoon, about an hour before my game."

I felt guilt radiating from him. My tears continued to fall, not for my own pain, but for his.

"Thad, I'm so sorry. I know I haven't talked about it much, but I do know that pain—the loss of someone you can never replace. And I've lost a parent too. Then not long after that ... Willow's dad." For some reason my lips couldn't say his name.

Alex.

He wiped both his eyes with his free hand and shook his head clear.

"One day I'd love to hear about them, when you're ready to tell me. But Eva, you didn't run away from your loved ones when they needed you. The way I treated my mom—well, let's just say talking about it brings back the guilt full force."

SAFE HARBOR

"I may have been there for them, but I hold a ton of guilt about a ton of things." The rain was the only outside sound penetrating the room. "Keep going. Finish your story."

A sob lodged in his throat.

"Dad was heartbroken over losing her, but also over my decisions. I stayed for my game, trying to be tough, played terribly, and flew home late that night. By the time I got here, Dad couldn't even look at me. He said again, 'I don't even know who you are anymore. But God does. He's the only one who sees your heart, the only one who can save it. You better get on your knees and cry out to him.' Talk about swiping the legs out from under me.

"At first I was mad, but God opened my eyes to the truth. It hurt, but I decided I would make some changes, be a better role model when I returned to California, be a better leader on the team, be a better fiancé to Becca, be faithful in all aspects of my life. I literally got down on my knees to beg God for forgiveness."

He scooted off the couch and went to the windows. "Turns out God's plan didn't include pro football or living in California."

I sat up and pulled my knees to my chest, watching him pace.

"Two weeks after the funeral, I injured my knee again. During the six months after surgery, I did a ton of soul-searching. It was a crazy time. Besides grieving, I had to recover and attend physical therapy, *but* I also started attending a local church and did a Bible study on my own every day." He turned to face me.

"I knew God was the answer, and he never let me fall. I never slipped into depression, but I had no direction. I didn't know what was next for me. There was no way I could work a normal desk job, so I just wandered. That's why I went to all those surfing spots. Remember I told you I searched the top ten beaches to surf?"

"Yeah, I remember."

"Well, it was on one of those trips, the eighth beach, that God finally gave me direction. I was in Fiji, watching the waves one peaceful morning, reading my daily Bible study pages, when a verse jumped out at me. I was searching, sure, but still really wrestling with guilt, sadness, and even anger that would creep up unannounced. I'd disappointed Dad, lost my mom, my career, my fiancée." He looked to see my reaction.

"Becca." I hid the hot, jealous blood circling my heart's well.

He collapsed back on the lounge. "Yeah, we broke up right before my search for the great waves." He said 'waves' like Brody from *Point Break* would have. "I knew it was for the best. I sought God's direction and stayed home every night, away from the party life. Turns out she didn't want to change." He grimaced. "I found out she was cheating on me with a teammate."

I couldn't help an angry gasp.

"I know." He locked eyes with mine. "Just so you know, I hadn't seen her in over four years until she showed up the other day. She came to make amends. I know she didn't go about it the right way, not at first. She did want me to tell you she's sorry for treating you the way she did."

"Really?"

"Yeah, she said she could see how much I was into you."

I hoped the dark of the room hid the sudden cherry color of my cheeks and neck.

"I didn't know it, but she's been dealing with some heavy stuff, and she was at a place where she wanted to make things right. In a way, it was a good surprise visit, but I'm sorry it catapulted us into a strange place. Knowing you were—are—angry with me was like acid on my heart."

Words spilled out of me like a volcano erupting. "Oh, Thad, I'm not angry."

I launched myself into his arms, arms he'd already made ready as the words left my lips. He pulled me into his lap. I tucked my face into his neck.

"How could I be mad at someone as great as you?" He started to say something, and I spoke louder. "Stop. Your past is your past, and I'm sorry I didn't take your calls. It's just—you know, being in a relationship and falling for someone was not in my plans, and it was easier to push you away. It was never about finding out you were once engaged to a supermodel or that you lived down the street. Though it is strange you changed your name. It was weird to hear you called Damien."

He laughed, his lips at my forehead. "To be clear, my name is Thad Damien Smith. My dad's middle name is Thad, so I'm named after him. Funny story, when I bought this house, the loan officer and closing attorney kept calling me Thad, since it's my first name. I just never corrected them to say I went by Damien and had gone by that name my whole life. When I got my license here, they called me Thad, and I just let it be. Kind of nice. Not as many people realize who I am with the name Thad."

"For what it's worth, I like Thad better."

He nudged my shoulders back so he could see my face. "Yeah?"

"Yeah. Thad means 'courageous heart,' which is exactly what you've got."

He leaned so close I felt his breath. "Really?"

I nodded as his hands went into my hair.

"Can I kiss you?"

His whispered words swirled through my heart as my mind flashed to our last kiss, the one that changed everything. The one that lingered still, replacing Alex's touch from so many years ago. His whisper fell softly, leaving peace and decisiveness. Alex would be happy seeing me move toward what I now accepted as love.

"Yes." The breathlessness in my voice stunned me.

He moved slow as dripping honey. His lips were soft, not urgent like before, but intimate and purposeful and cautious. I melted into his embrace, letting him know I was doing exactly what I wanted to do.

But it was over as fast as it started. He pulled back, then pop-kissed my lips again. He put his forehead to mine. "Okay, no more of that, or we'll fall into bad territory."

I smiled, still savoring his taste.

Probably true.

"Eva, everything I said the other night is still true. You can be sure the man here before you is the real me. I've left the selfish, arrogant person behind. I've allowed God to change me into someone much better than a good athlete who likes the spotlight."

"I believe you."

"Can we go back to our plan from two weeks ago? Before you found out, in a bad way, I was your neighbor? Can we agree to just let it be, let *us* be, and see what happens?" He caressed my chin, tugging it slightly to his.

"Okay."

He picked me up, sat me down next to him, and settled back into the cushions. Only this time he pulled me back to him. I wedged my shoulder up under his, molding myself to his side, as he wrapped his huge arm around my back.

"Hey, what was the realization you had on the eighth beach?"

SAFE HARBOR

THAD

"Ah, yes, the eighth beach. Fiji. Great place for hearing God. I'll take you there one day."

I squeezed her arm softly and inhaled a deep breath. "I'd read a devotion for the day and was looking up the verses that went with it. One of them was in Proverbs, and while I was stopped there, I just kept reading. A few down, in Proverbs 13, the seventh verse hit me smack over the head. It seems like a crazy verse out of all the other profound ones to have struck me so powerfully, but it did. It says, 'A pretentious, showy life is an empty life; a plain and simple life is a full life.'"

I was glad to be looking at the sky through the tops of my windows, even though the stars were lost in the rainstorm, instead of looking into Eva's eyes. "It was like something shifted, like my heart broke open to be filled with his Spirit. I know he never left my soul all those years. He was just waiting for me to return. And in that moment I felt him again, a full contentment I never had on the football field. I heard him whisper, '*Go home.*'

"So I did. Moved home, back into Dad's little empty house, and sold my place in San Diego. Dad was elated to have me. Of course, he's good at forgiveness, so our relationship was restored just like God's and mine. Then we ended up here, which doesn't lean on the side of simple, but we live a full life. And I closed on the property for the camp just after we moved here too."

"Wow. That was a lot of change fast, but I guess it's not much different than my recent move." She spun her finger in a circle on my chest.

"True. I'm finding we're more alike than I first thought."

"Agreed."

"The ease of our move here, how it fell into place, and the joy it gave us confirmed we did what God wanted. I hope you feel that way too." I interlocked my fingers in hers. "And that's my story."

I could almost feel Eva's brain churning.

God, what is she thinking?

I ran my free hand through her hair. Shifting it brought a wave of Skittle scent to my nose. The rain was the only sound as it lulled us into a hazy consciousness. The pitter-patter, God's lullaby to us, was my last thought before sleep pulled me under.

CHAPTER TWENTY-ONE

SATURDAY NIGHT

EVA

The smell of Thad, the sweet hickory, manly smell that entered my dream, registered before I opened my eyes. I told myself move, but my limbs wanted to stay tucked tight to his chest, smothered in the heat coming off him. It disoriented me.

C'mon, body, I need to know what time it is.

Willow sprang to mind, and my limbs went into action prying out of his embrace. She was safe with Mom, but had she noticed I wasn't home yet? Was she worried?

Where is my phone?

I sat up and looked around, realizing my phone was in my purse, which was still in his truck. I found a clock on his nightstand, its neon orange numbers bright in the darkness.

10:04 p.m.

Okay, not as late as I thought, but I needed to get home fast in case she woke up and wandered into my room as she sometimes did.

The rain had stopped, leaving the moon shining over the ocean, giving enough light for me to make out Thad's face. He looked younger in his sleep, and so ... content.

Everything he'd told me rushed back. He'd returned to God and started over.

I know he never left my soul all those years. He was just waiting for me to return to him.

My heart swelled a bit. Could it really be that easy?

He shifted.

"Thad," I whispered. He didn't move. I almost nudged his shoulder but remembered how close he lived. I could simply walk home and not have to wake him.

I crawled off the couch, or chaise, or whatever it was, and searched for my shoes. I was balancing on one foot to slide the other on when Thad spoke.

"You better not be trying to leave."

I'd be lying if I said the huskiness in his voice didn't give me butterflies.

"I didn't want to wake you. I figured I could just walk home," I whispered back.

He sat straight up. "Eva Elliott. I like your independence, but if you think I'm going to let you walk home at night by yourself, you don't know me very well." I slipped on the second ballet flat as he stalked over. "Let me take care of you. At least sometimes."

Yikes. He's hot when he's angry.

I stared at him, on the verge of defiance. "I've been on my own for so long, I just—"

He grabbed my wrist and held my arm out. "Not anymore." He put me over his shoulder. Literally. "Not anymore," he echoed.

I shrieked as I hung off him while he carried me out of the room, gripping the back of my knees. The wave of joy flowed out in my laughter as I drummed on his back. "Put me *down*."

"Not a chance," he shouted as he descended the stairs, not missing a beat with my extra hundred and thirty pounds.

"Thad! Seriously!"

"Shh, you'll wake Dad."

"Oh," I whispered. "Sorry."

"I'm joking. He sleeps through everything."

He grabbed my old sweatshirt as he passed it on the bar. I gave up trying and laughed the whole way to the Bronco. By the time he dumped me onto the seat, I couldn't catch my breath, having laughed so hard. He pulled my face to him and kissed me quickly on the lips, then shut the door to go to his side.

I knew then what my life with Thad Damien Smith would be like. It settled into my empty places, filling them perfectly.

CHAPTER TWENTY-TWO

SUNDAY

EVA

"Well, well, you girls are up kind of early for a weekend." Mom glided into the room, the tie of her fleece robe dragging the floor. "*And* making breakfast?"

"I'm washing strawberries." Willow piped up from her stool at the sink.

I took a step from the stove to peer into Willow's washing bowl. "And doing a great job."

Mom went straight to the coffee maker. "What's the occasion?"

"No occa—"

"Mama's going to church with us." Pride laced Willow's words.

"What?"

I scoffed at Mom's hanging jaw and stunned look.

"I just thought it'd be nice to go with y'all this morning," I said, "instead of staying in the house by myself." I didn't look up, just kept flipping the bacon, hoping Mom wouldn't make a big deal of it.

I've already got enough anxiety about stepping through the doors and not perishing in a puff of smoke.

Mom's gaze bored into my back, but I held strong. She finally said, "Well, want me to make pancakes?"

Willow turned to Mom, slinging water onto the floor. "Yeah! Can I stir the—the stuff?"

"The batter. And yes, you may." Mom went to the pantry. "So how was last night?"

"It was great."

Perfect.

Mom appeared next to me and retrieved a mixing bowl from the cabinet. "Hmm. Well, I'm very happy for that news." I chanced a glance her way, and she was waiting for it, smiling the satisfying smile of someone who'd gotten their way. Thankfully, Willow distracted us by pushing her stool to Mom's other side.

"Willow, after breakfast, we'll both need to shower."

"I don't like showers."

"I mean a bath for you. Then we've got to pick out something to wear. You know what'll look the best for both of us, since you've been before." I'd wear almost anything if it helped to coerce her into the bathtub more easily. "Deal?"

"Deal."

THAD

"Are we still on for next Saturday?" I asked Mike. "It's only a week away."

He poured cream into his coffee from the church lobby's coffee bar. "Yeah, man."

I came behind him and pushed the lever to send some of the hot stuff into my own cup. Its aroma awakened my sleepy senses.

"It may take all day to work on the list I've got going. I've already done a lot of work over there, but some things require more than one person, and the builder I've hired isn't starting until the new year. Are you sure you want to

SAFE HARBOR

give up our only free Saturday before the playoffs to do manual labor for free?"

"Sure. I'm excited about it. It's the start of something big."

I stirred a bit of creamer into my cup. "I hope so." I went to take my first sip and saw a blur of dark green pass by the windows of the church lobby. I looked past Mike's shoulder to see the brake lights of Eva's car.

"What is it, man?"

"Eva. That's her car."

We watched it pull into a parking spot. "I thought you said she doesn't come to church."

"I did." I stared out into the parking lot for a moment, coffee temporarily forgotten.

"Huh." Mike mumbled something as I ditched my coffee on the counter and sped through the front doors to greet them. Eva was undoing Willow from her car seat, and as Willow jumped down, she saw me.

"Thad!" She started toward me. She and Ellen hadn't been to church last Sunday, and her little voice hit me hard. I hadn't heard it in a couple of weeks. I'd missed her.

I picked up my pace, hardly able to withhold myself from running.

"Hey there, girl." I bent down as low as possible, ready to give her a high five. She bypassed my hand and threw her arms around my neck.

When she let go, she said, "Mama's here too."

"I see that." I stood. "Hi."

Eva was beaming. "Hi."

I looked over at Ellen. She beamed too. "Hi, Ellen."

"Hi, yourself. Let's get inside, out of this cold October wind." She grabbed Willow's hand to walk her into the lobby, leaving Eva and me to follow.

"You came."

"I did."

"I'm glad."

"Me too."

"What changed your mind?" I gestured for her to walk with me, hesitating only a moment before giving in to temptation and taking her hand in mine. She didn't pull it away.

"Let's just say I woke up believing there's hope for me and God yet."

"There is. C'mon."

EVA

We dropped Willow off at her children's area and found John in the sanctuary—though they didn't call it a sanctuary—and sat next to him. I had to catch my breath from dealing with the barrage of people greeting, hugging, and introducing themselves. Everyone treated Thad like a celebrity. All the attention and doting and singling-out would have normally given me an anxiety attack, but now, here ... it made me happy.

A woman came to the mic as the guitarist started to play. Thad squeezed my hand before he stood up. I followed, already curious about the music. Mom nudged me. "You're gonna love it."

When the singer belted the final song, a rendition of "Amazing Grace," my body began to sway to the music, even hum along.

Amazing grace, how sweet the sound, that saved a wretch like me.

She sang the words at the end—*I once was blind, but now I see*—over and over, the crescendo of the volume and intensity in the music building a pressure that, when released, brought clarity to my mind.

God, I haven't sought out your presence in a long while. But you're here now, in this place.

The song ended, and she invited everyone to take a seat as the pastor hopped up on stage. He was close to Thad's age, with black-rimmed glasses and Converse sneakers. Definitely the hippest pastor I'd ever seen. He set his Bible and bottle of water on a little table and spoke into his headset mic.

"Welcome! Today we're continuing our series called 'Established.' I'm sure many of you have seen little signs, usually made for families and marriages, that say 'Established 2010,' or 'Established 2008,' as a way to signify the joining of a relationship, or perhaps the beginning of a new family. This series talks about just that, only we're talking about a relationship with Jesus, and the beginning of our new life in his family." The pastor took a sip from his water bottle, giving me a moment to let his words settle.

Established.

"Last week, we talked about logistics. And about the elusive word 'salvation'—how when we break salvation down, it's simple. God didn't make it complicated." He held his palms up and laughed. "He *wanted* us to get it. That's how much he loves us. All we have to do is believe in his Son Jesus, ask him to forgive our sins, and receive his Holy Spirit in our hearts, therefore giving us the free gift of eternal life with him in heaven.

"Those are definitely the most important logistics to becoming established into Jesus's family. But today we'll talk about establishing your relationship with Jesus. I'm hoping at the end of the day, you'll be ready to 'open the door.'"

I lost track of what he said, because my brain froze on the words, *open the door*. I could swear he spoke them looking right at me. Chills sprouted on my spine and crept their way to my fingers, causing me to interlock them.

"We're going to look at the parable from Luke 15 about the lost son," the pastor said. "A parable is a story told to teach us something, a lesson. What's interesting about this parable is it's the longest one in the Bible. This tells me Jesus took special care in making it stand out. It has depth and significance.

"Now we don't have time to get into all the ins and outs of this story, but the younger brother asks his very wealthy dad for his inheritance. This was a very disrespectful thing to do. Basically, he was saying, 'Dad, you're not dying fast enough. Can I just go ahead and take the money I'd get when you do?'" The pastor made a face of shock and distain that we all mirrored. "Yeah, I know, he was rude. Now surprisingly, the dad gave it to him, or *maybe* it's not surprising at all. This dad loved his son, and his son thought life would be better without him. So, in order to make his son's life better, he gave over his inheritance."

I'd done this very thing to Alex a month after my dad died. I thought my life would be better off without him, that maybe our love wasn't as strong as it should be, that he'd loved me enough to let me go. I'd realized I was wrong, horribly wrong, and then he too was gone ...

The pastor went on. "And his son blew it." He raised his voice. "*Really blew it.*" His emphasis on those words rattled inside.

I blew it.

Had I done this with God too? Had I thought I was better off without him and blown it?

"This son spent every last dollar. And when he had nowhere to turn, guess where he went." The pastor cocked his head for responses from the congregation. "Yup. Home. He was certain his dad would not accept him back. He was certain he'd dishonored himself beyond forgiveness, and he was ready to become a servant in his father's household to receive shelter and food. But look what happened." He gestured to the big screen behind him where the verse popped up. "Luke 15:20 says, 'So he got up and went to his father. But while he was still a long way off, his father saw him and was filled with compassion for him; he ran to his son, threw his arms around him and kissed him.'"

I remembered this story from Sunday school.

The pastor looked up from his Bible. "Let's stop there a minute. The father was filled with compassion for his son. Another translation says *filled with tender love for his son.* Let's look on the screen to see some other synonyms for compassion and tender love." He gestured behind him again. "Kind, caring, softhearted, sympathetic, fatherly, motherly, gentle, generous, warmhearted ... this father was having all of these feelings. Well, all except maybe motherly."

Everyone laughed. Thad pinched my arm and leaned over to my ear. "That's definitely you." I smiled, but in truth, I barely heard him. I was focused on the synonyms still on the screen. The father had all these feelings toward his son, who'd dishonored him so greatly. How was that possible? My mind went to Willow, and I understood exactly how it was inconceivable not to have those feelings.

The pastor paced the stage. "Now, what's more is this dad plans a big party. And then the father says seventeen words that are the most important ones of the whole story. He gives instructions to his servants about preparations for the party and says, 'For this son of mine was dead and is alive again; he was lost and is found.' This father says these words twice in the story."

He nodded. "You know if God's word says something twice, you better take heed and listen. *For this son of mine was dead and is alive again; he was lost and is found.*"

My heartbeat intruded into the sound of his words as their truth sank down deep and latched on.

"Folks, the son went back. He was humbled, ashamed of his behavior, and in spite of those feelings, he still opened the door by taking that step. And what was the result? He was welcomed with open, compassionate, tender arms. It didn't matter to his father he'd strayed far, far away. What mattered was that he came back."

"Our relationship with God is like this. He's described as all of those synonyms we mentioned and so much more. He just needs us to open the door. Some of you were established long ago into God's family, but you need to return to him. He's already running to meet you, but imagine the door is locked from *your* side. You just have to open it and let him wrap his arms around you, establishing once more that *you are his*."

CHAPTER TWENTY-THREE

Sunday afternoon

Thad

I stuck my head out the door to the back porch, hoping the chill in the air had diminished some since church service. The afternoon sun had done its job, leaving a perfect fall day for an impromptu cookout. "Hey, Dad—can you go ahead and fire up the grill?"

"Sure."

He got up from his perch on his favorite couch as I shut the door and checked my watch for the tenth time. They'd be here any minute.

Now I just wait.

Dad came inside as I rounded the bar into the kitchen. "It's on. Shouldn't take too long to get good and hot. You got the steaks ready?"

I held up my tray full of raw meat. "Done." I set the tray down. "Baked potatoes are in the oven. I hope they get soft enough. Eva is bringing a couple of things. I even put juice boxes in the fridge for Willow."

"Quit stressin', son. You're actin' like a teenager."

Which is exactly how I sometimes felt around Eva. Dad went to the fridge. "But I guess ... well, this *is* a big step for you. We've lived here four years, and you've never grilled with anyone except Mike." He tossed me a bottled water.

"I know. Of the few dates I've had, none made it to a second one."

We both took a swig of water. Then he said, "Well, for what it's worth, I'm happy they're coming over."

The doorbell rang.

"I'm just glad she agreed." I set my bottle on the counter and took off to the door. "Well, hello, ladies. Nice of you to join us this evening." I winked at Willow, who laughed at my mock seriousness.

"Hi, Thad." Willow scooted inside and looked around.

"Hey, you," I said solely to Eva, unable to stop myself from looking her up and down. Her long, tapered, red and navy plaid shirt, navy leggings, and brown riding boots got my blood pumping.

"Hey to you too." She stepped inside, balancing two bowls and an aluminum-wrapped loaf of bread, while shifting her hip to keep the bag hanging from her shoulder from falling off. I took the bowls and bread, catching a whiff of her perfume. It didn't help my blood-pumping-out-of-control problem.

"Thanks."

"Where's Ellen?"

"She's at home. Said she wanted to finish reading her book. I think she just wanted the house completely quiet for a change."

She grinned and turned to find Willow, who'd wandered into the dining room. "Willow, let's go back this way." She looked at me. "You don't want her in these fancy rooms, or you might end up with some broken items"—one of her eyebrows went up—"even if you didn't pick them out."

I laughed. "She's fine. It's just stuff. But ..." I waited for Willow's attention to fall to me. "Like I told you earlier, I do have a heated pool."

"Yeah, Mama, you said I could go swimming."

"Yes, yes. That's why we brought this huge pool bag you helped me pack with toys." She gave an exaggerated tug of the bag.

"C'mon back." I led the way as we passed Dad, who stood by the couch flipping through the TV channels.

"Hey, John." Willow trotted to him.

"Well, hello, little lady. I hear you want to go swimming."

"Yeah, I wanna show Thad what I learned."

"Sounds great," I said on my way into the kitchen.

"Well, good," Dad said. "Somebody needs to get some use out of that pretty pool."

"True." I went to the fridge. "Eva, do these need to go in the fridge?"

"Ah, yes. Except the bread. I brought a salad and a bowl of fruit. I hope that's okay?"

"It's perfect."

I put the bowls in the refrigerator as Dad chimed in. "I agree."

Eva made her way to the living room. "Thanks for having us over, John."

"You are so welcome. We've been needing more visitors." I caught his wink at her as I rounded the bar with the tray full of steaks.

Willow stood at the windows looking at the pool, or maybe the beach, but turned with a perplexed look. "John, do you live here too?"

Dad's eyes flicked my way, but I was at a loss as to why Willow seemed confused. His forehead creased, and he got down on Willow's level. "Yes, I do live here, with Thad."

"Really?"

"Yeah. See, I'm Thad's dad, and sometimes, even when a child gets older, they still want to live with their parents. We're family. Like your mom chooses to live with *her* mom—Thad chooses to live with his dad."

Now Willow's forehead creased. "Hmm. I don't think I have one of those."

My throat closed immediately, but Dad hadn't caught on. "One what?"

"A dad."

I closed my eyes. Willow's words boomeranged between my ears.

Oh. No.

I slowly opened them. Poor Dad was still hunched over and silent. Eva grabbed Willow's shoulders.

"Baby, sometimes daddies can't be there or can't be around to see their children grow up. But not because they don't want to or because of anything the child did. They just can't sometimes."

I thought of my own situation as a child put up for adoption. *They just can't sometimes.*

"Why?" she asked.

"Well, lots of different reasons. When we get home later, can I tell you about them?" Eva looked at me and then at Dad, who had stood and backed away to give Eva space. "We're here to eat and swim right now. Later, deal?"

Willow studied her mom's features, considering, before saying, "Deal."

"Okay, let's go." She turned to me, and her face reflected the pain she felt but wouldn't let come out in her voice. "Thad, lead the way."

EVA

As she'd done her whole life, Willow's joy pulled me out of my grief. This time it was witnessing her sheer happiness at splashing around in a hot tub whose jets pumped full blast. And so, by the time I sat down at the table next to the grill, I'd recovered a bit.

Just a bit.

"Mama, we need one of these!" Willow watched her pool and beach toys float and swirl around in the water. I wasn't letting my eyes off her, but I was happy she liked staying on the bench in the hot tub.

"Well, baby, maybe we'll have to ask Gramma for an upgrade." I had to yell a bit for her to hear me over the bubbles.

"What's that?"

"Getting something fancier, nicer."

"Yeah, we need one of those," she said before going back to splashing.

Thad shut the grill's hood and turned his chair to face Willow too. I stole a glance his way as he sat down. The smile he wore for Willow wrapped around me like a warm comforter fresh out of the dryer. "Thank you, Thad."

He looked over, his smile toned down, but not gone. "For what?"

"Moral support."

He tipped his head and turned back to Willow. "You're welcome, but I didn't say a word. Hardly a help."

"No, you were. Are. I feel stronger when you're around." My words didn't even make sense to me. I couldn't explain the effect of Thad's presence. I took a breath. "I knew those kinds of questions were coming, that I'd have to sit her down and try to explain one day. I've run over possible words in my head a thousand times, but it never comes out right."

I watched Willow, oblivious to our discussion, happy and free.

"I'll be praying for God to give you the right words, Eva. I know you'll have them. You were meant to be Willow's mom, so I know he'll prepare your heart and mind."

"Thank you." I crossed my legs, needing to disappear from his gaze before tears fell.

After some silence, Thad spoke.

"Can I ... I mean, I'm here when ..." He hesitated, though I knew what he was going to say. I'd been waiting for it ever since I first told him Willow's dad had died. "I'm here when you're ready to tell me what happened with ... you know."

"I know." I smiled at his sincerity and compassion. It wasn't offered in place of mere curiosity like most people's questions or condolences.

He stood and pulled me out of my chair into a hug. "Until then, and after, I promise to be your moral support."

Thad kissed the top of my head as a little cry squealed out from the hot tub. "Hey, I wanna big hug too."

We pulled away, ready to accept a soaking wet embrace from Willow as she trotted to us.

CHAPTER TWENTY-FOUR

MONDAY

EVA

I put the picture of Alex and me face down on Willow's nightstand. "Baby, can we snuggle a while?"

"Yeah, Mama."

I pulled back the covers on her twin bed as she scooted over. I got under and pulled her close, hoping she couldn't feel my accelerated pulse. I kissed her temple. "Baby, remember yesterday when I said we'd talk more about why daddies can't always be around their children?"

"Yeah." She nodded underneath my chin.

"Well, I wanted to talk to you more about that. Would it be okay?"

She nodded again. I sensed she knew the importance of the conversation we were about to have. I'd run over the sentences I planned on saying all last night and all day. Even went over them with Mom, who I suspected was currently in the hall listening, but all my practice couldn't prepare me for the way my stomach felt, like ocean waves crashing over and over.

"Willow, I felt like I needed to wait until you were older to tell you this. But you're a big girl now, right?"

"Yeah."

"Good." I debated what to say, then figured I had to just get it out.

"Willow, you *do* have a daddy. But the thing is, he can't be with us because he ... he died right before you were born."

She gripped my waist tighter, and her voice was barely audible. "Like Nemo's mom?"

I closed my eyes and pinched my lips together so they wouldn't let tears and sobs escape. With her one movie reference, I knew she understood. "Yes, baby, like Nemo's mom. Your daddy was so excited you were coming. I had you in my belly, and he used to rub on it and talk to you. He loved you so much." Tears and sobs came. I was helpless to stop them.

Willow looked at me. "Mama, don't cry."

It was just like her to try and make me feel better. I wiped my eyes. "Okay, all better now." I forced a smile. "Do you want to see a picture of him?"

"Okay." Willow sat up so I could grab the frame, then leaned back on me again as I let her see Alex. "This picture's from *your* room, Mama."

"Uh-huh. See how handsome he was?" His short-cropped blonde hair and blue eyes stood in perfect contrast to my dark hair and even darker eyes. "You have his eyes. See how blue they were? Just like yours."

Willow's shoulder pulled up, and I knew she was smiling without even seeing her face.

"Baby, he wanted to be here. He just couldn't. But you do have a daddy, and I'll tell you anything you want to know about him. You just need to ask me."

"Do you have more?" She pointed to the frame.

"Yes, I do have more pictures. I'll get them out for us to look at tomorrow. It's too late to get them out now. But is there anything else you'd like to ask before bed?"

SAFE HARBOR

Willow considered this with her eyebrows pinched together. "Jessica, at my school? Her grandpa died." I nodded for her to continue. "And the teacher said he went to heaven. And that's like God's house, and it's pretty and fun, and everyone is nice and happy. Is that where my daddy is?"

I laid the frame in my lap and tugged her around to look at me. "Yes, baby, that's where he is. Just like my dad. And Gramma's husband. He died before you were born."

"Huh, the teacher says we can call God our Father too."

"That's right, you can."

"So we both have two dads in heaven. God, and your dad, and my daddy."

Words halted behind my tongue as the church service flashed through my jumbled mind. *Established into God's family. You. Are. His.*

"Yes." I forced the tiny word out. "Exactly right."

Willow smiled with a sense of relief, like those words had filled some of the hollow space in her heart, a space that had always been empty due to a situation she couldn't change. She hugged me and slid down deeper into the covers as I got out. I tucked the frame to my chest and pulled the string on her nightlight lamp to turn it on. I kissed her and whispered, "I love you, baby."

"I love you, Mama."

Willow closed her eyes, and I turned to leave then stopped. "Willow, would you like me to put this picture next to your bed?"

"Yes."

I set it on the nightstand, propped just the right way so she could see it if she looked from her pillow. Six months ago, moving Alex's picture from its permanent spot on my dresser would have caused me to go into cardiac arrest, but now, moving it into Willow's room—passing it on to her—felt right.

The broken pieces were mending.

I turned off her overhead light, giving her one last look as I closed the door halfway. Mom waited in the hall.

She could tell she startled me. "I'm sorry. I couldn't help it."

I moved past her and headed to my room, still talking. "It's fine. I figured you were listening."

I sat on my bed, and she followed me onto it. "You did beautifully, Eva. There will be more questions to follow. But you opened the door."

I knew she too saw the imagery in those words.

"You know what's weird? I feel better. It's like I was keeping a secret that was eating at me, and now I've let it out, so I'm free. Maybe I should've told her a long time ago."

Mom smiled. "God's timing, dear. You weren't ready before, but you are now." Her words reverberated. "Come here." She wrapped me in a hug. "I love you, and I'm proud of you."

"Thanks. I love you too."

CHAPTER TWENTY-FIVE

TUESDAY

THAD

"Okay, boys, last play. Then we'll bring it in."

They set up their formation quickly, ready to go home, but also found the rhythm of the snap with ease. They'd repeated it hundreds of times by this late in the season. Darren swung his body right to fake a carry to Jayden, then drew back to throw long to Bo. The ball went up, spiraling exactly the way it should, and landed smack in Bo's hands. He made it into the end zone, and the boys cheered for themselves.

"All right, simmer down and c'mon over." Dad sent his practice team my direction, and I waited for all the boys to jog my way. The hairs on the back of my neck pricked, and I turned to see what had caused it. Eva was just then easing down on one of the concrete bleachers. She saw me look her direction and waved. My soul always knew when she was around. I smiled as I turned back to my boys.

"Okay, good play just then. But no cockiness come game time. I know you're excited, and our plays are running pretty smooth, but the fans will see what happens on the field. No need to cheer for yourselves. Let your actions speak, okay?"

"Yes, sir," they all chimed in.

"Plus, you didn't have a full defense set up against you. It will be harder during the game in a few weeks."

"Yes, sir."

"I'll see you all tomorrow. Break on Falcons. One, two, three, Falcons!"

"Falcons!" The boys' shout bounced around the stadium. They all trekked to the shack, including Dad. But I made my way into the stands.

"Hey there."

"Hi."

"This is a nice surprise. I could get used to seeing you during the week instead of just the weekends."

Fire set to her cheeks. She wrapped her lightweight black jacket tighter around her. "You are so great with those boys, Thad. Really. They're lucky to have you."

As always, affirmations from her fueled my passion to keep going and gave me energy to complete the tasks God gave me to do in Palmer.

"Thanks." I sat beside her as the wind whipped by us. "This weather and my knee are telling me the hurricane is coming for us."

"What hurricane?"

I deadpanned her, then laughed. "Eva. It's all over the news. Hurricane Rowan. They're saying it will likely come ashore south of us. And with the full moon comes the possibility of king tides. We may need to get off the island come Sunday or Monday."

Eva shook her head. "Wait, what's a full moon tide?"

"Where the tides are extra high due to the moon somehow. Not sure how it works."

"You're making that up."

I chuckled. "I'm not—"

"And anyway we'll be fine. I'm sure it'll be just bad rain."

"Maybe. At least I hope it doesn't affect Saturday. Are you still able to make it for the camp workday?"

"I wouldn't miss it," she said. "I'm bringing Stacy, is that okay?"

"Of course."

She pulled one knee onto the bleacher, facing me, turning serious. "I was leaving and saw your Bronco still here. I thought maybe we could talk for a minute."

"Sure, what's up?"

A huge, sweet smile lit up her face. "I told Willow about her dad last night."

"Oh? By the smile you're wearing, I'm thinking it went well."

"Yes, I feel ... better. And I thought—I think—" She couldn't get the words out, and instead took a deep breath and looked to the sky. "I think I'm ready to tell you about Willow's dad. I may even *need* to tell you." Her eyes found mine. "But if this is a terrible time, we can meet up later—"

"No. Now's perfect."

No way would I let this opportunity pass by.

God, help her heal through this.

EVA

I relaxed against the bleacher. Thad put his elbows on his knees, giving me space to find the words.

"Willow's dad is Alex Hoovers. We were high school sweethearts. Started dating our senior year, and it was love at first sight. Well, maybe not first sight, since we'd run in the same crowd for years, but we never dated until high school was almost over. So, maybe it was love at first date."

I smiled at the memory. "He took me roller-skating, and I was terrible, an embarrassment. He skated circles around me but stayed by my side the whole time, holding me up, keeping me secure. Like I told you before, he signed on to play with the Dawgs. I followed him there. I guess he would have been playing at UGA while you were in San Diego."

Thad shifted, sat back some. "College football's the best."

"Definitely." I nodded, but found my courage fading as the story erupted from my lips. My eyes followed the fifty-yard line, its bright white standing out against the still-green grass, even though fall had settled in. The trees behind the visitors' bleachers made a beautiful mix of reds, yellows, and oranges, the sun's glow setting them alight. "Even this football field reminds me of him, of being on the sidelines cheering him on. We made a pretty good couple."

Except when his parents got involved.

"He was my first love, and our relationship was comfortable and easy." *Safe.* "We dated until the end of our junior year at UGA. My dad had passed that spring, and I think the trauma of losing him got to me. Suddenly, my relationship with Alex wasn't good enough. We weren't in love enough or something." I exhaled, trying to force the pain out with my breath. "I remember thinking about how in love my parents were. How their whole life had been full of sneaking kisses by the kitchen sink, dates every Saturday night, and surprise breakfast-in-bed moments."

I hated to admit my next words, words that hadn't been spoken aloud to anyone. I closed my eyes. "I mistook our comfortable, contented relationship for one that was lacking something, like we were missing a key element. I didn't see at the time that relationships are different, each unique, but still special. I looked past all the great things he did do. He never used to run around with the players, leaving me behind. He was protective and strong. He let me be me, a little nerdy and stubborn. But I was blind, and I broke up with him."

I looked to see Thad's expression. He seemed confused, like I knew he would. I could almost see his brain ticking, processing how I got pregnant with Willow.

Even still, he took my hand. "Go on."

"Well, we both came home to Chattanooga for the summer like we always did, but this time we went our separate ways. That summer was a disaster." I gulped down the saliva rushing to my mouth. I couldn't control my cringe. "It was like everyone found out I was newly single, and they pounced, and for a time, I ... liked it. I was around town with a new guy every week and partied every weekend. I can never make up for the stupid decisions I made during those two and a half months. Thad, I was awful."

And now he'll tell me to leave.

But he didn't. "Eva, nothing you say can top the awful I've done."

I sighed, this time to push out my shame. It didn't work, but I squeezed his hand for trying to put me out of my misery.

"I went back to school. It was the start of senior year. Alex had already been on campus a while 'cause of football, and soon enough, even though he'd heard all about my wild summer, he started calling again.

"One nigh,t he called late and wanted me to come see him. And I missed him and the security I found in him, so I went."

Embarrassed, I sat up straighter and pulled my hand away from Thad's. "About three weeks later, I found out I was pregnant."

Thad just nodded.

"I'd made plenty of regrettable decisions, but in this case there was no denying the baby was his, could *only* be his. I told Alex, and after about a week of shock, we decided we were officially getting back together. We'd raise the baby together, maybe—hopefully—get married and have a 'happily ever after' one day. And the thing is, we got excited. His parents weren't, but Alex and I were committed to trying to get it right.

"And so my whole senior year my belly grew and grew." I laughed. "Like, a lot. I was huge."

Thad laughed. "I would have loved to have seen you pregnant."

For some reason, his words caused tears to rush, and I had to fight back the ugly cry. "Thanks." I barely got it out. He sat back and put his arm around me, pulling me to him.

"Eva, you don't have to tell me the rest now. It's okay."

"No, I never talk about it. And I ... I need to." I swiped at my eyes. "We'd had our graduation ceremony and started packing to head home to Chattanooga, to wait on our little girl to be born. I was nine months pregnant. Alex left to meet up with some friends, and I didn't hear from him for the rest of that night. The next morning, I got a call from his mother telling me he'd been in a car wreck. An eighteen-wheeler had barreled into him. They airlifted him to a hospital in Atlanta. He was in a coma, and he died five days later without ever regaining consciousness." I covered my face to cry. "He never got to meet Willow."

I didn't know at first if Thad could make out what I'd said. I was frozen in time, stuck inside the memory of being in the hospital with Mom by my side, giving birth without Alex next to me.

Thad put both his arms around me. I turned to him, tucking my face in his neck. "I am so sorry, Eva. So, so sorry."

I melted into his embrace, feeling the warmth of his body and the beat of his heart, realizing I felt safe with him too. Maybe so much more than just safe.

SAFE HARBOR

"Eva, you've made a beautiful life out of tragedy. And I hope I'm not out of line when I say this, but think of what it could be like if you open the door for God to come in again. His plan never intended for you to do life alone, without him or without love. Remember from Sunday, *you are his*."

I pulled away. "I better get it together in case one of the students wanders this way." I wiped under my eyes, tempted to use the sleeve of my jacket.

"Eva, I see what you're doing. Don't avoid the topic of God anymore."

I stood, my feet wanting to walk away, my feathers royally ruffled. He'd touched a nerve.

Thad stood too, but didn't reach for me. "Is it so hard to imagine reaching out to God because you're angry with him?"

I wanted to fold away in my jacket and hide from Thad and God. I sighed.

"At first. Yeah, I was angry, but time showed me I was mostly angry with myself. I'd screwed up. I broke Alex's heart and had a wild summer that was supposed to be fun, only to realize I'd messed up a really great love. I ended up pregnant, certainly not planned, not making our senior year easy. Then he was gone." I shook my head over and over. "And I deserved it."

"Eva," Thad said with force, "that's not how God works. Remember the story about the lost son? You're afraid." Thad's words were firm, even chastising. "You're afraid if you run back to him, allow him to establish you into his family, you'll have to change. Be someone different than you are now. And guess what? You will, because that's how he works. He'll make you a better version of yourself, if you're not afraid to let him."

He was right. I *was* afraid. Afraid I'd have to come clean about Alex's parents, afraid I'd have to reach out to them, afraid I'd have to admit how wrong I'd been all these years.

"You're right." And with that whispered admission, my heart broke open. The lake that was my heart turned into an ocean, ruptured, wide, and never-ending.

God, is that you?

An immediate fog fell over me, bringing with it calm and peace. I relished in the subtle strum coursing through me because of him.

"Let's face that fear together. I'll help you when you're ready."

Thank you for sending him to help me, God.

"Okay."

"C'mon, it's getting dark, and these stadium lights aren't set to come on."

He grabbed my hand and I let him lead me, pushing aside— hopefully for good—the stubborn, scared Eva that had ruled so long.

CHAPTER TWENTY-SIX

SATURDAY

THAD

I slowly brought the tractor to a halt, letting it idle as I surveyed the circular area I'd just finished bush hogging. Now that it was free of all the tall grass and brush, you could see its fire-pit potential. It was positioned twenty yards from the lake, and at the right time of day the shade from three massive live oaks fell over it. The trees were the perfect backdrop, planted a hundred years ago with someone's foresight of being the perfect spot to relax by the water. Altogether, they created a scene better than the summer camp in the movie classic *Parent Trap*. By the end of the day, the spot would be magical.

As long as the rain stayed away.

I shifted in the tractor seat to look back at the barn. Seven cars were already parked next to my Bronco, with people milling around everywhere, chatting and drinking coffee. Mike was there, talking to a few guys, stepping in to give them direction. I checked my watch. It was already ten o'clock. The hour on the tractor had whipped by.

I shifted the lever to turn off the blade, disengaged the bush hog attachment, then rolled my way over to the crowd. Mike, now pulling coolers out of my Bronco and setting them on the ground, saw me and came out to meet me halfway.

"Man, that looks like fun," he yelled over the engine noise. "When is it my turn?"

I let the tractor roll to a stop and killed the engine.

"You wish. I'm not giving up this job anytime soon." I jumped down and winked as I punched him in the arm.

"C'mon, man. Please?"

"All right, I'll let you tackle the field. But first we gotta round everybody up."

"Yeah, the whole church group's turned out. Probably curious to see what you've been up to on this massive piece of property. They want to see what's kept you busy during the off-season."

I shrugged and looked at the hand-built barn I was so proud of. "Maybe. Or maybe they just think I'm a nice guy and want to help me out."

"Help you out *and* satisfy their curiosity, Hot Shot."

I was tempted to punch Mike in the shoulder again. He knew it and scooted away fast as we walked toward the crowd of maybe twenty people who'd gathered outside the barn doors.

As we approached, Pastor Andrew's wife, Jessica, strode over with a crockpot in her hands.

"I've brought the chili for the hot dogs tonight!" Everything Jessica said ended with an exclamation mark. It would be annoying coming from anyone else, but the joy radiating from her made it hard to be anything but happy around her.

"Thanks so much, Jessica. I'm sure it's delicious."

"We'll see! Where can I plug in this bad boy to keep it warm?"

"If you go inside, there's a little room with a table and an outlet somewhere."

SAFE HARBOR

"On it!" She and the crockpot disappeared into the barn.

I glanced around to see who'd showed up to give me free manual labor. Mike patted my shoulder in a "go-time" signal, and I raised my voice.

"Hey, everyone. Thanks for coming. If you could all gather around, I'll fill y'all in."

The rattle of gravel brought my attention to the road just in time to see Eva's car break through the trees. I focused, ignoring the part of my mind that wanted to watch her get out of her car. "Some of you may have heard bits and pieces of what I've started working on out here." I looked to Mike for support, but found him in a stare-down with Eva's friend Stacy.

Hmm.

"A few years ago, God gave me a vision for this place. Now the timing is right to begin breaking ground, literally and figuratively." I laughed, but no one caught my pun. I quickly added, "I hope you guys are ready to get dirty. Today, we start to make this"—I circled my hand in the air—"into a nonprofit Christian kids' summer camp. I've gotten almost all the permits we need from the county planning and zoning committee. A construction crew will get rolling at the start of the new year, but there are a few things we can do now."

Eva beamed, making my stomach flipflop. "Today, we'll build a fire pit complete with tree stump seating. Yes, the fire pits you're all envisioning right now from every summer camp movie you've ever seen. And we'll be cutting down trees. Joe, you're on that, right?"

Joe gave me a thumbs-up. "Yes, sir."

"Joe is a tree master. He already knows which ones we're taking down, and he'll need a couple of guys who are good with a chainsaw."

Randy and Pastor Andrew raised their hands.

"Perfect. He has extra chainsaws for you both." I raised my voice. "We'll also be clearing the brush and tall grass out of the pasture"—I gestured to where I'd left the tractor—"and raking the loads of sand we've had hauled in to make a beach entry into the lake." I looked at Mike. "Did I cover everything?"

"There are drinks in the coolers," Mike said, then held up his list to me.

"Yes. Drinks are in the coolers And both Mike and I have official lists of what I'd love to get done today. *And*, as a thank you, we'll have a cookout at the new fire pit this evening."

Everyone cheered and hooted their approval.

"According to the weatherman, the rain should hold off until tomorrow. Let's all say a prayer now, so our hundred hotdogs and Jessica's chili don't go to waste."

Everyone laughed and held up prayer hands.

Pastor Andrew spoke up. "Thad, I think I speak for everyone when I say this community is blessed to have you as part of it, and we're grateful God gave you your past to provide what's coming. This camp, the football program you're a major part of—even your surf lessons—they're all making a difference around here, and raising up our next generation to do great things. We—" he indicated the crowd, "—are super proud of you."

Every single person nodded, and I found myself overcome with emotion.

"Thank you all. Thank you, Jesus." Everyone clapped, making me eager to get out of the limelight. "All right, let's get started. Mike, you take a group for clearing and working on the fire pit. I'll take a group to the lake to shovel sand. And, Joe, you've got the trees." I handed Mike my tractor key. "Have fun."

SAFE HARBOR

His eyebrows wiggled up and down twice, after the manner of Groucho Marx. Then he moved out along with the crowd. I made my way straight to Eva. "Hey."

"Hi. This is Stacy."

"Nice to officially meet you. Thanks for helping today."

"You're welcome. It's really exciting what you plan on doing here."

"Thanks."

Eva said, "Mom is bringing Willow later for the cookout. I hope that's okay?"

"You kidding? It's more than okay." I found myself caught up in Eva's gaze, locked in a trance that was never easy to break.

Stacy said, "Um, I'll go help with the fire pit crew. Mike's got that, right?"

"Yeah." I was still lost in Eva's hold.

Stacy moved away, and all I could think of was pulling Eva to me.

"I haven't seen you since Tuesday, and I really want to kiss you right now," I said. Eva clamped her lips together, but her dimples exposed her mood. "But I'll hold off and not submit you to my sweatiness."

Her dark eyes flirted. "Well, if you must know, I want to kiss you too, and I don't care if you're sweaty. In fact, I kind of like the look."

"Well then, let me tote you off to the woods."

She broke out laughing. "So, Romeo, where's my shovel?"

"Huh?"

"My shovel. To help you with the sand?"

"Oh." I shook the fog from my head. "There's a pile over there. Come on." I put my arm around her shoulders as we walked toward the lake. "You know, I know we're both busy, but there's got to be a way to see you more."

"I'm open to suggestions."

After a few steps, I heard the tractor crank up in the distance. Mike was officially in hog heaven.

EVA

The muscles in my back burned, blisters formed on my palms, and even in the gorgeous fall weather, sweat dripped from my forehead. I hadn't felt so full of energy in years. I was beginning to think working, the physical work of getting my hands dirty, could be addictive. Which was a good thing, because helping Thad accomplish his dreams would take quite a bit of dirty work.

"Hey, young lady."

I stopped mid-swing and looked up to see John.

"Hi there." The sun was so bright I had to squint behind my sunglasses. "I'm glad you're here." I stood straight and propped myself up against the shovel.

"Yeah, I started a Bible study on Saturday mornings with my golf buddies. I didn't want to let them down." He looked around the area. "I don't see Willow. She coming later?"

"Yes, she will. Mom's bringing her."

"Great. Thad had hoped she would. Last night, he picked up marshmallows, chocolate, and graham crackers so we could all make s'mores tonight."

My heart skipped a beat. "Thank you. She'll love that."

John nodded. "Where're the shovels?"

I pointed to the tree line where a couple of extra shovels were propped up. When John had made it back over, shovel in hand, I met him at the sand mound.

"It was time to move those huge logs around the fire pit, so Thad went to help," I said. We paused to watch him as he heaved a ten-foot section of log into place with four other men, and then I turned back to John. "But his instructions were to get rid of this mound." I laughed. "Which looks about as high as it did an hour ago."

John huffed.

"See those pins with the flags on them? Near the lake?" I pointed. "We're to spread the sand between them and into the water." I waved to two of Thad's helpers who had waders on, spreading the sand into the water.

John called over to them, "Kallie, Ed, looks like you guys got the fun job." They smiled and waved back, then returned to their work. "Looks like an awful lot of work to do without a machine."

I grunted. "I know. Thad said he was hesitant to use a machine because of the damage it could do to the pasture." I leaned in closer. "I think he just likes manual labor."

John laughed. "Honey, you don't know how true that is." He gripped his shovel and stuck it into the sand. "All right, I'm following your lead."

Ten minutes later, John and I had a train going. He'd shovel directly from the mound and walk ten feet or so and dump it for me. I'd shovel from his pile and bring it to the water.

John hummed while he worked. I became lost in his tune, so much so that when he spoke, I almost missed it.

"How'd you like the service last week?"

"Excuse me?" I stopped. "Oh. The church service. It was eye-opening for sure."

"They always are."

I could only nod. I'd thought about it every day.

Establish your relationship with Jesus. You are his.

"No matter where your relationship stands with God," he said, seeming to read my mind, "you can always grow, open that door wider."

God, you sure use the Smith men to speak to me, don't you?

I scooped sand and walked to the lake.

"For some people," he said, "it may be hard to imagine a God who wants them to open that door—one they slammed tight long ago. But the story of the lost son is a good visual of the Father's love."

I watched rings appear in the water from the fish below the surface.

John came to me. "Eva, I'm really sorry for how I accidentally instigated that conversation with Willow last Sunday."

"John, it's fine. I knew those questions were coming. You did nothing wrong. I should've already discussed her father with her." I blew out a hard breath to show my irritation with my own lack of courage. "If anything, last Sunday helped me. I was able to sit her down and tell her she does have a father. He's just in heaven." *Along with Father God, who Willow so effortlessly pointed out to me.* "It ended up feeling good to talk about him with Willow, of course, but Thad too."

"Oh? Well, I'm glad. Thad's a good listener, so I'm not surprised."

"I know. It's strange how I fought so hard for so long to keep things simple and not change my life's dynamic. For years, it was just Willow and me. Then I moved here with Mom and met him. He seems to fit in so easily."

For so many reasons.

"Well," he said, and chuckled, "he feels the same about you. You have that boy pretty love-struck."

I quickly looked at John, and then embarrassment set in, and I turned back to the lake. "I'm still not sure why."

"He's been waiting for you, Eva. I mean, he didn't know it was you, but he was waiting for someone who saw him as the person he wanted to be. Someone who reminds him of his mom—devoted, caring. Stubborn."

"I'm afraid I'll let him down."

"You can't. Don't you see? How *you* see him now, he also sees who you are now. Whatever happened—whatever decisions you made and still regret—are from back then."

"What if I'm still making bad decisions?"

"It seems your mind just went to something specific. I'm not a counselor, and certainly not a pastor, but if you're convicted, then you're actually on the right track. You wouldn't feel that way if you hadn't opened that door again to Jesus. At least a little bit." His gaze wore me down. He smiled, satisfied. "Now you've just got to make a change. Make things right."

"You make it sound easy, but I can't turn back time."

"Maybe not, but you can stop the past from repeating itself."

I stuck the shovel into the sand.

"John, I've only been out here twice, but I couldn't help but notice we're not far away from Palmer Middle. In fact, the way the crow flies, it seems like it should be right over there, maybe through those woods." I pointed in the direction of the barn. I looked John in his chocolate eyes as he studied me, waiting for my next statement, or maybe question. "Thad's the anonymous donor of the football stadium, isn't he?"

John turned back to shoveling and gave a little harrumph. "Yes."

What doesn't Thad do?

"I'm not surprised."

"He did well in the NFL, but he made most of his money by being smart enough to hire someone to take care of him financially. He has a foundation set up that makes money, and he also personally donated to get it done. God just showed him the need, and he fulfilled it with what was already God's. Thad's just a good steward." I heard the unbreakable pride John had for his only son.

"Wow."

"Agreed. I've never been prouder of him than I have in these last couple of years."

THAD

Dad and Eva were engaged in intense conversation. I almost hated to interrupt them, but I'd told Eva an hour ago I'd be right back, so I moved faster. They heard my approach and turned to find me hugging five water bottles to my chest.

"Finally decided to make an appearance, huh, Dad?" I tried to remain serious but failed. "Just kidding. How was the group?" I handed Dad and Eva a water.

"Good as always."

"I'm glad. Kallie, Ed, come on in for a break." They laid down their tools and strolled over. I looked at Eva, still cute, even with sweat beading along her hairline. "Sorry it took me longer than I expected."

"You're fine. John's been keeping me company." Eva gulped down half her bottle, then held it up. "Thanks."

Kallie and Ed said the same.

"Of course. You know"—I cringed—"maybe I should've rented a machine for this." I stared at the still mile-high sand pile. "But there's just something about getting your hands dirty and doing the heavy lifting."

John and Eva gave each other 'told ya so' looks and guffawed.

"What?"

EVA

I couldn't take my eyes off Thad and Willow through the flames of the fire. Their smiles mesmerized me. I wished I was near enough to hear their laughter over the music playing from a truck. Willow held her hot dog stick over the flames under the guidance of Thad's fingers, which braced hers and showed her where to hold it the whole time. He was crouched down on her level. His knee was most likely killing him, but he didn't seem to care.

"Girl, you've found a winner." Stacy plopped down next to me.

"I can't even tell you how true that is."

"I'll say. Look at him."

"Stacy ..." I shot her a look of disbelief. "He's so much more than just looks."

"I know. I meant look at him with Willow. I could kill you for hunting for reasons why it couldn't work."

"Stacy, I'm not deserving of someone like him. God graced me with Willow, and she's one of the only things I've gotten right. Maybe my only redeeming quality."

"Girl, *please*."

I nudged her arm and redirected the conversation. "So what's this I see brewing between you and Mike?"

Stacy smiled. "He's cute, isn't he?"

Mike sat on a truck tailgate, singing with some guys to some country song. "Yes, he's definitely a cutie. I've seen him watching you. And it didn't go unnoticed when you joined his crew today."

Stacy's smile held tight. As if on cue, Mike jumped off the tailgate, met her eyes, and walked our way.

"Dance with me?"

Stacy couldn't hide her full-force blush. "No one else is dancing."

"Then we'll get it started," Mike said.

"Okay." Stacy grabbed his extended hand, and he led her to a clearing behind the truck.

I was happy for Stacy and gave her a thumbs-up when she looked over her shoulder.

Willow and Thad came to the table, her hot dog still on the stick. I started to get up and go help make Willow a plate, but Mom stepped next to them and grabbed the stick from her to take care of it. I relaxed and Thad came over, collapsing on the ground and leaning his back against the log, his long legs straight out in front of him.

"Thank you for helping her."

"You're welcome. Hard to keep the thing from catching fire." He took off his hat and dropped it in his lap, his long hair falling out of its tie in all directions.

"I'll bet. The fire is raging." I looked toward the blaze. "The pit turned out amazing."

"Thanks. It beat my expectations."

"What about the sand pile?" I laughed. My fingers moved into his hair on their own. I undid the tie and pulled the fallen strands back away from his face.

He closed his eyes and leaned into my touch. "The pile also beat my expectations."

"Liar," I said, as I finished putting his hair into a knot.

"Hey, you don't know. Maybe I always expected that pile to take more than one workday to get rid of."

"Sure." I could barely see the sand mound in the dusk lighting, but it was still there, tall and proud, having bested us for the day.

"Thanks." His eyes motioned to his hair. "Come down here next to me."

SAFE HARBOR

Exhausted, I slid right off the log to the ground, and he put his arm around me, relaxing back even more. "Rain's coming."

The leaves rustled in the wind, louder than the fire's roar, driving home the point that yes, rain was on its way. Thad hugged me a little tighter. "I'm just glad we had today and tonight."

"Me too," I said, for so many reasons.

"You joining us at church tomorrow?"

"Yeah, I plan on it."

"Good."

We both fell into weary silence, people-watching as more folks began to dance. Willow trotted over carrying her plate.

"Hey, baby. I saw you cook that hot dog, big girl. Come here and show me what you've got."

Willow grinned with pride, exposing a mouthful of half-chewed chips. She plopped down on my lap and snuggled into me while I helped balance her plate. After a few bites, Willow said, "I like it here."

I kissed the back of her head and whispered, "So do I."

CHAPTER TWENTY-SEVEN

SUNDAY

THAD

I stood and strained to see if Eva was coming as the worship leader hit the first note. I'd waited for her and the family in the lobby, but when the ushers began to close the doors, signaling the service was to begin, I went to Dad and the seats he was saving.

He leaned over and whispered, "Not coming?"

I shrugged. "Don't know."

I tried in vain to sing along and get myself worship-ready, but after the second song, I couldn't stand waiting any longer and retrieved my phone from my pocket. No missed calls. I was typing a text message to her when Dad elbowed me and inclined his head toward the aisle.

Eva, in a maroon sweater dress, stepped into our row still wrapping the tie around her drippy umbrella. Dad scooted back to let her through, and she sidled up next to me.

"Sorry," she said, soft enough so only I could hear. "I sent Mom and Willow away to Chattanooga ahead of the king tide issue and Hurricane Rowan. They're staying with my aunt. That's why I'm late."

I leaned into her Skittle-smelling hair. "It's okay. I'm just glad you made it."

She smiled. "I'm staying in case I need to go to work tomorrow."

"They'll probably cancel school," I whispered. "We'll talk about it later."

The look Eva gave me reminded me just how independent she was. Her attitude good-naturedly radiated *who do you think you are?* But it didn't matter. I was finally able to focus on praising God, because for the moment she was safe by my side.

A couple of songs later, we sat, and Pastor Andrew got up on stage.

"Good morning. We're so glad you chose to worship God with us this beautiful day. If you're a guest, we're currently in the middle of a series called 'Established.' To briefly repeat, as Americans who can't get away from our media mania, and who can't help but document everything, I'm sure you've seen signs made for families or marriages that say, 'Established 2010,' or 'Established 2008.'" He waited for nods from the crowd. "These signify the joining of a relationship, the beginning of a new family. And we've taken that word and asked ourselves, what does it mean to be established into God's family?" He let those words resonate, and again their power reverberated through my chest.

"Today," he said slowly, "today we are going to talk about one of the most hated words in the Bible—*repentance*."

You could feel a collective cringe shoot through the room.

EVA

I'd tried to remain normal during the sermon, tried to hide my shaking hands and the thunderous beat of my heart. But as the pastor spoke of Paul and the numerous times he called upon his fellow believers to turn away from their wrongs and instead turn to God, my throat constricted, growing tighter by the minute.

Pastor Andrew walked to the side of the stage closest to us.

"In Acts 25 and 26, Paul tells King Agrippa and the whole courtroom how God took hold of him and turned his world upside down. Remember, Paul was a hater. He discriminated against, tortured, and even killed Christ's followers. And yet God showed up in his life. He was a goner to God's love and did what God asked. He says in the twentieth verse of Acts 26, 'I preached that they should repent and turn to God and demonstrate their repentance by their deeds.' If you want to be established, firmly anchored in your relationship to your loving Father, then you have to show repentance for your wrongs. One with a repentant heart shows the strength of their desire to be in a close relationship to Jesus by their actions."

The words of Pastor Andrew mimicked John's words from yesterday.

You've just gotta make a change. Make things right.

"But guess what?"

I could swear the pastor looked right at me, and I thought I might be sick.

"Look to the screen and read this verse with me." He turned to the screen behind his head. "Acts 3:19 says, 'Repent, then, and turn to God, so that your sins may be wiped out, that times of refreshing may come from the Lord.'"

He gave the crowd a good once-over look, and the worship team stepped back on stage, quietly making their way to their instruments. Then he continued, "God is waiting to wipe out those wrongs and bring you a refreshing time—a healing time, a time of starting new."

He bowed his head and prayed. The music began, signaling the service was concluding, but his words were lost on me. Robert and Pamela flashed in my mind, and their words haunted me.

We want to reiterate how sorry we are for the way we treated you. Please give us a chance.

Words swirled—John's, Thad's, Pastor Andrew's—voices all mixing as Alex planted himself before me.

I got down on my knees and cried out to Jesus for forgiveness and restoration.

Open the door.

You've got to make things right. Make a change.

A time of starting new.

You are his.

I put my head in my hands to hide the tears. Thad stood, but I couldn't get my body to move as the worship leader sang.

The flood waters rise, trying to drown out everything in its path. I am dragged along through the newfound sea.

The storm rages above and below me.

I latched onto the words of the song, and their certainty punched me in the gut.

In the chaos, I hear my name. Through the noise, your voice is clear. You're the anchor in the rising waters. I reach for it. You've found me.

I looked up to read along with the words coming from the stage. They were true. I was tired and confused. I needed him.

In your embrace, the waters leave. In your closeness, troubles flee.

Hold me tight. Be my anchor.

I've come back to you.

I put my head back in my hands and whispered his name.

Jesus...

Thad let me have my moment. I sensed him, solid and still as the stones of a mountain, waiting for me to move, to need. When I chanced a look his way, I smiled, seeing his own smile waiting.

"You ready?"

I nodded.

We settled on him grabbing lunch and the two of us relaxing at his house to watch the storms roll in. I showed up in joggers and a T-shirt with a jug of sweet tea. In between the shattering thunderstorms ravaging the day, the weather was typical October-muggy in coastal Georgia—which, I'd been told, made for worsening flooding conditions.

John had stayed inland after church, having planned with Thad to meet at the barn loft in a few hours. Thad and I ate burgers, then sat on the couch, channel-surfing between golf and old episodes of *Dateline*. The hum of the television noise allowed me to process Pastor Andrews's words at length.

Thad caught me in a stare-off with the weather outside.

"Storm's getting angrier," he said. "You sure you don't want to get some sandbags for your house? I bet if we left right now, we could scrounge some up."

"Thad, it's not a hurricane—"

"Rowan is just below us, bringing in powerful storms that can—"

"I'm not playing into the fear."

"Oh, really?" Now, he teased. "You sent your mom and Willow away."

I nudged him in the ribs. "They'd been talking about going up for a few nights, and it just made sense. Plus I like the idea of being alone for a bit. And according to Mom, the house did flood once, like fifteen years ago. Not since. We'll keep the streak going."

"Well, you're coming to the barn with Dad and me if it gets bad. Promise me."

"I'm a ways off the beach—"

"Eva, that doesn't matter."

"I know you say it doesn't, but it has to mean something. I get why you guys are going to stay on your property. Less chance of flooding, and easier to get out of town if you need to. But you live *on* the ocean. Of course you need to get away from the big tide." I made sure to say those words really spooky-like.

Thad huffed. "Yes, the water might well reach my house. But I'm practically on stilts. My pool area can be cleaned up. The cars will be out of the garage. My mechanical hurricane shutters will be up—"

"Of course you already have hurricane shutters."

He shrugged. "We have hurricanes on this coast. Therefore I have hurricane shutters." He pointed with an index finger for emphasis. "*And* I'll be safe and dry at the property until my *house* is back to safe and dry."

He sat up. "You know what? This is crazy. School is going to get canceled. Either way, staying at the barn loft is closer to Palmer."

I narrowed my eyes. "You seem to have forgotten my need for peace and quiet."

Thad scoffed. "You madden me, woman!" But he was laughing before he finished the words.

I relented. "I *promise* to come to you if it gets bad, okay? Maybe we'll get lucky and school will be called off, and there won't be any flooding in Moanna or inland either."

Thad sat back and put his arm around me, satisfied for now. After a beat, he said, "Eva, are you okay? Since church you've been quiet."

"How do you read me so easily?"

I'd asked him the same question weeks ago. Something intimate passed over his features before he said, "You're avoiding the question."

I snorted with fake annoyance. "Let's just say words from you, your dad, and Pastor Andrew keep swarming in my brain. There's something I need to do, and it's certainly something I don't want to do. In fact, the thought makes me sick to my stomach, but not doing anything is making me just as sick." I sighed. "I'm rambling. I'm sorry."

"No, it's okay. Talk about it if you want."

"I'm too ashamed to even tell you. I wish I could go back, and I want to go back, but I'm not sure I can, not sure how." I knew I wasn't really making sense, but when he started to say something, I said firmly, "I don't want to talk about it."

"Okay."

I gripped his arm, so he maneuvered to face me. "I'm sorry. I didn't mean my words to sound so harsh. I just have some things to figure out, but they have absolutely nothing to do with you. You ... I don't deserve you."

He reached for me, slipping his fingers into the soft hair at the base of my neck, and pulled me to his lips. He kissed me slowly and I gave in, kissing him back fully. We pulled away a little, and he said, "I'm here whenever you're ready."

"I know you are." I pushed up to the couch's edge. "I'm going to go. Get my head straight, settle in for the night." This was sort of a lie. "You head on out before the tides rise. *If* they're even going to."

Thad studied me. "Okay, but keep me updated with the weather here."

"I will."

By the time I got home, it had actually stopped raining. I took it as my cue. With my rain jacket and boots on, I hopped onto my bike and peddled down the beach walk toward the wild ocean. Likely no one would be there, which was how I wanted it.

The humidity was thick, clouding my eyes as the gray sky seemed to draw closer. I shook off my awareness of the oncoming storm and pumped my legs faster. Nearing the dunes, I skirted to the left and ducked down a tad. Thad had probably already left his house, but I wasn't taking a chance he'd see me. I ditched my bike in the dunes and kept walking left. The beach was like a dead zone—a loud one, hauntingly vacant and yet furiously roaring to make itself heard. The sense of desolation, along with the strong wind that stirred up mist from all sides, brought me as close to God's elements as possible. Like I could touch him somehow, just as Thad had talked about with the jetty by the lighthouse.

I sat down and breathed in the thick air, not caring my backside would be wet in no time.

God?

I'm here. And I need you. I don't want to live this life any longer without you. I don't want to keep making mistakes. For so long I've thought Willow needed only me, and I'm realizing I'm so wrong. She needs more than just my love, and I'm so sorry I kept her tucked away from you, even though I know you were there the whole time. I'm sorry I've kept her away from Alex's parents, that I let anger and bitterness fester in my heart for so long toward them ... and toward you.

Time has healed parts of my heart, but I'm finding that time makes past regrets fester like an open gash. Give me the courage to go home, to Alex's home, and bring Willow to his parents. And give me the words to express to them the forgiveness that's grown in my heart since we've moved to Moanna. Give me the courage to ask for their forgiveness too.

The prayer bubbled out, and just as quickly, I felt the words wash over me.

SAFE HARBOR

You are mine.

Tears rushed down my cheeks. *Yes, I am yours ... again.*

A raindrop fell, hitting my face and mingling with my tears. With each one that followed, a supernatural cleansing took place. His grace carried away my shame. The song from the morning tumbled out, *In the chaos, I hear my name. Through the noise, your voice is clear. You're the anchor in the rising waters. I reach for it. You've found me. In your embrace, the waters leave. In your closeness, troubles flee. Hold me tight. Be my anchor. I've come back to you.* I sang the verses over and over until my tears dried, because my soul was new. Gone was the stain of my past, and I would not let my sin repeat itself.

Thank you, Jesus, for ... everything.

Even through the rain still poured, I bicycled my way slowly home, resting in the somberness around me. There were likely people home, reluctant to leave for a *possible* high tide that *could* flood the island, but if they were there, they hid in their darkened houses as the nonexistent sun moved further west.

After I took a hot shower, my bed called to me. I went to Willow's room, grabbed the picture of Alex and me along with Willow's plush stuffed elephant, and took them to my room. My phone dinged. It was the school system calling off school for Monday. The joy of being able to sleep in made me smile.

After texting Mom to let her know I'd call after my nap, I curled up with the picture frame and elephant as the rain drummed on the roof. *God's lullaby to us*, Thad's voice in my head reminded, and it put me right to sleep.

CHAPTER TWENTY-EIGHT

SUNDAY EVENING

An alarm startled me awake.

Total darkness enveloped me, momentarily disorienting me until I felt the wood frame of the picture next to me and remembered I was in my room.

My phone. The noise was coming from my phone.

I shuffled the covers in search of it, and finally a flash of light under Willow's stuffed animal caught my eye. Its message panicked me more, as the weather alert system warned of a flood occurring in my area. I silenced the alert. It was eleven p.m. I'd slept quite a while, and if a flood warning had been issued, it was probably time to head to Thad's.

I stumbled to the light switch and—nothing.

The power was out, explaining why the house felt eerily darker than normal. Using my phone's flashlight, I ran to the front door and hauled it open.

Below the first step, black water waited, maybe a few inches deep. The whole front yard glistened in my small light. And it was still raining. It was happening as Thad had said it might—the perfect storm of high tide plus heavy rain. As if in agreement, lightning flashed somewhere just past the road, followed immediately by thunder so loud my body shook with it.

Slamming the door, I hustled back to my room, calling Mom as I grabbed a duffle bag.

It wouldn't go through. I had no indicator bars. The storm had knocked out the phone service.

Get it together, Eva.

But my heart wasn't listening to my mind. I hurriedly threw some clothes and a phone charger in the bag and hustled to the bathroom to get my toothbrush, of all things, because, well, a person still needed to brush their teeth in emergencies. Using the light from my phone, I went to the mudroom and sat on the bench. I tried to call Mom again while sliding my feet into my tennis shoes without even untying the laces.

It didn't go through. Again.

"C'mon!" I screamed into the pitch-black house. I would just keep calling on the way off Moanna. What choice did I have? Leaving this house, this road, this island was the best I could do. Maybe I'd see others doing the same thing. *Right?*

I slung the bag over my shoulder and found the garage door opener button.

But nothing happened. Of course it wouldn't. The power was out.

God, help me, please. I took a breath.

Think, Eva.

There's a manual release for the garage door. *Right.*

I stepped down the two stairs. The concrete floor was already soaked. Water gathered, coming in from who knew where. Using the phone's mini flashlight, I tossed my bag inside my car and went around to the back. Climbing on top of the trunk, I pulled the red cord, releasing the garage door from the power option. Pulling the garage door up manually was harder than I thought it'd be, but once up, it stayed. Looking out into the night for only a moment made it clear I was alone.

SAFE HARBOR

No car headlights or flashlights scanned the area. The blackness was so thick, I couldn't see past the phone's small beam of light.

My movements blurred as I got in the car and cranked the engine. The dashboard lit up, so I turned my flashlight off and tossed it in my passenger seat. I put the car in reverse, and a thunderous crack pierced my ears just before I fell into a black well of emptiness.

CHAPTER TWENTY-NINE

SUNDAY, NEAR MIDNIGHT
THAD

"Something is wrong, Dad. I feel it in my gut."

"Now don't overreact, son." He tried to slow my pacing by gripping my shoulder, but it only stopped me momentarily. "These storms've got everybody riled up."

"The emergency alert woke you up too. And I haven't been able to get hold of Eva all night. She's stubborn, but she's not irresponsible. She wouldn't ignore a weather alert, and she hasn't called to come here. She promised she'd come here."

"I bet she has no service. She'll probably pull up right outside any time now."

"I have to do something. I wish I had her mom's number." I snapped my fingers. "Wait, can't you get on your social media and message her or something?" Dad knew more about Facebook than I did.

"Yeah." He started tapping his phone. "I think I can even call her."

"What?"

Dad shrugged. "I don't know how it works, just know it does. My buddy Ted called me once that way."

"Whatever." I ran my hand through my hair. "Just please ..." Words failed.

A few more taps, and he gave the phone to me. One look at the screen told me it was ringing somehow to someone—Ellen.

"Hello, John?" Ellen fumbled a minute until I saw her on the screen. Realizing it was some sort of FaceTime call, I held my screen so she could also see me. Her eyes came into the frame.

"Oh! Thad! Thank God. I've tried for hours to figure out how to get hold of you. Is Eva there?" Her evident worry made mine worse.

"No. You haven't heard from her?"

"Not since this evening. She texted, saying she was laying down for a nap, and she never called back. I can't get through."

"Me neither."

"It's all over the news. The weather channel talking about the king tides, and the governor's been on TV, and oh, something is wrong." Her voice rose five octaves in those two sentences.

I pulled out my own phone. "What's your cell number? I'm going to text you from my number so you'll have it."

She rattled it off, and I texted her my name quick. "There. It should come through now. I'm going to Moanna. I'll find her."

"Thank you." Behind her words was a sob.

"I'll call you back soon."

I went straight to the door where Dad already stood with my raincoat.

"Find her," he said. "But be safe. Don't do anything crazy, Thad."

"Crazy would be me doing nothing."

He nodded, caving to my will.

"I'll call you *when* I find her." I trotted down the loft stairs and into the storm.

CHAPTER THIRTY

SUNDAY MORNING

EVA

You know when you *know* you're in a dream? Flashes of Willow, Mom, and Dad played behind my eyes, but they weren't real. I knew this. My body just wouldn't wake up. Even as the pain in my head and legs cried out for relief, my mind wouldn't open my eyes. And a constant ticking annoyed me, like an out-of-rhythm metronome.

Wake up, Eva!

The angry twin version of myself did the job, because my eyes fluttered. I *knew* I was in my car, but it all felt off somehow. The movement of my eyelids was painful, so I opened just one.

Everything is dark and cold and loud.

I moved my fingers and they trailed through liquid, which was enough to wake me up fully. I tried to shift—screamed as my lower half fought back, and my already throbbing forehead hit something inches away.

I'm trapped. And sitting in water. The car is flooding.

My breath came erratically as I assessed my body, trying to understand why I couldn't move and why steady rain kept hitting my face. Then lightning flashed, illuminating both the open sky above and the live oak—the one from the edge of the driveway—where it pierced the garage roof, dissected my car and crushed the hood. My legs were trapped underneath in the cold, rising water.

Why hadn't I listened to Thad? I could be dry and safe with him right now. He and Mom were probably trying to reach me.

My phone!

I stuffed my hand through the branches and leaves that raked and scraped my arms, until finally I touched the softness of the passenger seat. I stretched and found my phone's edge. Pushing down on the corner caused its weight to shift my direction, and I slid my fingers along its glass until I could grab it. I ripped it through the brush. It was wet but lit up.

Still no service.

Worse, the low battery message popped up. I growled as I sent the screen to dark and held it to my collarbone, hoping to shield it from the rainwater.

Think, Eva.

Save the battery. I didn't need any light right now. Lightning would flash periodically anyway. The storm had to stop at some point, and the sun must rise.

But the water kept rising too.

A shiver overtook me. I could also freeze to death.

God! Where are you?

"Help!" I cried into the dark sky, but I couldn't hear my own voice above the rain. Tears began to flow freely into the water, and my exhausted body started to give out. I was so tired ...

THAD

The bridge onto Moanna was still open. The headlights of a few cars passed me, going inland. I was the only one traveling outbound into danger.

SAFE HARBOR

Less than a quarter-mile down the main road of Ocean Oaks, a police cruiser sat parked in the middle of the road with his lights flashing. Flooding covered the road past him, blocking off any chance of driving to Eva's house, or mine for that matter.

He stepped out of the car with his poncho on and approached my vehicle as I slowed to a stop and rolled down my window.

"You can't go any further." He shined his flashlight into my car. I squinted and he moved the light away.

"I have to get through. I need to check on someone. I can't contact them."

"Phone service is out. Most people evacuated earlier. We had a steady group of cars leave between eleven last night and one-thirty this morning. Whoever you're looking for has probably left already. And anyone still on the island, at least in that direction"—he pointed toward Eva's house, and coincidentally mine too—"is stuck until tomorrow. At dawn, we'll get out there and at least fly over the area. Once the rain stops, we think the water will go down pretty quickly."

That wasn't good enough. My intuition, or maybe God, told me so.

"I *have* to get through. You can't stop me."

He frowned at my challenge. I didn't care. He deliberated a moment and then said, "Look, I get it. You've got a loved one who may be in trouble. All I can say is you can't get through right here. If you turn around and, say, go toward the gate and the bridge and find a way to get where you need to go, I can't stop you." He clicked his tongue. "Just don't leave me out here searching for you at dawn, understand?"

"Yes, sir. I won't." Before he changed his mind, I rolled up the window, reversed, put my foot on the gas, and turned down a side street to the left that wasn't flooded.

I glanced back and forth across the street, hoping an idea would take shape. Eva's road would be a few blocks over and to my right. Not too far away. I could walk there. Swim if I had to. As I approached a cul-de-sac and was about to park and trek it through the rain, my headlights flashed onto a small covered johnboat sitting in a dark driveway.

I turned off the truck and ran to the small boat, ripping the cover off to see if it was a possibility. The boat was only maybe seven feet long by three and a half across. The tiny engine had a pull crank like a lawnmower, and it folded completely over into the boat bed when needed so that it wouldn't hang down below the floorboard. Perfect if I wanted to, say, pull it through floodwaters.

I could drag it behind me until the water got too high and then motor the rest of the way.

Thank you, God.

I unlatched the bungee cords securing it and heaved it off the trailer. I started in the direction of Eva's, knowing I needed to find the golf course behind the houses around me. That golf course would lead me right to her.

CHAPTER THIRTY-ONE

SUNDAY MORNING, PRE-DAWN

EVA

The pain in my legs was long gone, along with any warmth I had left. I'd waked to extreme pinpricks in my fingers.

Hypothermia.

Instinct told me my body was shutting down. The urge to fight, to struggle and tug my legs, was fleeting. My battered body was bruised and scraped, but in my numbness I felt no damage. Eventually the pain in my fingers would dissipate too, allowing me to drift away into an enticing sleep from which I'd never wake.

That is, unless the water kept rising, and I simply drowned. That would be a horrible death.

The water was up to my chest now. A steady stream poured in from my broken window. But the rain had stopped. Surely the full moon tide would go back out to sea, and with the rain gone, the water would recede.

But it might not matter by then.

Willow will have lost both her parents. The pain of her having to deal with such tragedy broke me.

A sob retched out. The motion made my chest heave, and the phone dropped into the water. I searched for it, but my frozen fingertips had no feeling. And reaching for the phone brought rancid water to my mouth, the filthy liquid rushing in as though taking a shot at damaging me even more. I choked out the foulness and stopped searching. The phone was gone, along with my last urge to hold on and fight.

I closed my eyes, and like a movie reel playing on super speed, memories of my life with Willow passed like a dream across the screen inside my mind. Willow was when my life began—everything before her was just filler, until she lay in my arms. Her baby feet, tiny and soft, the smell of her Baby Magic bald head. The toothless smiles, the blood dripping from the small nick on her hairline above her right eye from when she fell onto the coffee table's corner, learning to walk. The bows in her wispy hair, until she decided she didn't want them anymore. Her self-assured voice letting out a *'please.'* The way she flopped like a fish in bed, never still for longer than fifteen minutes. The hugs around my neck, the running into the garage to greet me every day with her pint-sized but powerful joy, the *I love yous* ...

Oh God, please send someone who will help Mom take care of Willow, someone who understands her past. Someone who will take her to meet Alex's parents, someone who will love her more than life. And thank you for bringing me back to you before I die, and for showing me it was okay to love again.

We'd almost had it figured out.

Thad.

The first time his smile shot through my heart like an arrow flashed before me, when I held my baby in my arms after he saved her life. I smiled through my tears.

"Eva?" The memory was so clear, I could almost hear his voice.

"Eva!"

SAFE HARBOR

I was delirious. I had to be. Still, just in case, I pushed out the word as loud as I could.

"Help ..."

"*Eva!* Hold on. Talk to me!"

Thad?

This was no more than a cruel, near-death dream. Even so, I strained to see anything, anyone coming to me from behind the car in the pitch black.

Moments later, a light appeared, then a figure.

"Eva. I'm here."

THAD

"Thad?"

"It's me."

I'd nearly had to swim to her car. The downed tree covered the whole area, making her Honda look like an ant.

"I'm getting you out of here." I tugged on the door handle. To my surprise, it opened easily.

"I didn't open the door. I was afraid more water would come in." Her voice sounded so calm and almost angelic. "My legs are caught."

I touched her arms. "You're freezing." I pulled her face to me. She could barely keep her eyes open. She was not calm or angelic. She was lethargic, deep in hypothermia. She would die if she slept.

"Eva. Don't go to sleep."

"My legs are stuck," she repeated drowsily.

Fear had never so overrun my mind, or fed my determination so fiercely. I shined my light on her legs. The tree had crushed her car's entire front end.

"I'm going to slide your seat back. It might hurt, but I think it'll give me more room to get you free."

She mumbled what I took to be an okay. Her slurred words were those of someone nearly asleep.

"Eva," I said sternly, searching for the seat release lever, "you have to wake up."

Her head lolled to one side, her eyes closed. I was in no mood to let her give up.

"*Eva!* You wake the sam hill up and *talk* to me!"

Maybe discomfort wouldn't be such a bad idea. I adjusted the seat backward, and she cried out, but only for a second. At least now she was awake, and the seat's movement seemed to release some of the pressure on her lower half. I shined the light there but couldn't see because of the murky water. I stuck the flashlight's end in my mouth and felt around.

"There's some kind of metal bar over your feet." Maybe the pedal. "I think I can move it up, then we can get you free."

"Okay," Eva looked at me. Heartbroken. In pain. Like she thought I was a dream.

I held her face between my hands. "I'm getting you out of here. Can you hold the flashlight for me?"

She nodded. Barely.

I gave her the flashlight, then felt down her leg. She jerked, and I could sense her pain beneath my fingers as they brushed past battered skin to her ankle. "I'm going down, and when you feel your feet free, pull up fast."

"Okay," she said, as the light bounced around from her weak hand.

"Forget about the pain, okay? Just do it." I took a breath and went underneath the water.

God, please! Move this!

I found a grip, braced a foot on the car's edge to leverage my weight, and pulled against the entrapping metal bar with all my might, though I knew it wouldn't be enough unless God stepped in.

SAFE HARBOR

It didn't budge. I moved my hands closer to her left ankle and pulled as hard as humanly possible.

Jesus, please!

This time it shifted, and suddenly Eva's feet slid past my arm. She was free.

Thank you, Jesus.

I shot out of the water and tugged her to me, dragging her out of the car as she cried uncontrollably. She did what she could to help me wade through the waist-deep water, still gripping the flashlight and pointing toward our exit, but by the time we got out of the garage, she was lethargic again.

"Come on, Eva. Stay awake!" I screamed. The whites of her eyes shone as they shot open. "Good. Keep those eyes awake and blinkin', okay?"

I put her into the tiny boat and crawled in after her. It would be better to use the small engine, and the boat would keep her out of the frigid water as we made it back to my truck.

I put her body practically between my legs once I got the engine cranked. We headed out at full speed, which wasn't nearly fast enough for me.

"Eva, where do you hurt?" She wasn't waking up anymore. Hypothermia was painful once you began to warm up. Her extremities would be on fire. Why wasn't she writhing in pain? "Eva, talk to me. Where are you hurting?" I yelled, not recognizing my own voice.

I grabbed the flashlight she'd dropped on her lap and scanned her body with it, while the other hand guided the boat. We were afloat over the golf course now. Not much further.

And that's when I saw it. Red like a crime scene, or a haunted house's fake massacre. Blood, oozing out her left ankle and dripping into the boat. And white bone, visible underneath the ooze.

"Oh, God, no."

It wasn't just the water making her hypothermic. She'd been bleeding, maybe for hours. More urgency lit in my core. I didn't know I had any more to release.

We were close to the house where I'd entered the golf course. The water wasn't as high. I ran the johnboat aground and clicked off the engine. Then I was out of the boat as fast as I could move, carrying Eva through the now ankle-deep muddy water. We made it to my truck in minutes.

She hadn't said a word the whole time.

Once I got the side door opened, I sat her gently in the seat and reclined it back. "Eva. Stay awake," I said, even though she clearly wasn't. I checked her pulse. It was still throbbing, but slower than it should be. I ran to open my back hatch and found a handful of beach towels, rushed to her side, and wrapped one around her left ankle, tight.

She screamed. Without her lungs' normal force behind it, the sound came out as a squeak.

"I know it hurts, baby. I'm sorry."

She mumbled as I clicked her seatbelt into its lock and blanketed her with three more beach towels, then slammed the door.

After cranking the truck and turning the heat on high, I sped off the island. Driving to the hospital, located ten miles over the bridge on the deserted road, took what seemed a million minutes. I kept checking my phone and finally got service a few miles out from the hospital.

"Hello, 911, what's your emerg—"

"I'm on the road on Highway Sixteen, just off Moanna. My ... girlfriend is injured, soaking wet, hypothermic, bleeding—I don't know what all. Maybe a concussion too. A tree fell on her car. I'm five minutes out from the hospital. Please tell them I'm coming."

"Yes, sir, I'll have them ready—"

SAFE HARBOR

I clicked off, only then realizing I probably should have stayed on the line. But Eva started mumbling.

"I cried to God ... bring someone for Willow ... and thanked him for showing me ... it's okay to be ... in love again." Her head fell to the side toward me. "Then you came."

She hadn't said so many words since I found her. She was definitely in shock.

"Yes, I came, baby. I came," I said a little louder than I needed to, but what if she couldn't hear me through my pounding heart and the straining engine?

An eternity later, I screeched to a stop at the emergency room's doors, shifted into park, and jumped out of the truck. By the time I made it around to the passenger side, a doctor, two nurses, and a paramedic had the gurney at her door, carefully easing her out and laying her down on it.

"Her name is Eva Elliott." I told a nurse who caught my eye.

She looked lifeless.

"She's passed out again," I said, though they didn't hear me. I stayed on their tail as they rushed through the automatic doors, talking fast to one another, while she lay unmoving, oblivious.

I followed them through the heavy doors into the triage area, where the doc gave the nurse a look. She turned to me, putting her hands on my chest to halt my step.

"Sir, you're not allowed back here. Go to the waiting room. Someone will come out with an update as soon as possible." I watched the gurney with Eva disappear around the corner. The nurse put her hand against my back and pushed me lightly into the lobby. Once I'd gotten far enough into the waiting room, she gave me a sad smile and retreated quickly down the hall before the doors had a chance to close.

A woman rounded the reception desk. "Sir, I'm sorry, but we need you to move your truck to the parking lot."

I looked out at it, still running, Eva's door still wide open. At least the rain had stopped.

"Oh. Sorry."

On autopilot, I relocated the truck in a proper parking spot and made my way back to the waiting room. My adrenaline was wearing off and fatigue—mental *and* physical—settled in. I ran my hands down my face.

"Sir?" The lady behind the reception desk stood to get my attention.

"Yes?"

"Can I get you anything? Some towels? A blanket?"

I squinted, confused, and then followed her gaze to my damp clothes. "Oh, yeah, uh, I mean no. I'm fine, thanks."

"No problem."

"But where's your bathroom?"

She pointed, and I hauled it to the men's room, bursting through the doors and into a stall. Luckily, I was by myself, because I stared into the public restroom toilet and dry-heaved too many times to count.

What's happening? Am I sick?

No, this was *fear* sickness, plain and simple. I'd almost lost Eva, maybe could still lose her. She'd only just wisped into my life, and could be taken from me just as fast. And I was terrified.

I love her.

There was no question now. The words that popped into my head, the words I'd brushed off, not ready to utter them aloud, were confirmed by this sheer panic.

I went to the sink and turned on the water, the mirror holding me in its grip.

I knew tragedy. I'd lost a parent, a career—even lost my fiancée to someone else, but this? The one you loved as a soul mate, maybe to lose her to death? No tragedy I'd endured came close to this torture. Now I understood some of what Eva had been through with Alex. The pain she'd had to pull herself out of.

Oh God, heal her, body and spirit. Please.

A verse I'd memorized from Isaiah to help me climb out of sadness brushed across my mind.

When you pass through the waters, I will be with you.

I blinked, breaking my stare-down with myself, and washed my hands. God had done an overhaul on me years ago, and now he was working on Eva. He had her in his arms. I had to trust him.

I walked back to the waiting room and crashed down into a chair. After one too many minutes, I pulled my phone out, texted Dad that I'd found her and made it to the hospital. He texted back that he was on the way. I needed to call Ellen but didn't know what to say. I tapped her number anyway.

She picked up quick. "You found her?"

I told her the short version of the story and could hear her tears through the phone. "No one has come out here yet to fill me in on her condition." I started toward the reception desk to bug them when a doctor entered the waiting room.

"Eva Elliott's family?"

"Hold on, Ellen." I approached him. "I'm her ..." I stammered again over the label. Friend wasn't enough. I loved her. "... boyfriend. Uh, and this is her mother on the phone." I turned on the speakerphone.

He nodded, like that was enough to qualify. A natural disaster *was* happening outside.

"My name is Dr. Rimer. Eva's been through some trauma. Our first concern was hypothermia. We gave her warm IV fluids, and her body temperature's now at a more normal level. She hasn't shown signs of any head or internal injuries, and all her scans were negative. Her legs and left foot are bruised and scraped, but otherwise uninjured.

"Her left ankle is the biggest problem. She does have an open fracture. We've splinted it and started antibiotics. We did a type and screen as a precaution in case she needs blood, but we think she'll be all right without any transfusions. She'll be going into surgery to take care of that ankle as soon as we know her body can handle the anesthesia and the surgery, probably within the next few hours."

Ellen released a breath over the phone. "So she's gonna be okay?"

"Yes, she's going to be okay. She looks to be an otherwise healthy, strong, young woman. She should do fine." Dr. Rimer smiled, the lines around his eyes and lips creased. He had probably given loved ones the same smile a million times in this same waiting room, but when he gave it to me, I wanted to kiss him.

Ellen cried out, "Now I can breathe."

"Me too." I addressed the doctor. "Can I see her?"

"No, since she'll be heading straight from the trauma room to surgery. We've got an orthopedic surgeon coming in for her. Reception will let you know when they take her up, and they'll get you to the surgery waiting room. When she's out of surgery, you'll be able to see her."

"Thank you, Doctor," I said.

"Yes, thank you, Doctor," Ellen chimed in.

The doc disappeared behind the heavy doors.

"Thad ..." Ellen sighed. "... thank you for saving her life."

"You're welcome."

"I'll head south as soon as Willow wakes up. It'll take me five or six hours, I guess. How's the weather there?"

"On Moanna, it's pretty bad. But you should be able to make it to the hospital just fine."

SAFE HARBOR

"Okay. See you soon."

I hung up just as Dad walked through the automatic doors. My throat caught. My eyes dripped without permission as I was overwhelmed by my need for my own strong man to hold me up. I stood, and he embraced me like a little kid.

"You did good, son."

"She's going to be okay."

He pulled back to see my confirmation in a nod. "Thank you, Jesus." He smiled. "And thank you to your gut."

CHAPTER THIRTY-TWO

MONDAY

EVA

I knew the machine sounds well.

beep beep beep

I was dreaming, reliving Alex's last days by his hospital bed. But this nightmare wasn't like my other one.

Great. A new nightmare.

I opened my eyes, expecting to see Alex hooked up to the machines, or the beautiful angel by my side. Instead, I saw Mom slouched in a chair.

It took effort, but I rolled my head to look up. Everything around me was cloudy, like fog was moving through the room. I squinted into the fluorescent light above me.

Me.

I was the one in a hospital bed.

beep beep beep

I looked at Mom. No dream. The water—heavy, cold, unforgiving. My smashed car. My crushed legs. It all rushed back. I'd almost died, almost left Willow without any parents.

Willow!

"Mom," I tried to yell, but it came out a harsh whisper.

She startled awake. "Eva." She rose and stumbled to my side.

"Where's Willow?" I could get out no more than a dry rasp.

"She's fine. She's with John."

I nodded, initiating an immediate headache. I tried to bring my arm up to rub my pulsing head, but the arm was too heavy to lift.

"They're probably at the barn loft by now, watching cartoons," Mom continued, "having filled up on Whataburgers and ice cream like she made him promise to do since he couldn't take her fishing today." She stuck a straw by my lips, and I drank. The water was cold and tasted good. "How are you feeling?"

Tired, delirious, confused. And everything hurt. But the fog began to lift. "I'm tired."

"I'm sure. You went into hypothermia, and you lost a lot of blood to top it off." She patted my hand.

"How'd I get here?" As I asked that question, my brain released the memory. "Thad."

"Thad," Mom said with me. "He found you with your ankle trapped underneath something in the car."

I nodded, remembering his frame appearing out of nowhere. Then he was beside me.

I'm getting you out of here.

Tears ran down my face.

I'd been crying out to God to send someone who would take care of Willow, love her with their whole life, and thanking God for bringing Thad into mine, and there he was, in the flesh. God sent him to rescue me.

Oh, thank you, God.

Mom swiped her thumb over my tears. "Once you were stable, they took you into surgery to repair your ankle."

I looked at my foot, completely wrapped and propped up on two pillows. The other leg was bandaged too. "That doesn't look good."

SAFE HARBOR

Mom laughed. "You'll heal just fine, but you do have a metal plate somewhere in there now." My eyes widened, and she smiled. "You won't be going through metal detectors easily anymore."

A chuckle escaped. I was alive. Willow still had a mom. Mom still had a daughter. And I was in love. Who cared about an ankle that would heal in time?

Mom held the straw in front of my lips again. This time I sipped more, my throat already less dry, and my senses waking up more each minute. Mom read my mind like always. "You're probably still groggy from the blood loss and the anesthesia."

I was able to move my arm now. I rubbed my temples, processing everything.

"I'll go get Willow in a little while. She wants to see you, and I think with the state-of-emergency thing still playing out, they'll let her."

My heart started pounding. "Mom. Your house ..."

"It's fine. It will be, anyway. We can't get back on the island yet, but we will in a day or two. The news says the water is pretty much gone already, but some of the roads are washed out, and the bridges have to be inspected. But either way, we'll rebuild and repair the water damage. Thad has already offered to put us up in the barn loft—sounds super cool, by the way. He and John are going to stay with Mike until they can see the damage on their house."

I sighed and pushed away tears. She was right, but it was ... a lot.

Wait. "Mom, if John has Willow, where's Thad?"

My hero.

Mom grinned. "He stayed here the whole night in his waterlogged clothes. I told him to go home, sleep, change. But he wouldn't listen, wouldn't leave this hospital."

I exhaled. "Really?"

"Really. He went to get something to eat from the cafeteria."

"Mom, I love him."

"I know, honey, I know."

I tried to sit, but it was too much effort. Mom found the button and began to mechanically move the bed upright. The small movement made my ankle scream. I grimaced, and she stopped.

"Thanks, that's better. Mom, I have so much to tell you. I went out to the beach to talk to God. And you know what? He showed up."

"I know, honey. I've been feeling him tug you to himself for quite some time, so it doesn't surprise me."

There was a light rap on the half-open door, and Thad appeared, lighting up when his eyes caught mine.

"Hey, sleepyhead." He grabbed my hand as soon as he got to the side of the bed.

"Hey." I couldn't help the tears that overflowed my eyes and ran down to my chin.

"Don't do that." He swiped my cheek.

"Thank you for saving me." I pulled his hand against my face and kissed the back of it.

"You're welcome. Don't ever scare me again though." He smiled.

I nodded. A nurse appeared behind Thad. "Oh, I see you're awake. I'm Jamey, your nurse. How are you feeling?"

"Tired. Hurting."

"Well, you should be after what you've been through. Your ankle had a bad open fracture." She pointed along my ankle but didn't touch it. "The doctor will come in soon to give you more information, tell you when you'll be able to leave …"

"Which will be?"

She seemed pleased by my awareness. "Probably tomorrow. We'll want to make sure no infection has had

SAFE HARBOR

a chance to set in, since your ankle was submerged in floodwater. He'll keep you on heavy antibiotics a little longer. You'll be tired. Your body got pretty beat up." I couldn't see the bruises under the hospital gown, but I knew they were there. "You were really lucky."

"Yes, I know. Thank you."

"I know you just woke up, so I'll come back in a bit, let you guys talk a while." We all nodded and thanked her, and she smiled and left, but Thad's eyes never left mine. Our intense stare-down must have made Mom uncomfortable.

"Well then," she said briskly. "I'm going to go get some coffee. Need anything, Eva?"

I didn't take my eyes away from Thad's. "No, thank you."

"Okay." She disappeared.

Thad carefully sat down on my bed, pulling my hand into his lap. "You really scared me."

"I know. I'm so sorry. And sorry I didn't listen to you. I fell asleep and woke to the evac alert on my phone. By then, the flooding had started, and ..."

"What all do you remember?"

I swallowed with great effort, my throat already dry again at the memory of the water at my mouth, so close to drowning me. I sighed.

"Water. Lots of water. Being crushed. Thinking I would either drown or freeze. I was dying. I could feel my life slipping away. Then you showed up." I laughed. "I'm really grateful you have those superhero muscles."

"It wasn't me." He leaned in to kiss my forehead. "God definitely moved that metal."

I started to cry again. "Earlier. Before the power went out and the flooding started, I biked to the beach—"

"Eva!"

"I was safe *then*. I wanted a special place to talk to God."

He put his hand on the other side of the mattress beside my hip and leaned on it. "Okay ..."

"And I think I've been set free." My heart fluttered at those words, making my shoulders straighten and rise, and my lips shape themselves into a smile. "I'm his again."

Thad's features showed his joy. "Established."

"Yes. But my talk with him also solidified something I've got to do. And before I tell you this, just please know I'm really ashamed."

Thad squinted. "Okay."

I took a deep breath. "It's about Alex's parents. They're not in the picture because of me."

Thad's head tilted, one eyebrow quirked upward in a silent invitation to continue.

"They weren't supportive of the pregnancy. At first, they didn't want me to keep the baby, and then, they wanted a paternity test. Alex was always on my side, and he *was* supportive . He didn't want a test because he knew Willow was his, but he couldn't sway his parents. And then—" A rush of emotions took over, and my throat closed up.

Thad finished my sentence. "And then Alex's accident."

"Yes." My sore throat tried to gulp down the saliva that rushed into my mouth. "I knew they were grieving, but they continued to demand a paternity test if they were going to be involved in her life. At the time, I was furious and offended. I refused. Willow was born without an appearance from them at the hospital.

"Then the letters started. Over and over, they wrote to me, begging me to give them a paternity test, angry I wouldn't cave to their demand." I looked out past Thad's shoulders at the sunlight coming through the blinds, too embarrassed by my own behavior to look at him. "I was mad and hurt."

"It sounds to me like you had every right to be."

"Well, maybe I did at the time. Whenever a letter came, I'd read it and tuck it away. I never responded to them. But over time, the words in their letters changed from anger to regret, and they began asking for forgiveness. They wanted a chance to make their wrongs right, to be a part of their son's only legacy." I wiped the tears away with the back of my hand. "And I denied it to them. Denied it to Willow. I've never responded to them."

Thad kissed the back of my hand where the tear had been, only making more fall as he waited patiently for me to continue. "Maybe the most shameful part is I moved out of town without telling them. But because the mail was forwarded, a letter arrived a few weeks ago, and I've been a mess."

Thad sighed. "A mess because you've got to take Willow to meet them."

He already knew me so well. "Yes."

"Last night," he said slowly, "when I was sick with worry, God reminded me of a verse. 'When you pass through the waters, I will be with you ...'"

Fitting. My waters were literal and figurative.

"He's there to help. And, baby, I'll help in whatever way I can."

His eyes locked onto my wide ones. "What?"

"You called me *baby*."

He sat back a little. "Uh, I did. Is that okay?"

"Yes. Come here." He went in to kiss me. "No, wait. I just realized how awful I must look."

He rolled his eyes. "You've never been more beautiful."

My turn to roll my eyes. "Liar."

He kissed me anyway. I hesitated against his lips.

"I need to tell you I'm sorry for being so stubborn. I've always felt Willow would be neglected in some way if I fell in love, but last night God made it clear it's okay that I've fallen in love with you."

He teased, "Oh, you have?" He put his forehead to mine.

"Yes, and I think I have been for quite some time."

"Really? So you're saying you love me?"

I bit my bottom lip. "Yes."

He pulled back to look in my eyes. I cupped my hands on his cheeks.

"Well, good, because I love you too, and I also think I have for quite some time. Last night, seeing you hurt—" He shook his head. I reached to touch the scar over his eye, tracing it with my finger. He leaned into my touch. "It was horrible. I think now I know a little of what you went through with Alex. And I am so, so sorry."

"It's okay." And it was. My sadness seemed to be gone. It'd been replaced with happiness over memories of our time together and ... hope. I cocked my head.

"You know, we both just uttered the words 'I love you,' but we've never been on a date."

He leaned in to brush his lips over my collarbone and moved them to my ear.

"Dates are overrated. What we've had is way better than any date. We've fallen in love on chance encounters and scheduled get-togethers."

CHAPTER THIRTY-THREE

THURSDAY

EVA

I'd put off calling Alex's parents long enough.

If I were able to walk without crutches, I'd be pacing in the barn loft staring at my phone. Mom had left to take Willow to preschool, which reopened this morning after some cleanup around its building. Thankfully, its distance inland had protected it from any real storm damage. And Willow needed to get back into the week's normal routine.

I hadn't wanted to call Alex's parents while I was in the hospital, because I was never alone. This fact baffled all logic. Three months ago, I moved to Moanna, and the only people who cared for me were Willow and Mom. I was in a hospital bed only forty-eight hours, yet Thad never left my side, Mom left only to care for Willow and bring her to me, and John, Stacy, Mike, my principal, *and* Pastor Andrew, along with his wife, came to visit. When the doctors released me, we'd had to tote home six vases of flowers, which we'd spread throughout the loft.

Now, there were no more excuses. The silence hovered, waiting for my fingers to type in the number I still knew by heart from my teenage years. I sat up a little straighter in the bed, trying not to disturb my foot and cause the shooting pain that came if I did. The foot was propped up just as the docs told me to do for the next few weeks. Already, I was annoyed with the whole idea of bed rest.

God, speak for me, please.

I took a deep breath, typed the numbers, then held that breath in as the *brrrt* of the ring tone began.

"Hello." Pamela's voice came through after the second ring.

My hand shook the phone at my ear, and my voice sounded just as shaky. "Hi, Pamela."

She sucked in a harsh breath and hesitated for what seemed like a millennium. "Eva?"

"Yes."

I heard her inhale sharply again, and I forced my practiced words out. "I know it's early, but I didn't want another day to pass without calling you. To apologize."

I swallowed, resisting the urge to throw up over the side of the bed. She hadn't made a sound, and I could only imagine her frozen in time, hoping my next words would forever change her life.

I cleared my throat. "Pamela, I'm, um—"

Get it together, Eva.

"I'm truly sorry for keeping Willow from you. The moment I read your letter saying you wanted to meet her, I should have dropped everything and come right over. I regret—have long regretted—that decision. You and Robert didn't deserve that behavior. I know you were devastated after Alex"—his name leaving my lips broke me, and tears gushed before I could finish—"after Alex died. And I only added to your pain."

"Oh, Eva, we're so sorry too." Pamela's sobs between her words broke me even more. "You and Alex were so young, and we were so angry at first when he told us about the pregnancy. We wanted his life to be ... well ... happy.

SAFE HARBOR

And we didn't see how a baby right when he graduated college—before he'd even found a job—could fit into that plan, especially since the two of you'd broken up. But we were so wrong, because now we look back and see how happy he was in the months leading up to his—" Her voice was shaky. "To the accident and his death. He was so excited, and we should have shared in the happiness with him—and with you. We should have trusted him from the start."

We both fell silent. I relived one of my last nights with Alex. He'd kissed my huge belly and spoken to it, telling Willow about her name and its meaning.

You, my precious one, will be graceful and elegant as your name says, but also strong and resilient. Just like your mother who gives you life, which is very fitting since that's what her name means. 'Mother of life.'

Mother.

That thought brought me back to Pamela. "Can you ever forgive me? Please?"

Pamela let out a sigh with joy packed into it. "Eva, we already have."

The weight I'd lugged around for four years crashed to the floor. "Really?"

"Yes, honey. Can you forgive *us*?"

I smiled. "Yes." My words choked me up. "I already have."

"Wonderful."

"Pamela, I know we have a lot more to talk about. Could Willow and I come see you and Robert next Saturday? A week and a half from now?"

"The happiness your question brings me is more than I ever dreamed it could. What time will you be here?"

CHAPTER THIRTY-FOUR

SATURDAY

CHATTANOOGA, TENNESSEE

THAD

"Are you sure you're okay going by yourself?" I held open her driver's side door, bending to peer into Eva's rental car. "I mean, I don't even have to get out of the car. Well, I could just get out of the car to help you and Willow get out of the car." I gestured to her crutches in the passenger seat.

Eva adjusted her driver's seat and laughed. "I can't even reach the pedals. You almost don't fit in here."

I laughed too. "Don't avoid the question."

She looked up, still pulling the lever, her seat moving slightly back and forth as she tried to find the right spot. "Yes, we're okay. Willow and I have to do this alone."

"Yeah, I know. You're right."

"But I am already over this whole injured foot thing."

"Well, that stinks, 'cause you've probably got at least another month on those crutches."

"Thanks." Her tone was exquisitely sarcastic.

I shut the car door and leaned in the window. "At least, you're checked into your room, and it's located right next to mine."

"Yeah, the big bed is like Gramma's," Willow screeched from the backseat.

"Yes, it is." Eva looked at Willow through the rearview mirror. "And those sheets and blanket are so soft and fluffy."

"Yeah, I know. I already jumped on it." Willow's expression was one of confident defiance.

Eva looked at me with pursed lips. "Yes. She did."

I looked around Eva's head to lock eyes with Willow. "Maybe I can jump on it with you later."

"No." Willow giggled.

"What? Why not?"

"You're too big."

I grabbed my chest, pretending she'd wounded my heart, which only made her laugh more.

"Well, I guess I'll just have to watch you jump on it." I looked back to Eva. "I plan on walking over to one of these restaurants to get something to eat." I spun my finger around in a circle. There were restaurants everywhere. We'd decided to book rooms in a downtown Chattanooga hotel, right by their famous Tennessee Aquarium. The Tennessee River was a block away, an old bridge across it. The city had turned the old structure into a "walking bridge," connecting it with the North Shore community.

That was where Alex's parents lived, so it wasn't too far away.

"Sounds like a plan. I'll call you when I can, but I have no idea how long we'll be. It could go really well, and we might stay for—"

I put my finger to her lips. "It doesn't matter. You and Willow stay gone all night if you want to. Just please tell me before that actually happens." Thoughts of the flood on Moanna rushed back.

"I will, I promise. Will you pray for us?"

I nodded. "The whole time." I didn't kiss her. Not sure she'd be comfortable with Willow watching. I just brushed my fingers down her cheek like always and backed away to watch her drive out of the parking lot, already proud of her.

EVA

I kept glancing in my rearview at the man I loved until he faded out of sight. He stood motionless on the sidewalk watching us fade away too. The strain of his Carhartt button-down against his bulky arms and chest, with his dark jeans and heavy boots, easily intimidated anyone who passed. That is, until you looked at his face and saw his huge smile. That smile gave me courage to keep pushing the gas toward Alex's house. Strange how I straddled my new love with my old, and it was okay.

Willow sang along to the tunes from the radio, and before long we entered Alex's old neighborhood. Even though the homes were at least fifty years old by now, they all looked freshly painted and their lawns were pristinely landscaped. They looked exactly the same.

"Mama, are we there now?"

"Almost, baby. This is the neighborhood. Just a few more turns."

I couldn't tell if she was nervous or just wanted to get out of the car for good. I was leaning toward her desire to be out of the car. We'd left after Thad's early morning football game, having cheered them to another victory, but seven hours in the car were more than enough for her.

I made the last turn onto their street.

"Here it is." I rolled to a stop and turned the car off. My stomach chose that moment to take a turn for the worse as nausea rushed through me. Willow shifted in her car seat to get a better look out the window, but I couldn't move.

God, please help me get through this.

My nausea fled instantly, and I took a breath.

Thank you.

I chanced a look out the window, and instead of anxiety, nostalgia washed over me. Not grief, not pain, not anger, but joyful longing as memories rushed back of our summers at home. We'd take his dad's convertible to the lake, thinking we were hot stuff and so much more mature than we were. Those were great memories, and thinking of them didn't hinder my state of mind. They made me smile. I chuckled under my breath.

Willow cried, "Mama ... c'mon." A second later she added, "Please?"

"Okay, okay." I grabbed the crutches and carefully pulled them to my side to help me to get out of the car. When I was out, which took longer than I cared to admit, I stuck the keys in my pocket and went around to the other side to get Willow. I helped her down onto the pavement.

"Let me grab your bag." I snatched up her bag of toys, not knowing what we'd need and turned to find her frozen, staring at the house.

She's nervous.

I put the bag on my shoulder and maneuvered my crutches into position.

"You ready, baby?" She nodded, her expression telling me she was determined to be brave. She gripped onto a few of my fingers as I tried to grip the crutch. For a moment, we gaped at our destination.

Their house sat on a hill with a stately front porch, white siding, black shutters—a classic design that would never go out of style. The grass had gone dormant, but yellow and blue pansies still lined the sidewalk. Pink camellias spread out across the front. Both added some color to the dreary fall day.

SAFE HARBOR

I squeezed her hand as best I could, and we started up the walk. By the time I navigated the stairs, I was shocked to find I was still okay. Nervous, but okay. I reached to ring the doorbell, but before I could press the button, the porch light came on, and the door pulled back.

Both Pamela and Robert appeared, and my throat constricted.

Pamela took a step onto the porch, Robert close behind her. Their eyes locked on Willow. Both seemed to hold their breath.

I swallowed with great effort. "Willow, these are your grandparents. This is Grandma Pamela and Grandpa Robert."

Willow squeezed my hand a little tighter, but said, "Hi."

Pamela reached an unsteady hand to Willow, her eyes misty and unblinking.

"She ... she has his eyes." Her trembling body rotated slightly to me, and I nodded. She dropped to her knees. "Hi, Willow." She took a moment to recover. "I've been waiting to meet you for a very long time, and I've got to say you are even more perfect than I could have ever imagined."

The compliment got a smile out of Willow.

"Your dress is beautiful."

"It's Princess Tiana's dress." Willow's voice was soft but there.

Though tears rolled down, and I fought the urge to ugly cry, I said, "It's her Halloween costume. A Disney Princess. She insisted she wear it to meet you since it's her most beautiful dress."

"Oh my, I agree." Pamela cocked her head. "I don't know Princess Tiana, but I'd love to hear all about her. Do you think you can tell me her story?"

Willow's nod must have struck Robert out of his trance like lightning because he squatted in Willow's line of sight.

"Thank you for coming to join us this evening. We were wondering if you'd like to stay for dinner? We thought we might have pizza."

Willow looked at me for an answer, and I nodded. She turned back to Robert. "Yes," she said in the matter-of-fact, confident way she had about her.

They both stood. Pamela held out her hand to Willow. "Let's go in, and you can tell me your favorite toppings."

Willow let go of mine and took hers. "Just cheese, please."

"Cheese it is." Pamela guided Willow toward the kitchen, and Robert turned to me.

"Eva, Pamela told me about your accident." He gestured to my foot, still tightly wrapped and booted. "Thank you for driving up here in your condition."

"Thank you for having us. I didn't want to let any more time pass." The tears that had dried came back as I locked eyes with Robert. Alex had his eyes, and so I could see both Alex *and* Willow as I looked into his.

They now held a look of hope. "I'm glad you've come." He smiled nervously. "Thank you. Thank you for coming home." Before I could speak, he hauled me into a hug.

I cried in his embrace while I did my best to hug him back and not drop the crutches. His hug told me what words couldn't, that he'd truly forgiven me. I whispered, "Thank you for letting me."

He let go but kept his arm around my shoulder and led me into the house. "C'mon, we've got a lot of catching up to do."

"Yes, we do."

Thank you, Jesus.

EPILOGUE

A YEAR AND A HALF LATER ...

THAD

"Okay, little lady, take the paint roller and go up and down." I rolled mine in demonstration against the last wall left to paint in the nursery. "Someone told me if you want to look good, make a capital 'N' with the paint roller, but you wouldn't know how to do that."

"Yes, I do. I'm in kindergarten." Willow started to make an "N" on the wall with the blue paint.

"Oh. Well, then, you'll have no problem getting that wall looking amazing for your baby brother."

"Hm." Willow turned back to the wall with intensity and satisfaction, while I chuckled as quietly as I could.

After a few strokes, Eva came in.

"Okay, worker bees, I brought you drinks and some of the cookies Mom made last night."

"Yum," Willow said. She'd picked up her roller three minutes ago, but she haphazardly dropped it into the tray to get to the cookies. The extra time it took to doubly line and tape the plastic drop cloth had been worth it.

Eva put the plate on the little table we'd moved into the room and held out a juice box for Willow. "Here ya go." She turned to hand me a glass of ice water.

"Aw, man! I wanted a juice box too." I pouted as Willow laughed.

"You would," Eva said through her smile. "Okay, where's an extra roller for me? I can help knock out that last wall before we've got to get ready."

"Nuh-uh." I took a swig of water. "You are *not* painting."

"Thad, we got nontoxic paint so it wouldn't be a big deal for Willow or me to breathe it in. It's totally fine. *We're totally fine.*" She patted her pregnant belly and handed Willow a cookie, then took a bite of one herself.

"Okay, I'll let you stay in here for ten minutes, but only so I can look at your belly that's finally poking out."

She scoffed.

"Liar. My belly's poked out for a long time now."

Willow laughed and nodded.

I wiggled my finger. She was not going to change the subject. "Ten minutes. But then"—I hitched my thumb over my shoulder—"you're outta here."

She rolled her eyes. "Okay. Willow, you take a cookie break. I'll work on your spot for a bit."

"'Kay." Willow plopped down on the floor.

Eva and I picked up rollers. "So what is this color again?" I asked.

"Shadow Blue."

"What does that even mean?"

Eva laughed. "I have no idea. We'll just call it a medium, deep-water-gray-blue."

I snorted. "Yeah, 'cause that's easier to understand."

"Well, no matter the color's name, it's gonna be beautiful."

"I know." I found Eva's eyes and gave her a wink, wishing I were close enough to kiss her and rub on her tiny sixth-month pregnant belly.

"I need to ask you something." Willow spoke up behind us.

Eva said, "What is it, baby?"

Willow squinted her eyes in thought. "Well, I know I have a daddy in heaven, and I know God is a daddy to everyone too, but do you think it's okay to have three? Three daddies?"

Eva's gaze shot to me, and her gaping mouth froze a moment before she recovered.

"Uh, yes, I think it's okay to have three daddies. It can never hurt to have more people who love you and who want to take care of you." Eva put her paint roller in the tray and sat down on the floor facing Willow.

I put down mine too, but hung back. With the new baby coming, we'd been wondering when this conversation might come up.

"Well then, is it okay if Thad's one of my dads?" She searched Eva's face for the answer in her reaction.

Eva leaned closer to her. "I think it's more than okay. In fact, I think it's a great idea." Eva turned to me. "Don't you think it's a great idea?"

I walked over. "Willow, I would love to be one of your dads." I sat down. "It would be the greatest honor of my life to be called Dad by you and your brother."

"Yeah?" Willow's eyes brightened.

"Definitely."

Eva patted Willow's knees. "Plus, it may be best. You don't want to confuse your baby brother." Eva spoke sarcastically to Willow, though her eyes were misty. She was trying to pretend Willow calling me Dad wasn't as big a deal as it was ... to both of us.

"Yeah, true." Willow agreed with a nod.

"Willow, you call me Thad, Dad, or both, and I'll answer to any of them, okay? Whatever feels right to you, because I know it could get confusing to try and change what you call me."

"Nah, it's easy."

"Oh?"

Willow narrowed her eyes, perhaps because she thought I was having a "duh" moment. "Yeah, 'cause *Thad* rhymes with *Dad*."

Eva and I busted out laughing. I recovered and said, "You're right. Maybe it won't be too hard then."

Ellen appeared in the doorway. "My goodness, all my loves in one room. How'd I get so lucky?" Mom was dressed, but her hair was still wet from the shower.

"Do you like the color, Mom?"

"I do, I do, but this will have to wait. You guys better get moving and get ready to go."

"What time is it?" Eva asked to whomever. I looked at my watch. "Eleven-o-eight a.m."

"Already? We gotta hustle."

I jumped up and pulled Eva to her feet.

Ellen motioned to Willow. "C'mon, honey. I'll go get you changed, then we'll fix my hair." She pretended to toss her hair over her shoulder, but it was too short.

"Thanks, Mom. Her clothes are on her bed." Eva began wrapping the brushes in plastic while I made sure the lids on the paint cans were secure.

"Okay," Ellen said, just before I heard Willow tell her she was going to call me Dad.

EVA

"Okay, guys, it's game time." Thad nodded to the men who'd accumulated by the little stage—Mike, John, Palmer's mayor, Pastor Andrew, and even our local House reps. We'd set it up under the oak trees next to the fire pit we'd constructed many moons ago. "You guys go take your seats."

Any nervousness Thad had didn't show on his face as he bent down to kiss me on the lips. He lingered there for a moment, so I grabbed his face to keep him there, kissing him one more time. Then I whispered, for his ears only, "I can't wait to see my sexy man up on that stage." I pulled back a little. "I'm so excited for you, for Palmer, for the kids that will be coming here in a few months. What God's got you doing is amazing."

"Thank you," he said as he stood up to his full height, dwarfing me as always.

"C'mon, everybody, let's go sit."

Robert nodded. He held Willow's hand, and they led the way to our reserved row in the front. Mom and Pamela stopped their conversation and followed. Stacy was already there, sitting on the far edge, her eyes on Mike as usual. She noticed us coming and gave a jittery wave.

I waved back and took a seat between Mom and Willow, with Robert and Pamela on the other side of her. They'd made the trip down to celebrate the summer camp's ribbon cutting and were just as ecstatic about it as we were. In fact, they'd helped on the camp's volunteer workdays numerous times. Ever since the Halloween we showed up on their doorstep, they'd made a habit of coming to Moanna at least one weekend a month.

After Thad and I got married last summer, Mom had tried to stay in her house, tried to live alone after her home was repaired from the flood damage. We'd offered to move her in with us, to live as one big happy family in Thad's big house, to fill it up with love. At first, she refused, but soon enough she began staying over more and more. When we found out I was pregnant, it sealed the deal. She was now with us permanently. She didn't sell the house on White

Egret Drive but began renting it out. It ended up being a perfect spot for Robert and Pamela to stay when they came to visit.

It was a wonder to watch how God shuffled people around, in and out of our lives. Two years ago, Willow had just one grandparent. Now between Mom, Robert, Pamela, and John, she was more spoiled than any other child on the planet. And crazy enough, Alex's parents were viewing my pregnancy as if they, too, were about get another grandchild, which suited all of us just fine.

But what was even more incredible, Willow went from no dad to three, and God showed me it was okay. And it was okay to love again and to still love a person who was gone. As long as God was in the picture, everything fell into place perfectly.

Thad moved his head into my line of sight, pulling me out of my reminiscing trance. He mouthed, "I love you."

"I love you too," I mouthed back as the men took the stage. Thad stayed back, waiting for his introduction.

Mike tapped the mic to test it, then spoke. "Thank you all for coming on this glorious day." He gestured all around him. The pasture-turned-ball-field, bunk cabins, outhouses, and mess hall in the distance, the barn now full of toys for the lake and land, the quaint chapel tucked into the woods with floor-to-ceiling windows, which all could be opened to allow the fresh air to flow through, the lake behind Mike—all picture-perfect. Everything fit into the grooves of the property like it was meant to be a summer camp from the beginning of time. Which it was, on divine authority.

"Today, we're here to celebrate the official opening of Camp Fun." The whole crowd laughed. "Well, there will be a whole lot of fun going on here, but that's not its name. The official opening of Camp Formations!" Everyone clapped. "This camp has been my best friend's dream-in-

SAFE HARBOR

progress for a long time, and I'm honored to bring him up here to talk more about it. Around here, he's Coach, but sports fans remember him as Damien Smith, tight end for the Chargers. Let's welcome Mr. Thad Smith."

I couldn't help but stand in excitement to clap him on, but it turned out everyone felt the same way, because the whole crowd stood with me. When he arrived on the stage, he motioned earnestly with his hands for everyone to sit down. "I don't know anyone who calls me Mr. Thad Smith, but thank you, Mike, for the kind words. And thank you all for coming today."

He took a breath. "It's true this camp has been a long time in the making, but I wasn't alone in my dream for this place. God gave me a vision of what it could be, and I can only hope it meets his expectations, since he's so good at surpassing mine.

"God's been diligent in showing me over and over how he can make something beautiful out of tragedy. Some of you may know parts of my story, but for those who don't, I was adopted as an infant, and my birth mother's tragic loss turned into my adoptive parents' greatest gift. My amazing parents and I lived in rural Georgia." He gestured to John behind him. "That's my incredible earthly father right there." The crowd, full of former and present players and their parents, gave a loud round of applause peppered with cheers.

"Yup, he's awesome. My parents were both schoolteachers, teaching classrooms full of kids every day, but most importantly teaching me about Jesus. I was blessed to play football for the University of Iowa. Any Iowa fans here?"

Nothing but crickets in the crowd. Thad laughed.

"Just kidding. It's pretty far away, and not part of the SEC, so you guys have probably never heard of 'em." Everyone nodded.

I smiled at watching Thad work the crowd. He was such a natural leader and showman, a perfect person to be God's messenger.

"After that, I was drafted into the NFL to play for the Chargers. I led a crazy life then, did a ton of dumb things, and after a few tragedies, including the loss of my mother and a busted knee, I had to retire young. Too young, I thought at the time.

"But God had more in store for me than playing football in the big leagues—an unexpected life that would bring me more joy than playing football on TV ever did. He used my tragedy to bring me back to him. Then he brought me to this area, brought me to this property, and brought me to my wife and new family, growing bigger by the minute." Thad threw up his hands. "My dad and I were just minding our own business, and bam! God moves *three women* in with us."

Mom called out, "And you love it!"

"Yes, I do. I do love it." He pretended to talk just to the crowd. "Most of the time. But if you look at my beautiful wife's adorable belly, you'll see we have a new addition coming, and guess what?" I laughed and shook my head, knowing what was coming. "It's a boy! The house will soon be on an even playing field."

After the hooting crowd calmed down, he said, "See, out of tragedy, God brought such joy, and this camp is part of that. We'll be having a ton of fun here. But it's my hope the kids don't just have fun, but also learn how to get—and maintain—their lives in the right formation, creating the ultimate success. We'll have many athletes here for football camps, and I hope they learn more than just formations on the field. I hope they learn God's rightful place in the formation of their lives."

He pointed to the right of the stage where a large red ribbon was pulled between two trees.

SAFE HARBOR

"In just a moment, my family and key staff members are going to cut the ribbon signifying Camp Formations is ready to go. Afterward, we'd like to invite you all to join us in the mess hall." He pointed behind where we were sitting. "We're serving a feast to celebrate, and you'll be able to mingle with all the staff members who've already been hired. You're welcome to quiz them about what we've got in store for the kids. Again, thank you for coming."

Thad stepped away from the mic, and Mike jumped back on it as Thad walked offstage toward the ribbon. "Let's give Mr. Thad Smith a hand." Thad shook his head at the formal name again, and I could tell Mike loved every bit of Thad's fake annoyance. "All right, let's get this photo op." Mike gestured for the men on stage to go to the ribbon. "And if Thad's family will go on over for the photo as well."

Our whole row stood. I reached over and grabbed Stacy's hand to bring her along too, and as I passed Mike, I said, "C'mon, bud. You're totally in on this."

Mike hesitated only a moment, then said into the mic, "Okay, folks, we'll see you in the mess hall." He jumped down to get in the line behind the ribbon next to Stacy.

Thad handed me the extra-large scissors and picked up Willow, making her the very center of the picture. John was on the other side of Thad, Mom on the other side of me. Robert and Pamela huddled with Mike and Stacy after Mom. Palmer's mayor and Pastor Andrew stood next to John. We were one crazy bunch as Thad held his free hand over mine, and we cut the ribbon. The crowd cheered, and cameras flashed like we were famous, but even in the chaos, my peace was strong and sure and joyful.

I could picture Alex looking down on this moment—happy for the way his loved ones had turned a tragedy into something beautiful and full of joy, happy for the way I'd let God back in, for remembering I was *his* all along.

Thank you, Jesus.

Kristen Terrette

"Shout for joy to the Lord, all the earth. Worship the Lord with gladness; come before him with joyful songs. Know that the Lord is God. It is he who made us, and we are his; we are his people, the sheep of his pasture. Enter his gates with thanksgiving and his courts with praise; give thanks to him and praise his name. For the Lord is good and his love endures forever; his faithfulness continues through all generations."

—Psalm 100: 1-5 (NIV)

ABOUT THE AUTHOR

Kristen Terrette is passionate about storytelling and helping people take their next steps in their relationship with Jesus. She lives forty-five minutes outside of Atlanta, GA with her husband and two children. She's an author of Christian fiction, and also a literary manager with Martin Literary & Media Management. She gets to work with writers, editors, words, and stories every day and loves every minute of it. To find out more, go to www.kristenterrette.com.

Made in the USA
Columbia, SC
27 October 2023